Summary

A cocky professional dancer who has been thrown off his own TV reality show is forced to teach a class of wheelchair ballerinas under the protective eye of Livia, a shy young woman with a forbidden past.

Get emails or texts from Deanna about her new releases:
Deanna's List

~*´♥`*~

*For my husband Kurt.*

*Every love story is your story.*

**Book 1 of the Lovers Dance Series**

---

**by Deanna Roy**

Six-Time *USA Today* bestselling author of

*The Forever Series*

*The Lovers Dance Series*

---

Sign up to be notified about new releases via email or text.

Casey Shay Press
PO Box 160116
Austin, TX 78716
www.caseyshaypress.com

E-ISBN: 9781938150623
Paperback ISBN: 97819381506-6

Library of Congress Control Number: 2017901093
eBook version 3.0

## Chapter One

This is my happy place, pretty much my only one.

I check the form of my *plié* in the mirror and straighten an arm, then slide out a foot. I've been doing ballet for two years, ever since Dreamcatcher Dance Academy opened and accepted students who couldn't afford classes.

But it's time to start working toward toe shoes and begin dancing *en pointe*, and my instructor Betsy says I'm not ready.

I want to be ready.

The next song on the playlist begins and I move to *demi-pointe* for a free dance. As I turn and whirl, feeling the sheer pink fabric of my dance skirt whispering against my thighs, I am free.

My wretched home life disappears.

No overbearing father.

No forced homeschool that has now extended a year past graduation.

No rules about where I go, who I see, what I wear.

It's just me and the dance and the form I'm trying to get perfect.

I'm surrounded by life-size images of ballerinas I admire, including Juliet, who is performing the famous entrance to *La Bayadère*'s Dance of the Shades. Her mother owns this academy, and they have changed my life.

After four years of house arrest by my family, I get a small measure of freedom when I'm here.

I practice my *pirouette*. I've chosen parts of *The Nutcracker* to dance to, since Christmas season is coming and I want to get in the mood.

Besides, the girls in the beginner ballet class I help with are using the song in the holiday recital in six weeks. I want to know it inside-out. It's how I give back, something in return for my free lessons even though it's not required.

I started too late for serious study of dance. At nineteen, I would normally have either joined a ballet troupe or given up by now.

But I only began learning at seventeen, and not without a fight. My father took one look at the body-hugging leotards and voiced his strenuous opposition.

No matter that I was a heartbeat away from legal adulthood and could leave home anytime I wanted.

He knew I wouldn't. I have nowhere to go. No skills. No way to earn money, at least not enough to support myself. I don't know anything about living on my own. I'd never make it.

The music speeds up as the Nutcracker Army marches into the scene. I increase my pace, adding leaps and spins. My glossy black hair is braided into a circular crown, one of the few ways I can distinguish myself with no makeup and the plainest wardrobe imaginable. At least my hair can be beautiful.

The leotard was another victory. When I finally convinced my father to let me try ballet, he attended every single class for six months, forcing me to wear baggy pants and T-shirts. But finally he recognized the beauty and elegance of the dance, far more structured and demanding than anything he could dream up. Plus, no men anywhere. So he allowed it.

In dance attire, I look like everyone else. I fit in. I'm not talented, and this passion of mine can go nowhere, although maybe, if I stick with Dreamcatcher, I can eventually graduate to teaching toddlers, like Aurora does.

That's one goal I have.

But first, toe shoes.

I spin, arms in, so tight, so fast, then extending up over my head. The world is a blur. I'm both giddy and fierce in my concentration, happy and determined at once. I will get those shoes. My late start in life is a problem, but I will overcome it.

I slow the rotation and circle to the floor, my arms splayed out across the glossy wood planks.

"That's beautiful," a low male voice says.

I leap to my feet, my heart racing, as startled as a deer.

The door is open and a man leans against the wall beside it, one foot crossed over the other. He's clearly a dancer, wearing sleek pants, black jazz shoes, and a loose white tank.

"Who are you?" I ask. I haven't been alone with a man anywhere close to my age since I was fifteen. My father has made sure of it. The only male instructor here is Jacob, and he is gay. All the boy students are very young.

"The more important question," he says with an impossibly sexy smile, "is who are *you*?"

I resist the urge to find something to cover myself with. I'm a dancer. This leotard is standard issue, and I've done recitals in front of an audience wearing them.

But somehow I feel naked when this man looks at me.

His chiseled jaw is shadowed with just the right amount of scruff. He's outrageously handsome. I can feel the pull of his sex appeal all the way across the room. I'm not scared of it. I knew it once. Knew it better than anybody.

But now that is forbidden.

"I'm only a student here," I say. "Practicing." I don't want him to know my name. I can't have him saying it out loud to someone. No one can know we met.

He seems extremely pleased with the situation. "You do ballet beautifully," he says. "It was a pleasure to watch."

The way he rolls out the word *pleasure*, his voice a rumble, wakes up parts of me I've forgotten about. He pushes away from the wall.

I take an uncertain step back, glancing at the open door. I'm ready to bolt.

And yet, I'm riveted to his face, his glittering mischievous eyes. He's larger than life, pure charisma.

His approach is graceful and predatory in equal measure. I'm frozen in place now, finding it hard to believe that I've come to this moment after so long in hiding.

"Can you show me an *arabesque?*" he asks. "I've never taken ballet. My father thought it was too feminine. He didn't want me to take dance at all. I had to force it."

My shoulders relax. I definitely know all about that. "My father didn't want me to take dance either," I say.

"So we have something in common." His smile draws my eyes like a hypnotist's charm. His mouth is beautiful. I can already feel his lips on mine.

I shake that thought away. "I've only had two years, but I'm happy to show you an *arabesque*," I say. I gesture to the oversized photographs on the walls. "The perfect examples are all around you. It's a beautiful extension, but fairly strenuous to hold for long."

"Try me," he says.

I move into an *arabesque*, my belly quivering a little as his gaze travels along my body.

I return to standing. "You try," I say. "Keep your chest high and lift your back leg."

He leans over too far, and I touch him lightly to lift his chest. He is muscled and hard. He must work out a lot.

"Now your arms," I say.

He lifts them, and I adjust his form. The touch is electric, sizzling through me. I've forgotten what this feels like.

"You've got it," I say.

He straightens. "I want to do more of this. I haven't had a chance to take an actual class in years."

"Well, we have a few adult classes, but I think you'll find they are mostly older women. It might move too slowly for you."

"How about you teach me?" He moves into a

lunge, one leg behind him, his arm outstretched as if he wants me to take his hand.

His form is perfect on this. He obviously has a lot of training in something. Jazz, maybe, judging by the outfit. Possibly contemporary.

"Who are you again?" I ask.

"Benjamin," he says. "And I am so glad to meet you..."

He pauses, expectant for my name.

I relent. "Livia," I say. "But I really think you'll be better off with Betsy. She does the advanced ballet here."

He stands up from his lunge. "All right, Livia. Well, thank you for that recommendation." He bows at the waist, a gesture so old-fashioned and charming that I almost regret turning him down.

"Suze is at the front desk," I tell him. "She can help you with that."

Benjamin nods at me. "It's been most enjoyable meeting you. Perhaps if I hang around a bit, we'll cross paths again." He takes my hand, and before I realize what he's doing, he's kissed my knuckle.

"Oh!" I exclaim. I'm completely overwhelmed by this gesture. Who is this guy? Can he be for real?

He releases my hand and I immediately clutch it against my chest as though my own fingers are a prized possession.

Then he's gone.

I turn back to the mirror and look at myself. It's still plain old me. Pink leotard, a little worn, and the pale pink sheer skirt. My threadbare ballet slippers, dirty at the toes. I clasp my hands to my cheeks. What just happened?

Aurora dashes in.

"Holy cow, Livia, did Blitz Craven just kiss your hand?"

I turn to her. Her face is bright red. She's the toddler teacher, petite and adorable in her sunny yellow leotard.

"He said his name was Benjamin."

"Oh my God." She turns in a circle, hands on her head. "You really don't know who that was!"

I want to calm her down. She looks like she's ready to explode. "He didn't introduce himself as Blitz anybody. But he does look like a dancer."

"Livia!" Aurora puts her hands on my shoulders. "That's THE Blitz Craven. The host of *Dance Blitz*! The reality TV show!"

"I don't watch TV, remember?" I say. "And my dad thinks the Internet is evil."

I've never had a cell phone or a computer. If we need to know something, Dad gets a book about it at the library.

Aurora lets go of me. "Well, he's huge. Like, bigger than huge." Her eyes go wide. "And he's here. That means Danika let him in!" She turns in a circle. "This is so crazy! Blitz Craven at Dreamcatcher!"

I grab her arm so she'll stand still and explain things. "Why is this such a big deal?"

"This academy is going to be famous!" she says. "Blitz is going to help out around here! We could end up on his show." She gets thoughtful. "Well, I wouldn't. I have Samuel. But you could! And Suze! And all the single dancers!"

"Why does it matter if we're single?"

"It's like the *Bachelor*, Livia. Blitz has been looking for the perfect dance partner for two years and hasn't found her." She frowns. "Though I can't believe Danika let him in here after the scandal."

I have no idea what the *Bachelor* is and can't imagine what sort of scandal that old-fashioned romantic boy could get into. But it's all pointless for me.

"It doesn't matter," I say. "And PLEASE don't tell anybody he kissed my hand. If my father found out, I couldn't come here anymore."

Aurora's eyes get sad, an expression I'm used to when people realize my situation. "Livia, you're nineteen. Can't you just try to get out of that house? Live your life?"

I've heard this too. "I will," I say. "I just have to figure things out." I head to the corner and pick up my bag. If this Blitz guy is going to be here, I should probably avoid the academy except when I'm in class. My dance is important to me, and the last thing I need is some reality TV Romeo jeopardizing it.

Even if he is the most thrilling thing that's happened to me in a long time.

# Chapter Two

I'm a frazzled mess of nerves as I wait in Studio 3 the next morning for the little dancers to arrive. I pray nobody has talked about me or Blitz. I want all that to go away.

I lift my ankle to the barre and lean into a stretch. I don't really need to warm up for this class. The girls require a lot of help, and I do more encouragement than dance. But it passes the time.

The first dance student arrives, Marissa, a six-year-old with a riotous head of honey-blond curls. Her mother wheels her in, smiling to see me.

Marissa sits up a little straighter, but I can see by the strain in her smile that she's had a rough night. She's weaker than usual, listing against one side of the wheelchair. She has cerebral palsy, and some days are tougher than others.

"I've got her," I say to her mother.

"I'll be outside," she says. "She's not quite one hundred percent today."

I don't ask questions, just push Marissa to the center of the room and face her to the mirror. "We'll start with some arm positions while we wait for the others," I say. "I'll turn on the music."

As I head to the corner, Janel, the instructor, rushes in. "Thank you, Livia," she says as the music fills the room. "Marissa, how are you today?" Even though she asks, I see by the concern in her expression that she also recognizes Marissa's lack of energy.

"I'm okay," Marissa says, but we know better.

"I'll help her with arms today," I say to Janel.

Two more of our students arrive at the same time, one powering her chair, the other pushing the wheels on hers. They are all smiles and excitement, bright in hot pink and vivid purple tutus that explode off the seats like blossoms.

Janel greets them and helps them fall into line beside Marissa.

The fourth and fifth girls also arrive. I struggle to pay attention to our warm-ups as well as the open door to the studio. I can't help but wonder if Blitz is still here somewhere, if he's doing whatever got Aurora so worked up.

I try to shake him from my mind as I adjust the

girls' arms to mimic Janel's position. Marissa can't lift her right arm at all today, so I gently hold it in place.

When the first song ends, I realize Gabriella isn't here yet, and all thought of Blitz is eclipsed by my concern over her absence. Janel continues to take the girls through a simple dance, turning in a circle. The whir of electric motors and squeak of rubber on the floor punctuates the whimsical tune of the music.

When we pause for a moment, I ask Janel, "Did we hear from Gabriella's mom?"

Janel shakes her head no. "Let's practice our recital number!" she announces.

I have to rush to line up the girls in their spots. They will be dancing to "Flight of the Sugar Plum Fairy" in the Christmas show, their first public appearance together. I'm beyond excited. I fought for the class, pestering Danika about it until she relented, and personally made fliers and sent them around until we filled a class.

But the little girl I did it all for isn't here today. Gabriella's mother didn't enroll her right away, and I had begun to despair she would ever show until one day, she wheeled in. That was pretty much the best day of my life.

Where could she be? I always fretted over these girls. They were so vulnerable to illness, complications, and setbacks. Gabriella's spinal cord injury was caused by a car accident a year ago, and she's grown stronger as she's taken the class. But I worry. Always.

I've just gotten the last girl into place when I hear, "So sorry to be late."

My shoulders relax in relief. It's Gwen, Gabriella's mother. I turn to them, Gabriella merrily pushing herself into the room. She's four years old and a spitfire. Her hair is exactly like mine, dark and thick. Gwen has twisted it on top of her head and fastened it with a sequin scrunchie.

My heart clenches as it always does when she arrives. I hurry over and wave Gabriella into her position in the line. Gwen heads out. The music begins, and time flies as I help the girls maneuver into their places.

Janel has been clever in the design of the dance so that the girls who can't propel themselves are situated at the heart of the formation and don't need to move their chairs to make the choreography work.

My pride surges as I watch Gabriella curve her arms and turn her chair in time with the song. She's smart and quick to learn. I wonder how different her life would have been if she had not gone to live with Gwen, if she hadn't been in that car with her adopted father when it crashed into a semi, killing him and injuring her tiny spine.

None of that would have happened if I had been stronger. If I'd stood up to my own parents.

If I'd never let them take my newborn daughter away.

## Chapter Three

We're only halfway through the song when Blitz arrives.

I'm lifting Marissa's arm for her, keeping her in time with the others, when I see the movement in the mirror.

Janel spots him too. She stops, momentarily shocked into stillness. "Is that Blitz Craven?" she asks. "In my dance class?"

I gently lower Marissa's arm. I can't say anything. My voice seems to be stuck.

He's wearing black jazz pants and another white sleeveless shirt. Every muscle in his body is defined.

He hesitates when he catches sight of the wheelchairs. He steps back outside the door and glances at the painted placard outside that reads Studio 3.

Janel breaks out of whatever paralysis she's in and

asks, "Are you lost?" The music plays on, but the girls all falter without prompting from their teacher.

Blitz realizes he's interrupting. "Danika told me Studio 3. Beginner ballet."

"Well, this is it," she says. "Do you have a dancer to enroll?"

He steps back inside the room, his grin sheepish. "I don't have any kids."

"He's from *Dance Blitz*," I hiss. At least my voice is back.

Blitz snaps to me, seeming to just now notice I'm there. He looks disappointed. "You know?" he asks.

"I do now," I say. "I'm sorry I've never seen your show."

This amuses him. His smile is like the sun coming out from behind a cloud. Even the young girls turn toward it, as if they are flowers seeking light.

Danika, the owner of Dreamcatcher, swishes inside, her skirt fluttering behind her. The lights overhead brighten her short buzzed blue hair, a style she's kept since fighting cancer a few years ago.

"Ah, you found it," she says and claps her hands for attention. "Janel, Livia, girls," she gazes fondly at all the dancers in their chairs. "This is Benjamin."

I realize Blitz must just be a stage name. Of course. Nobody names their baby Blitz.

The girls chorus a hello.

"Benjamin will assist as you prepare for the

holiday recital. He's a professional dancer, and very excited to help you all with your performance."

The girls giggle. Blitz looks at each of them, his expression carefully neutral. I don't know what he's thinking. If they are a waste of his time, or if Danika is out to make him miserable.

Fire burns in my belly. In my book, this is the most important class at Dreamcatcher Academy. He better not upset these girls, most of all Gabriella. I resist the urge to move closer to her. Nobody knows she is my daughter. No one in the entire world, not even my best friend Mindy, knows I found her and set up this class just to be near her.

No one *can* know. It's the only way I get to have her in my life at all.

My throat is so tight that I can barely swallow.

Blitz takes in all the girls, and then his gaze rests on me. Something ticks in his jaw. I have that naked feeling all over again as he scrutinizes my white leotard, pale yellow skirt, and white tights. Now I understand why my father forced me into baggy clothes for so long. He anticipated a moment like this.

He's ignored Janel, who is way more beautiful than me, so I guess I'm more his type. He's bound to be very experienced if he's on television. Women probably fall at his feet.

But I don't feel alarmed or concerned. I'm not

totally naive. I might have been fifteen when Gabriella was born, way too young for all that transpired, but her conception did not come about by anything traumatic or painful. Wrong, perhaps, the worst kind of wrong by most books, but I still hold those memories close.

And they are coming forward now. Skin. Heat. That buzz of attraction and need in my belly. Blitz's interest burns into me, heating up key places I was forced to forget about.

But now there is Blitz. Apparently he's staying.

Danika moves forward. "I'll be here today as we get started." She takes Blitz by the arm and turns him, as if he's a child in need of guidance. I can see in her expression that she might be questioning her decision to bring him close to me, possibly thinking of my father and his overbearing protectiveness.

"These are some of our most prized pupils, Benjamin," Danika says. She introduces each girl. When she gets to Gabriella, my heart squeezes. "Little Gabby is our newest ballerina. She's a quick study and already knows all the basic positions."

Gabriella beams up at Blitz. Little sprigs of black hair frame her face, tiny curls that escaped the sequin-wrapped bun. Sometimes I'm shocked other people don't recognize how much she looks like me, but maybe it's only because I know. Everyone else assumes Gwen is her biological mother. She never mentions the adoption and Gwen's dark brown hair seems close enough.

But Blitz looks down at Gabriella and back to me and back again. I see him noting something and I wonder if he's guessed. Panic rises in my belly, but then he moves on and I shake it off. Nobody would guess that someone as young as I am could have a four-year-old child.

I flash for a moment to the hospital, the ripping pain, the fear, the clucking disapproving nurses, and my parents' embarrassment and shame. I have to shove it from my thoughts.

"Let me start the music again," Janel says. "Girls! Back to your starting positions!"

I help settle the dancers. Danika and Blitz stand near the mirror, watching. We run through the entire routine. I rush from girl to girl, having to let go of Marissa to make sure Daisy moves aside before she blocks Gabriella's turn.

When the song is done, Blitz claps heartily. "That's great," he says. He approaches the girls. "You're Daisy, right?" he asks.

Daisy beams that he knows her. "Yes," she says. "Whose daddy are you?"

"Well, if you ask my lawyers, they'll tell you I have defended fifteen paternity lawsuits," Blitz says.

"Benjamin," Danika says, a warning note in her tone.

"Right, right," he says. "I am no one's daddy. May I take your arm and show you something?"

Daisy holds out her arm.

Blitz encircles her wrist with his fingers and shakes her arm gently. "Wiggle your sillies out," he says with more goofiness than any of us expected. "Turn your arm into a noodle, and then you will get a beautiful curve." He lifts her arm into fourth position.

I wonder if he knows more ballet than he let on, or if he's just picked up some form from his show. I'll have to find a way to watch it. I'm desperately curious.

When Daisy makes her arm go straight, he grasps her wrist and jiggles it again. "Beautiful relaxed curve," he reminds her.

His voice is like a drug. The girls are all rapt, just listening and watching, even though this is the sort of correction we've all done a thousand times to beginning ballerinas.

Daisy's arm bends slightly, this time too angular. Blitz shakes her arm out one more time.

The curve falls more naturally.

"That's it!" Blitz says. "Now drop your arm."

Daisy lowers her hand to her lap.

"Now back," Blitz says.

Her arm isn't quite right, but after a quick shake, she's in position again. They do this several times until her arm goes into a nice curve straightaway.

"Keep practicing," he says. "Your arms are your superpower, so make them shine."

He turns to Gabriella and my breath catches. "You next?" he asks her and she nods.

Behind me, Janel asks, "Is he in charge now?"

Danika says, "Only as much as you want him to be."

Janel steps forward. "We'll have individual ballerinas work with Blitz — Benjamin — while the rest of us continue practicing our timing with the music," she says.

The other girls turn back to Janel. I come up behind Gabriella. "You want to move over near the barre?" I ask her. I can't manage to frame a direct question to Blitz. I'm running hot and cold, torn between protecting her and my secret, and the memory of the charming boy he was yesterday.

It's a lot to manage.

"Great idea," Blitz says. He moves as if to push Gabriella by the handles, but she snatches her wheels and darts forward.

He straightens, surprised, and catches my eye.

"She's a zoomer," I say with a shrug.

We walk toward her, away from the group, as alone as you can get in a room full of girls. He quietly asks, "So none of these girls can walk?"

"That's why they are in wheelchairs," I say.

"But they can use their arms."

"Each girl has a different level of movement and control," I explain. "We choreograph around it, same as you'd play to the strengths and weaknesses of any dancer."

He stops walking and waits for me to pause and turn back to him.

"This is a really special class," he says.

"Of course it is," I say, maybe a little more haughtily than I intend, and head toward Gabriella.

He rushes to catch up. "Is this one your sister?"

That panic rushes through me again. Behind us, the music restarts and Janel begins talking the girls through their movements. I take this as my cue to ignore his question.

When we get to Gabriella, Blitz says, "Show me the arm movements, and I'll stop you when I see something we can work on."

"Okay," Gabriella says shyly. She maneuvers her chair so she can see Janel and picks up the dance in the middle. I'm proud of how she can just pop in and still fall into the flow of the dance. She's smart.

Her arms sway left and right, and she reaches down to turn her chair at the right moment, then lifts her arm again.

Blitz watches, his hand on his chin, rubbing his cheek with his fingers. I find myself staring, wondering about the feel of that stubble, when he stops Gabriella.

"Okay, I see a couple places where you can choose a slightly different moment to reach for your chair in the turn, and get a little more arm movement in."

I step away, realizing I can be better used with the main group. But I feel a little in awe of him. He's actually saying things that make sense, and the dance will be better with his close attention, whether he really knows ballet or not.

Even as I walk toward the other girls, I watch the two of them in the mirror. Seeing my daughter with this man does something to my heart that makes it feel like it's only just now started to beat again.

## Chapter Four

As the mothers enter the studio to fetch their daughters, I hang back in the corner near the sound system. Some of them know Blitz and stop to talk with him and indulge their curiosity. His star power is striking. Almost all of them get flirty, tucking their hair behind their ears and giggling like girls half their age.

I have to turn away, although I do glance surreptitiously in the mirror to see if Gwen is like that. She's actually single, unlike the others. It's been well over a year since the accident, and she hasn't dated anyone, at least not as far as I can see from stalking her Facebook page. She's still deeply mourning her husband.

But she is the most straightforward of the mothers, thanking Blitz for spending time with her daughter and following a glowing Gabriella out of the room.

Janel sets up for the next class, and Danika heads to the foyer to greet the parents, as is her custom during the transition. Blitz stands at the door, watching the girls wheel out.

I linger in the corner, not feeling brave enough to pass by him. I'm done for today, and Blitz has already been too observant, asking if Gabriella is my sister. Hopefully seeing her with Gwen will end those questions. I have the poker face of a dandelion, and there is no doubt in my mind that he'll guess all my secrets in five minutes if he asks me anything directly.

A few dancers file in, part of Janel's beginner ballet for preschool-aged girls. They are adorable and look up at Blitz with giggles and smiles. Even if they don't recognize him as a famous person, his charisma tugs on their young hearts.

Janel motions them inside. "Warm up at the barre, girls." She notices Blitz is still there. "Are you working with this class too?"

He shakes his head. "I don't think so. Danika only gave me one per day." His eyes meet mine and I quickly look away, tugging self-consciously at my skirt. It's sheer and has a tiny mend in it that I always try to hide.

"We meet again," he says, his voice as silky as melted chocolate.

I risk a tiny glance and regret it, as his earnest attention is like a powerful potion. I want more of it, all of it. "Yes," I say, my own voice soft and nervous.

He holds out his elbow in another old-fashioned gesture, as if I would ever have the courage to take it. "Can I interest you in a tour? I need to know my way around."

When I don't move, he lowers his arm. "Unless you're assisting in this class too."

I shake my head no.

Janel looks between us. "That shark will definitely bite, Livia," she says. "I don't blame you for staying out of the water."

Blitz places both hands over his heart. His fingers are long, and I'm shocked at the places I imagine them going. My face flames red. But I'm not an innocent girl, not like everyone here thinks. I've felt what fingers can do.

"I'm injured," he says to Janel. "My intentions are strictly honorable."

Janel snorts, sending the ballerina girls to giggling. "Livia, can you at least get him out of here?"

I nod and head toward the door. It's easier to follow the command of an instructor than to say yes to Blitz. There's no guilt involved, no worry.

Blitz holds the door open for me. I slip through it and move past another mother-daughter pair about to go inside. This woman recognizes Blitz instantly, and despite the oversized diamond on her finger, she sidles up ridiculously close. "Blitz Craven? From *Dance Blitz*? Oh, my lucky stars!"

Her drawl is never that thick on ordinary days. She's so close to him that her rather impressive chest brushes against his dance tank.

"We were just heading out," Blitz says, although he's grinning as if making every female forget her husband is the stuff his good days are made of.

Despite the fact that I'm just as smitten as the rest of them, I manage to keep my chin high and flounce to the other side of the wide hallway.

Dance Mom doesn't really want to let Blitz go, and her fingers trail along his muscled arm as he follows me. But her daughter is mortified, five years old and already sick of how her mother acts. She pulls her away and into the dance studio.

There's a rush of girls and moms as the transition goes into full swing. "Probably not the best time for a tour," I say. "You might get mobbed."

"Where does that go?" he asks, pointing to the double doors at the end of the hall.

"Just storage," I say.

"Sounds perfect," he says, just as another mother recognizes him and looks ready to pounce. He jerks open the door and grabs my hand to pull me through.

I'm startled to the core to feel his fingers on

mine. It feels so forbidden, so daring, like the love I once felt and lost. Like Gabriella.

My chest goes totally tight, making it hard to breathe. As we pass through the door and Blitz closes it behind us, I jerk away from his hand. I can't let him think he's affected me, even though he has. Just not for the reasons he might believe.

My breath comes in wheezes. The dust doesn't help. Soon I'm sneezing and coughing. Blitz hammers my back.

"You okay, Princess?" he asks.

Princess? Where did that come from? I force my breath to slow until I can take in air easily.

The light is dim, just the shafts beaming in from the high windows along the back wall. "The switch is over there," I tell him.

He looks around. "I sort of like it this way."

He wanders among the ghostly shadows of the equipment. Small trampolines, stacks of mats, props, and racks of costumes fill the space. He picks up a top hat from a shelf and tilts it rakishly on his head.

"It suits you," I say.

Of course it does. Everything does.

He rummages through costumes in clear plastic bags, then triumphantly holds up a scarlet corset. "This has you written all over it."

My face flushes. I'm glad for the low light, as my cheeks probably match the color of the fabric.

"I don't think so," I say.

"Oh, but I insist." He heads toward me, expertly unhooking the ornate fasteners down the front.

Everything about this sets me on fire. His expression. The hat. His bare arms, the shadows of his cut muscles in the half dark. He circles behind me to fit the corset around my middle, and I'm burning up from the heat of his nearness.

The boning fits snugly against my ribs. When he latches the first hook, his knuckles brush the undersides of my breasts.

I'm completely on fire. I want to back away, but my feet refuse to move. My breathing is shallow, and he has to know how I'm feeling. He's so experienced. There is no telling how many of the women on his show he's been with.

He grins at me as he works his way down. He's so close, I can study his face, the shadowed jaw, firm lips, dark brows. His hair has a little curl to it, just enough to make the short cut fall in a wave. He concentrates on the hooks, his eyes down. He's touching me. Blitz Craven has his hands all over me.

The corset tightens around my middle as he works, sending another rush of heat on a path to my belly. When he's finally done, he goes around to the back to tighten the strings.

I want to ask him where he learned to fit a corset, but my throat is too tight for words. I'd sound like a strangled mouse. So I just stand there, listening to the whisper of the cords sliding through the metal grommets. It's sexy, him dressing me, as if we're a couple and he's preparing me to go out onstage to perform.

Or maybe to wear something just for him.

He pats my shoulder. "All set, Princess."

I inhale a deep breath and realize he hasn't cinched it too tight. I can take in air.

"I need something more formal," he says. He rummages through the rack again and comes up with a jacket with tails in the back. When he slips it on, my heart speeds up. He's really something in the formal getup, even with the jazz pants. Or maybe *because* of the jazz pants, tight around his waist and thighs, loose around the ankles. Black as night, a complement to the jacket.

But he knows it. He whirls in a circle, his shoulders a blur, the tails flying, then halts, arm out, hand reaching for me.

"I only do ballet," I say. I don't know steps for contemporary dance, or jazz, or anything else. I've never danced with a partner.

"And you're amazing," he says. He runs forward, arm still outstretched, and takes my hand.

The world spins as he turns me around, then suddenly I'm in his arms, leaning on my back. He holds me inside the crook of his elbow.

I look up, and that's it. I get it. His star power, why he has his own show. It's that look. That grin. God, he's sexy. You can forget everything when somebody holds your gaze like that. As if you're the only woman in the world. The most beautiful. And he has eyes for no one but you.

Except I did that before. I fell just like this. And it was more forbidden than this. The most forbidden thing that exists. It destroyed my family, wrecked my carefree life.

I swallow hard, my grip on Blitz's arm like a vise.

He recognizes the change in me and lets me up. "The corset really suits you," he says. His eyes drop to my cleavage.

I look down. I do actually have cleavage. That's not usual. I'm sort of slight, but the boning pushes out what little is there so that it seems to be overflowing. The sight of it sends another zing through me. Blitz is admiring me. *Blitz Craven. Me.*

Now that I'm vertical again, I unfasten the hooks on the corset as fast as my fingers will let me. My family expects me home to check in before doing a volunteer shift in the church office. I can get away with a small delay, but I've used it up.

"I can't really do a tour right now," I say. I fold the corset nervously. "I'm expected somewhere."

Blitz removes the top hat. "Can I take a rain check on that?" He holds his arm out for the corset and I pass it to him. But his eyes never leave mine, keeping me in their gravitational pull.

I have to look away before I can force my feet to move me toward the door. "I — I won't be here again until Friday afternoon," I say. It's only Tuesday. "You'll know your way around by then."

He carefully sets the costumes back on the rack and shrugs out of the jacket. "I'll save myself for you."

"O—okay." He can't mean that. And he can't be interested in me, of all people. There are tons of beautiful dancers here. Suze is single. And Betsy. He can have flings with them. I can't afford to lose the little freedom I've gained by being caught with him. Even the storage closet was a bad idea.

So I don't even say good-bye. I just turn and jerk open the door to fly home.

## Chapter Five

I spend lunch with my parents, trying desperately to shake free of the feeling of being in Blitz's arms. By the time I start the short walk down the block to the church for my volunteer work, I've given up trying to change the subject in my head.

I'll just have to mindlessly file papers and obsess about him.

The weather is warm and beautiful, a perfect fall day. San Antonio has been a good home these past four years, away from the memories of Houston and all that happened there. I give in to the urge to spin in a circle, arms outstretched.

An elderly lady walking her dog smiles at me, probably amused by my energy and youth. I feel young today, like I'm supposed to, despite the heaviness of my life.

I have very little contact with the outside world. Even now, walking down the street to the church with fewer than one hundred members, my father is undoubtedly out on the porch, ensuring that I don't bump into some miscreant boy on the way, as if someone could impregnate me with a greeting.

But I can't be contained. I'm happy, excited, charged up by my encounter with Blitz. It's so rare I meet someone new. I half walk, half skip as I circle around to the side of the building and go straight into the church office.

The secretary is the only person in the building on a Tuesday afternoon, as it's the day the priest visits shut-ins, mostly elderly parishioners in nursing homes or who no longer leave their houses. I'm in charge of much of the paperwork, and I know from filing it that we have as many members who can't make services as we do those who actually show up on any given Sunday.

When I arrive, Irma is digging through the bottom drawer of her desk, her chestnut hair in a sloppy topknot. She's forty or so and always dresses in paisley pastel dresses. I know her entire wardrobe.

She rolls her chair back the moment she sees me and says, "I'm forwarding the phone to the back, I have to run to the dentist!" She shoves the drawer closed with her foot. One thing Irma has going for her, she always looks busy, even when there is absolutely nothing to do.

"That's fine," I say. "I'll hold down the fort."

Irma punches the buttons to send calls to the telephone in the library storage room.

"You'll get two calls if you're lucky," she says.

"Has Crazy Eddie already checked in today?" I ask.

Irma laughs. "Yeah. Ten minutes of telling me about the Virgin Mary on his toast this morning."

"He used that one again?" Eddie is eighty-five and loves to find holy images in his breakfast food.

"Yes, he's recycling," Irma says. She slings her purse over her shoulder. "I'll be back in an hour."

As she leaves, I'm torn between actually doing my work and sneaking a search for Blitz on the Internet. There's really nothing I do here that has to be done on a deadline. Of course I'm going to look him up.

When she's out the door, I jerk open her top drawer and pull out a set of keys to the electronics cabinet. It holds the wireless microphone the priest uses during Mass, a projector, and a laptop.

I pull out the ancient Dell and hurry back to the storage room. Then I remember the alarm and go back to the office and set the small console on the door to beep in the back room if someone comes in. I'm supposed to do this anytime there's no one at the front desk, but it also keeps me from being discovered with the computer.

When I'm safely in the storage room, hidden between two shelving units, I crack open the laptop. It's not used for much as far as I can tell, but it still connects to the Internet. I'm forbidden from anything like this at home, but my friend Mindy, who is sixteen and also volunteers at the church, showed me how to turn it on and do searches.

I type in "Blitz Craven." I'm instantly rewarded with dozens of pictures, links, and video clips from his show. Where to start?

There are images of Blitz with all sorts of women. Blond. Brunette. Every skin color and body style. He definitely doesn't seem to have a type.

There are stills from his show, a stage lit up with colored lights, him dancing with all manner of partners. I recognize some of the girls in dance costumes and out in street clothes, always on his arm. So he dates the women on his show too, sees them off camera.

I guess I can start at the beginning. I click on the Wikipedia entry for *Dance Blitz*. It says:

An American reality show where the star, Blitz Craven, auditions women to be both his dance partner and his future wife.

Wife?

Whoa.

There are references to the *Bachelor*, which Aurora mentioned, and *Dancing with the Stars*. Apparently they were templates for the new show. Each season of *Dance Blitz* starts with twenty-five dancers. Blitz trains each of them to be his partner and eliminates several each week.

At the end of season one, he got down to three girls and decided none of them would do. The show was so popular that he got a second season to try again.

So why was he at a small dance academy in San Antonio?

I see a section titled "Twitter Scandal" and scroll down. Now my heart is hammering.

Just weeks before the big finale to season two, which was supposed to be a live televised event, Blitz's Twitter account posted a photo of a naked woman with the caption "Ate me like a gorilla."

My face flames. I can't imagine the Blitz I met saying or doing any of these things.

The woman was one of three final contestants scheduled to be on his show. She filed an invasion of privacy lawsuit. The Tweet went viral. The show's sponsors pulled out, and every feminist group in the world called for his head on a platter. He apologized publicly, but it did nothing to stem the damage. The network suspended the show indefinitely.

Yikes.

I compare this description of Blitz to the charming man who held out his hand to me and it doesn't fit. But then, there was the corset in the storage closet. That definitely seemed like a Blitz move.

There's another tab that draws my eye.

"Censored episodes."

I click on the link.

It's a video of the second episode of season two. I glance around the room. I'm at church of all places, watching *Dance Blitz*. But I can't help myself.

I press play.

A black stage is suddenly illuminated with a single light on a red satin bed. A woman is sprawled on it in a black gown.

Blitz arrives and they begin a dramatic dance on and around the bed. They do a dang convincing job of simulating sex and in a flash, Blitz jerks the dress off her, revealing a black bra and a very tiny pair of underwear with no back.

They dance a little more, then the video abruptly ends.

What happened?

I go back to the Wikipedia article.

Apparently in a bid to avoid being eliminated, this dancer continued to strip all the way, but naturally that part hadn't been aired. A few images were leaked, but the article doesn't have any.

I want to see them, not because of her, but for him. I want to see his expression. How he felt about her.

If it was the same way he looked at me in the storage room.

I type in "censored Dance Blitz" and click on a few links. I don't get anything useful right away, but finally buried in a thread I find some embedded images that haven't been deleted.

These were taken by cell phones of audience members watching the show as it was recorded. Heat rushes to my face to see the naked woman, arms in the air, flaunting herself in front of Blitz.

He looks ready to eat her up. His expression is wolfish, his eyes devouring her. Parts of me burn that I haven't paid any attention to in a long time. I wonder what happened after this moment and scroll through the comments. Someone came and wrapped her in a robe, apparently, but there are no images. The people posting are only interested in the naked woman.

And no, that isn't anything like how he looked at me. He was mischievous, charming, cute. When I moved away, he was a downright gentleman. He never pushed.

I scroll back up and look at him, then her, then him.

I sit back, my breathing faster than I expected.

My body is so hot. Images of Blitz collide with feelings I once knew, ways I once felt. I was so young then, though, barely figuring out what went where. But the urgency is the same. The need.

The beep beep beep of the door opening sends me into a panic. It's only been fifteen minutes! My hands slam the laptop shut and slide it under the shelves.

Assuming Irma has forgotten something and might pop her head through the doorway, I snatch a box of newsletters and begin flipping through them.

After a moment, I realize it could be someone else coming in, so I stand up to investigate. I'm almost to the door when Mindy charges through, nearly running smack into me.

"Oh!" she says. "Livia!"

I press my hand against my chest and laugh. "What are you doing here on a Tuesday?"

"My mom told your mom that the secretary was going to be gone while you were here. Naturally, they sent me to make sure you didn't do anything naughty!"

We both dissolve into laughter at the thought of Mindy making sure I stayed straight. She was the only reason I ever defied my parents' orders.

Mindy looks around the storage room. She's dressed a lot like me, loose jeans, plain sweater, no makeup, simple hair. Hers is light brown. She's home-schooled too.

"At least Mom didn't come up here herself," I say. "You are not going to BELIEVE who showed up at the dance academy."

"Blitz Craven!" she says.

"What?" My face floods with shock. "How?"

"It was all over the local news. He's helping underprivileged dancers realize their dreams!"

"What did they show?"

"Just him talking at some press thing. He wasn't at the academy yet."

My elation collapses. "Did your mother tell mine about that?" My mind races. If my parents find out about Blitz, they might stop me from helping with the wheelchair ballerinas. Then I won't get to see Gabriella!

"She didn't," Mindy assures me. "I don't think she knows. She doesn't pay attention to stuff like that."

"They'll take me out of dance classes for sure if they know someone like Blitz is there," I say.

"I get it," she says. "I know."

Mindy doesn't know about Gabriella. I've considered telling her a dozen times, but I just can't. It's too big a secret. My parents have never spoken of their granddaughter and have forbidden me to bring her up. I love Mindy and being rebellious with her, but giving my baby up for adoption is not something I can talk to anybody about.

"Are you sneaking Internet?" Mindy asks, glancing around for the telltale laptop.

"I was!" I say. "I found censored images of Blitz Craven!"

"You didn't!" Mindy plops onto the floor. "How?"

I sit next to her and pull the laptop back out from beneath the shelf. "There was a dance they had to edit because the dancer stripped naked," I say.

"Show me, show me, show me."

Her eagerness is childlike, and I know we're being immature and silly. We're both sheltered, living in a bubble of homeschool and church created by our families. Mom found Mindy's mother through a homeschool group and eventually recruited the family to our church. Mindy also has a younger brother, so they can all congratulate themselves on socializing us even while keeping us away from the evils of public school.

But while Mindy has more access to media and the outside world, I had the benefit of a normal life up until I got pregnant. So we can swap stories, her regaling me with current movies and world news, and me explaining what it was like to have P.E. and sit next to boys in darkened classrooms.

I show Mindy the image and she squeals. "Oh my God, look at those boobs!" She presses her hands against her chest. "Is there anything showing more of Blitz?"

I hadn't even thought of that. My fingers click back up to the search box and my body flushes as I type the words "Blitz Craven naked."

Results begin appearing. Blitz has done a million nude shoots, it seems, although they are all proper, for magazines. Still, we click on one after the other, Blitz stretching on a stage in nothing but his own skin, leg carefully blocking the goods. Laughing as he's surrounded by women in leotards, probably contestants on his show. They cover him with their hands. And one particularly sexy one on a black leather sofa, a satin sheet wound across his hips.

I can't take my eyes off him. This man was dancing with me just an hour ago.

"Man," Mindy says. "He's really something. So what happened?"

I tell her about meeting him, and the ballet class and the corset in the storage room.

She starts fanning her face. "Oh my God! You were alone with Blitz Craven in the dark?"

I nod, the memory of it flooding back to me.

"Are you going to see him again?"

"I guess," I say. "I don't know which classes he's doing. But next week, for sure."

Mindy stands up and paces back and forth. "This is incredible! Imagine! My friend and Blitz

Craven!" She drops down beside me again. "How old is he?"

I check the Wikipedia entry. "Twenty-six," I say.

"You're nineteen," she says. "That's not bad."

I shove her shoulder. "Blitz Craven and I are not going to be a thing," I say.

"You don't know that," she insists. "It sounds like he was flirting with you pretty hard."

"I guess." I don't know. This is where my experience is definitely lacking. I've never had a proper boyfriend. I couldn't call Gabriella's father that. I've never been flirted with, not by anyone as old and experienced as Blitz, for sure.

"He probably acts like that with everyone," I say, gesturing at the pictures. "He's known for liking tons of women."

Mindy takes the laptop and types in "Blitz Craven girlfriend."

The hits go on and on. Picture after picture of him with one woman or another. Getting out of limos. Walking on red carpets. Dancing. Kissing. Holding their hands up as if to ward off the photographer.

"Look at this," Mindy says. "Rumor is that Blitz slept with as many as twenty of the contestants on his show." She looks up at me. "Twenty!"

She leans back against the cabinet, her knees tucked to her chest. "I wonder if he's any good or if they flock to him no matter what because of who he is."

I can't think about this. The idea of these other women makes me a little crazy.

Mindy sits up suddenly. "You could find out!" Then she frowns. "Except you have nothing to compare it to!"

My face heats up. I want to tell her I do, but I can't do that. She'd want more details than I'm prepared to provide. I don't want to risk getting caught by looking any longer, so I type in "Most famous hymns" in the search box. I click and click on a bunch of links like Mindy taught me. When everything in the recent history looks good, I shut it down and close the lid.

"Blitz Craven," Mindy says with a sigh. "This is the most exciting thing that's ever happened to me, and it's not even happening to me."

I lie back on the flat carpet of the storage space and stare up at the water-stained ceiling. "I don't know anything about how long he'll be there or if he'll even look at me again," I say.

But I do know one thing. I'm not supposed to have class again until Friday, but I'm going back to Dreamcatcher tomorrow.

## Chapter Six

Danika keeps a studio room open most mornings for dance students who want to use a space to work on their recital routines. That's where I was on Monday when Blitz found me.

So the next morning, I dress in my best light blue leotard and skirt — one without any mended tears — and head to the living room to tell my mother I want to get in an extra practice this week.

It should be fine, because my father always meets his friend Larry for lunch on Wednesdays, so he won't be home asking what I did that morning. Mom is fanatical about telling the truth and prefers the answer to be "some chores around the house and studied for her SAT." This gets an approving nod.

I'm not sure I'll get to go to college, but I like

studying for the test and thinking about a future away from my family.

And there's Gabriella to consider. My situation is perfect for seeing her.

There's no need to change things. The transition from home high school to studying for the college admissions test has been seamless. Other than a cake with a graduation cap on it six months ago, my life has been no different for four years. Only the grade levels on the booklets ever changed anyway.

Mom looks up from the pie crust she is rolling out. "You're dressed for dance. You going up there?"

"Just getting a little extra practice in. I really want those *pointe* shoes."

She pauses. Her hair has bits of gray in it, twisted in the elaborate braid that she favors. She wears an old pair of jeans and a Houston Rockets T-shirt. Seeing the shirt sends a bolt of nostalgia through me. Our old life. Watching basketball games on TV with other families. Picnics. Movies. Going to the beach at Galveston.

Dad flipped so hard after the baby, after everything. He became a different person than he was before. Controlling. Angry. Disturbed. It's hard to blame him. We all lost so much.

"How long will you be gone?"

"Just an hour, probably, less than two for sure." I pick up an apple from the fruit bowl and take a big bite. Mom watches me, her hands on the rolling pin, the dough still thick on a cloud of flour.

"All right. Just be sure to come back in time to do some studying. Your dad will ask."

I nod in agreement. I think my mom probably wants to end my house arrest, but she doesn't go against my dad. I think she has plenty of reason to, maybe even to leave him. But after the baby, our whole family took a turn for the religious, as if getting our church on would erase all the terrible things that happened.

It's a small church and very old-fashioned. Mom has fallen in step with everyone there, deferring to Dad as the "captain of the ship." The Rockets T-shirt is possibly her only form of protest, although I'm betting she put it on after Dad left for work and will change it before he gets home. She doesn't like confrontations. The last big one in our family almost destroyed it. She's careful. She teaches me to be careful, too.

My eight-year-old brother Andy comes in, arms full of books. "Science test today," he says with a grimace. "Will you help me?"

I ruffle his hair. "After lunch, okay?"

He looks at Mom. "Can we take it after lunch?"

She gives him a half smile. "Only if you study hard until then."

"Do a good job, Buddy," I say to him.

I pick up my bag by the door and leave the house.

I'm out. Free!

The walk to Dreamcatcher is exhilarating. I feel so full of joy and energy. I wish I hadn't panicked so much when Blitz took me in his arms. It was just a dance move. I could have kissed him! Imagine! We were safe enough in the storage room. What could happen at a dance academy?

I'm determined when I see him today to be bold and not freak out. In fact, I tug at the pins holding my hair in a tight dance bun and let it fall free. It floats against my shoulders and tickles my arms. I feel different, less trapped. Lovely.

I picture dancing alone with him again, and this time accepting his kiss, and I squeal loud enough to disturb the squirrels in the tree overhead. They treat me to a shower of brown leaves.

"Sorry!" I call out, but I'm not the least bit sorry at all. As I approach the academy, my feet fairly fly up the steps to the front door.

Suze looks up from the desk. "Extra practice today?" she asks.

"Yes," I answer, my face falling at the empty foyer. But of course Blitz wouldn't be out here. If he's at Dreamcatcher at all, he'll be in one of the rooms. I just have to go look.

"How full is the practice room today?" I ask.

"Just Cassidy and Allen, going over their ballroom routine."

I didn't know Cassidy had a partner now. Another man at Dreamcatcher! Thankfully they wouldn't be at the recital for Dad to see.

But their dance will take up a lot of space. I'll be confined to the barre to avoid bumping into them. "Anything else open?"

Suze clicks on the keyboard. "The other three studios are in use. But you could go on the recital stage if you want. Danika is in there so the lights are on."

Hmm. I definitely want to go down the hall and peek into the other rooms. Maybe I can warm up in the studio and then move on to the recital stage.

"Thanks," I tell Suze. I grip the strap of the string bag that holds my ballet shoes. I should ask her if Blitz is here, but I can't bring myself to do it. I don't want to be disappointed, but more than that, I don't want to tip Suze off that I'm interested in him. They will talk.

The hall is quiet in the middle of the hour. I peek into the window of Studio 1. Aurora is there with her baby ballerinas, toddlers in tutus who mostly roll around on the floor. The moms all sit against the wall, ready to redirect their child, kiss a boo-boo, or change a diaper.

I don't see this class often, as it's my off day, but

today I pause, watching the mothers snap pictures of their little girls. I missed this part of Gabriella's life completely. I didn't discover where she was until she was almost three. Then it was another year before she arrived for the wheelchair ballerina class. She couldn't know who I was. That would be the worst of all.

I cherish my one hour a week with Gabriella and I won't endanger it. My parents would flip for sure, maybe even move us again. That alone is enough to keep me quiet about who I am.

I just wish I had been there for the years I missed. When Gabriella learned to smile, crawl, and take her first steps. And her last ones. I'm not sure of her condition exactly, but if she isn't walking a year after the accident, I can only assume she never will again. That doesn't mean I don't pray for miracles.

I move across the hall to Studio 2. This is a jazz class taught by Jacob. He's something to behold, a frenetic ball of energy. He's showing the students a move that involves a leaping turn in the air, arms outstretched. These children are also small, boys and girls approaching kindergarten age. It's morning on a weekday, so all the older kids are at school.

In fact, it's a little unusual for all the studios to be full at a time like this. I glance at Studio 3, where Cassidy and Allen are sweeping through the room in a dramatic tango. If Blitz isn't in Studio 4, he's not here.

I stifle a giggle when I approach the window. It's the Tappin' Grandmas group, nine ladies in black leotards and tights, gray hair puffed up or braided down. They look awesome, dancing in a line, but the thing that is making me laugh is Blitz.

He's at the front in shiny tap shoes and black tights, no shirt, and a red bow tie. He looks like a waiter at a strip club, or at least what I imagine one would. It's hilarious. The woman on the end is wearing a white tank remarkably like the one Blitz had on yesterday, and I have a feeling she's the reason he's shirtless now.

They can't see me with the mirror on the other side, so I lean against the window and take him in. The familiar heat burns through me as I watch him dance. Either he's learned their routine or he's teaching one of his, because they are all together, legs out, legs in, tap tap tap. Well, mostly together. Some of the ladies are more coordinated than the others.

I'm not sure who the regular instructor is. Probably Danika herself. It's the sort of class she would put together. Maybe once she saw Blitz had it under control, she went on to work in the recital hall. If last year was any indication, I should be able to get a lot more time up at Dreamcatcher to help, especially with the new class. More freedom. More time away from home.

More Blitz.

"How's he doing?"

I'm startled to hear Danika's voice. She walks through the halls like a ninja, graceful and silent after a lifetime of dance.

"They seem to be enjoying his company."

She peers through the window and huffs out an abrupt laugh, no doubt the moment she realizes one of the Tappin' Grandmas has stolen Blitz's shirt.

"I think he's found his calling," she says. "I somehow doubt he can break all their hearts."

"I don't know about that," I say. "He leaves a swath of destruction wherever he goes."

She looks at me with surprise, and I wish I hadn't said anything. Everyone here is used to bright naive Livia, not the one who sounds jaded. "So I read in the grocery store tabloids," I add.

She laughs a little more naturally. "I was definitely concerned about bringing him here," she says. "But I owe Bennett a favor, more like a thousand, and for some reason he thinks this joker got a raw deal in the press."

"Is this all about a Tweet?"

Danika shakes her head. "That was just the part that blew up," she says. "He stands for everything we should hate. Cheap fame. Exploitation. Shock culture."

"He's a good dancer, though," I say. Blitz is doing a free-form tap routine for the women now. They are clapping and cheering, even though we can't hear what's happening from outside the soundproofing.

"There are a thousand dancers just as good," she says. "But he's got some sort of magic charisma." She leans against the window. "He's charmed all these ladies. He'll get his happy publicity to offset the bad stuff. This is gold."

"How is anyone going to know he's here?" I ask. I realize camera crews might come in and the academy could hit the news. It will be impossible to hide all this from my parents. It's so close to home. They'll notice with their own eyes if the media starts blocking the street. It's less than a mile to my house.

"I'm not going to let him take over my academy," she says. "But he'll have some small promo videos done, only with dancers who sign a waiver."

I wonder if Gwen will do that. I guess it doesn't matter. Even if the wheelchair ballerina class gets visibility, nobody will know who Gabriella is.

"I can't sign one," I say.

She squeezes my arm. "I know. That's fine. We'll work around it." She watches the grandmas take turns dancing with Blitz. "Did you talk to him?"

My face flames. "Only about the girls," I say. "He wanted to know about their limitations."

She nods. "I'm really throwing the works at him. He's got the wheelchair class, these Tappin' Grandmas, one toddler class, the boys' hip-hop, and the advanced jazz girls, who I felt could really learn from him."

"You think he'll be okay with the babies?"

"I am hoping one of them spits up all over him."

We laugh together as the lights blink twice in the hall, signaling the five-minute warning until the transition begins. A few mothers trickle in to stand outside the windows of the jazz class.

"Were you going to dance this morning?" Danika asks. "This isn't your usual day."

"I'm working toward my toe shoes." My eyes dart back to Blitz.

"Ahh," she says. "And to take another gander at wonder boy."

I shrug and fiddle with my skirt.

She turns to me. "Please take care with someone like Benjamin," she says. "If something were to happen to you, I'd be devastated."

"What could happen?" I ask. "It's just dance."

Danika peers back through the window at the grandmas. One of them has tricked Blitz into getting close to her face. Suddenly she plants a kiss on his lips.

“That is what I’m talking about,” she says. “He makes women act crazy.”

Blitz sweeps the elderly woman up in his arms and turns in a circle. A silent whoop goes up, the women all gesturing wildly, mouths open. I can’t tell if the others are excited or jealous. One thing is for sure. His charm isn’t limited to any age.

## Chapter Seven

As the grandmas reluctantly file out, taking Danika with them, Blitz puts his shirt back on and strips off the bow tie. When he heads toward the door, I panic, flooded with shyness, and dash for Studio 3 to do a warm-up.

But he comes out before I can go in.

"Livia?" he asks.

My hand is on the door handle. "Hello, Blitz," I say.

"You practicing with them?" he asks, gesturing at the window where Cassidy and Allen are still doing a tango.

"Oh, no, I don't know ballroom. Just ballet." My face heats up at my ignorance.

"I could show you."

Now my heart is racing. "We'd all crash into each other."

"We can check with Danika about this room." He points back to Studio 4. "I don't think anyone's in it."

He's right. It looks like we're about to hit a lull in the schedule. Aurora has another batch of tiny ballerinas headed into Studio 1, but nobody is coming to any of the other rooms. And Studio 4, the Dance of the Shades room, is where we met.

"Okay," I say. "But I'm not a very quick study."

"Oh, I bet you are." Blitz holds out his hand, and maybe because of where we are, or my promise to myself to be bold, I don't hesitate in taking it.

His expression is earnest, as serious as I've ever seen it in real life or on what I saw of his show. It's like he's another person entirely, as if there is Blitz and then there is this man, Benjamin. Maybe that's why Danika insists on calling him by his real name. Maybe she sees it too.

As soon as my fingers brush his, he grips my hand and somehow, without my knowing a single step of couples dancing, he whirls me into a perfect turn.

I stop just inches from him, my face outrageously close to his, and he spins me out again. It's effortless, like we've practiced this a thousand times.

He reels me back in, and this time, moves his hand to my back, where the pressure there must push some button, because I'm taking steps with him, long strides to the door of Studio 4. I feel like Ginger Rogers, rushing across the movie screen with Fred Astaire in one of the few movies my parents allow to be shown at home.

"See, Princess," he says as we break our dance hold to pass into the room. "I knew you were a natural."

"How did you do that?" I ask. "I've never danced with a partner, ever."

His grin is wicked and sets my pulse jumping all over again. "Then I am honored to be your first."

I blush furiously as I follow him into the room. I never can tell with Blitz exactly what we're talking about. Every word out of his mouth feels like a sexual innuendo.

My gaze darts to the mirrored window. Anyone could watch us and we wouldn't even know. But that makes it safe, more so than the storage closet. And I do want safe. As much as I'm a moth to his flame, I'm afraid too. This man could charm the panties off a nun.

He heads to the corner where the sound system is stored. I close the door and turn away from the window. Despite knowing no one is out there, I feel on display.

I set down my string bag and kneel to switch out shoes. Blitz is on the other side of the room. There are a half-dozen unfurled ribbon sticks piled near the door, so once I have my shoes on, I roll them up. It keeps my nervous hands busy as Blitz fiddles with the music, scrolling around looking for something in particular, I guess.

I focus so hard on making the bright ribbons a perfect coil that I don't notice he's come close until I see his jazz shoes beside me.

"Ready?" he asks.

When I look up, I feel dizzy. It's like a dream. Blitz Craven isn't just someone on the television set. He's here. And extending his hand to me. *Me*. A nineteen-year-old homeschooled wallflower.

I have to swallow over the lump in my throat. He looks so handsome, so devilishly roguish, that I'm momentarily stunned. I take his hand and allow him to lift me up.

"You look devastatingly beautiful in pale blue," he says.

I glance down at my leotard and matching skirt. It's now officially my favorite outfit.

"What are we going to dance?" I ask.

"We'll take it easy," he says. "A waltz, like the name of your academy."

"It's named after a waltz?" I ask.

"One of the most famous ones there is."

I realize the music he's playing has three steps per beat. "Is that what you're playing?"

"No," he says, leading me by the hand to the

center of the room. "It's Nocturne in B Major by Chopin."

"It's beautiful."

"One of my favorites."

He steps in close to me and takes my right hand in his. "Left hand just below my shoulder," he says.

His muscle there is strong. I've never touched anything like it. He places his free hand lightly on my shoulder blade. A tingle runs up my spine.

"We're going to go backwards for you," he says. "Step back, then to the left, then feet together. Ready?"

I nod, although my mind is racing. Are my hands sweaty? What if I step on him? He's going to think I'm a terrible dancer. I flirt with the idea of sprinting for the door.

But he counts us in, and something in the squeeze of his hand and the pressure on my back tells me when we're going to move. We step back, left, and together, and then he pauses.

"See, you're a natural," he says. "Let's do it again with the opposite foot."

We do the step again, starting with the left. "Perfect," he says. "Now you know it all. We'll do them both in a row and keep going."

He starts us off again, and this time we move around the room. I can't believe it, but I'm waltzing!

"You're amazing," I tell him, and I mean it.

"You learn quickly," he says. His steps become longer, more exaggerated, and suddenly we're turning, and I'm keeping up somehow. There's communication in his touch, in the pressure of his hands, some small clue in his posture and position, and my brain gets it. Take this pivot, lean here, stretch out the step.

The music is intoxicating and the beauty of the dance overwhelms me. I've loved ballet these two years for its grace and precision. But this dance in his arms is like a revelation, a miracle. I really do feel like a princess at a ball.

The song comes to an end. I'm so overwhelmed by what we've done that I can't speak. My calves ache from standing on tiptoe, and my arms burn from holding myself in position. But it feels amazing.

"Now you need to just relax into it," he says. "As you learn a partner, the distance between you decreases." He takes a step in. We're no longer a foot apart, as we have been, but almost touching.

"Should I wiggle my sillies out?" I ask, remembering him working with the wheelchair ballerinas yesterday.

His laugh is like water splashing in a fountain, bold and refreshing. "Princess, you are a balm for my jaded soul."

"You, jaded?" I ask. "It seems like you have the world at your feet."

"No," he says. "I have the wolves at my door."

I had forgotten that he was disgraced, his show suspended. It seems impossible that he could be vile when he acts so charming.

But I don't have another moment to think about it. Another waltz comes on. His hand grips mine, and then we're off, sweeping across the floor.

Now that we're closer together, there are more points of communication between us. His hips, his thighs, his knees, the turn of his shoulders, his chest. We glide across the floor like one person. This waltz is faster, more demanding.

My skirt flutters around my thighs. I spot us in the mirror, spinning and turning, the steps long and beautiful. My hair swings, black as night against my pale blue shoulders. We're a sight.

"Let's try a turn," he says.

Fear stabs me. I know I'm going to ruin this moment with a stumble, but when he releases my shoulder and changes his grip on my hand, I just go. I unfurl like the ribbon stick, like a flower blooming.

His arm lifts high and I turn beneath it, the world spinning. I'm glad for my ballet training, as I know how to work inside the rotation without getting dizzy.

Although I might be anyway. I've never drunk alcohol, but I think this must be what it's like, giddy and lightheaded.

He turns me again, too quickly after the last one, and this time I do lose my footing and crash into him. He laughs and crushes me against his chest. We stop dancing, breathing against each other, his face above mine. But the spinning doesn't stop just because we're still. It whirls around us as if we are the center of the world.

"Livia, you are a breath of fresh air after all the contestants on my show," he says. His grin is infectious, happy and full of charm.

I'm completely lost in it. But we're so close, pressed all the way tight. I can feel each part of him. Chest, belly, and below.

Fear stabs me. Twenty women, I remind myself. He slept with twenty women from his show.

I'm not afraid of things that could happen, I remember them too well. I'm afraid of the after. How many paternity suits had he mentioned? Fifteen? How many were true? He says he has no kids, but how does he know?

I step back. "I'm pretty clumsy," I say.

"Are you kidding?" He still has my hand, and he twirls me. "Look at you. Dancing like a pro."

The music is still going, and he walks with me, not pulling me to him, but holding only one hand. His steps are still in waltz time, one-two-three, and I instinctively walk with him, matching his stride.

We remain apart, and I calm down from my

thoughts about paternity suits, falling back into the dance, turning in, then out, facing, apart, following his guide. He's an amazing teacher, but of course he is, guiding all those contestants week after week, taking dancers of all skill levels into competition with each other for his approval.

"How would I do?" I ask without thinking.

"You're doing fine," he says.

"On your show, I mean." I want my mouth to shut up, but it just keeps talking. "If you were teaching me to perform with you."

His expression is thoughtful. "Well, I would be impressed by your ability to follow me so soon. But..."

Without warning, he turns, slides his hand beneath my back, and takes me off balance. I'm in a dip, weight on his arm, my face inches from his again.

"We'd probably dance more like this," he says.

He holds the position, and I've forgotten how to breathe. I'm completely at his mercy, gripped by him, my hair streaming toward the floor.

His lips are paralyzingly close. He's going to do it. He's going to treat me like the women in his competition. Kiss me. Give a good show.

"For the audience," I say.

This breaks the spell. He lifts me back to standing. "For the audience," he says, a confirmation. "It's all about the ratings. It has to seem as though every girl has a chance or they won't keep watching."

He releases me and heads back toward the stereo.

"Do they all have a chance?" I ask. "Or is it scripted?"

He stops the waltz and the room goes silent. "You're asking trade secrets," he says.

Of course he wouldn't tell me things like that. For all he knows, I'm the type to sell my story to one of those sketchy magazines at the checkout line. Blitz is a favorite topic. He frequently makes the cover. Now that I think about it, I'm pretty sure some of the links I saw yesterday involved the paternity suits.

I wonder what a story like that is worth. Enough to get an apartment of my own?

God, I'm horrible. I could never do that.

Could I?

Blitz puts on a tango, and I think about that scene from his show with the girl on the red satin bed. How she stripped for him.

"This is a more challenging dance," he says. "Latin dances have so much more passion. It's a good test for the, well, compatibility of a woman with my style."

Now he looks like Blitz. His walk has that predatory quality, as though he is coming for me, and there is no escape. The song begins, and he circles me, stepping in time with the music. First slow, then fast. Slow, then fast.

My heart hammers. There are so many sides to this man. Are they all real? Or are some an illusion, such an integral part of his image that he no longer separates it from his real self?

I'm no different. I'm naive, I know, about culture and current events and how to act in social situations at my age. But I've seen plenty, done plenty, broken some of the most powerful rules of society.

I tap into that person, the Livia of four years ago. Young as I was, I knew what I wanted then. I took it, same as he had. I was headstrong, bold, none of this shyness. No fear.

My circles match his and we walk in tandem, apart, but following the same rhythm. When the music rises, he reaches for me, arm outstretched.

I accept his hand, and within a heartbeat, he has whirled me into him.

This time, our positions feel natural, and our bodies come together without distance from the first try.

"This is trickier," he says. "But just a little. Lean into me. Shift into a close embrace."

My hand goes around his back, and his arm fits against me much more tightly. I can feel his breath on my hair.

"First we walk slowly together," he says.

We take the steps, me backward, him forward.

"Then to the side like the waltz," he says.

We accomplish that. "Now you must take two steps back, then one foot across the other, then back to the side."

My mind jumbles at all of that, and I have no idea what he means by across, and I trip on his feet. He catches me easily.

I laugh shakily. "Not so quick on this one," I say.

"It's a trickier step," he reminds me.

He slides me behind him. "We'll do your step together."

I pause and look down at his feet.

"Two steps, the cross, then step and slide." His feet glide effortlessly across the floor.

But I see it now. I do it a couple of times alone.

"Now you have it," he says. We return to the tango embrace. "Let's walk a bit first."

The steps are slow and deliberate, one step to the beat. I can't relax yet, concentrating, and I sense when we shift to the side.

"Now the new steps," he says.

I go back, step across, and back into the slide. Then we're just walking again.

"Perfect!" he says.

We continue this basic step until the end of the song, but it doesn't feel like the waltz did. It's tricky and I have to concentrate. I don't love it as much. I've probably failed his sexy dance test.

Blitz releases me and heads back to the stereo.

"Can we waltz one more time?" I ask. "I don't want to forget it."

"Of course," he says. "You have more time today, I see."

My face heats up again, remembering how I chickened out yesterday. Maybe I'll get that kiss yet.

Except, the windows.

"I do," I say. "We could try the storage room again."

He stops what he's doing and turns around. The wolfish look is gone, and he's back to Benjamin, the sweet charmer. "You sure about that?"

Now I'm not. What does he mean by that? Does he not want me after all? Or does he think I'm propositioning him, that we'll have sex back there?

I suck in a breath and a piece of hair sticks to my cheek. I push it away. "I — I just meant we could finish the tour. Unless you already got one."

He hasn't put on any music, but he heads toward me anyway. Now I remember why I panicked yesterday, why I ran. When Blitz Craven comes at you like a full-on wolf aiming for prey, it's more than any woman can handle. I fight the urge to startle away again.

Within seconds, he's crazy close, his lips near my

ear. “Princess, I’ll follow you anywhere,” he says, his voice low.

My knees are wobbly. I can’t breathe. His face is so very near. I look at his lips. They are full, with a defined edge. The scruff of his unshaven jaw looks rough and sexy.

“There’s a recital hall. And the staging area.” My voice isn’t very confident now.

“Show me,” he says. “I want to see everything.” His tone tells me he isn’t talking about the academy. His fingers reach for a lock of my hair and he twists it around his thumb.

The door flies open. Danika storms in. “Benjamin Castillo, lay a hand on my dancer and I’ll throw your ass right out of this academy!”

I forgot. The windows.

Blitz sighs heavily and lifts me back to a standing position.

“I’m okay,” I tell her. “I was just learning some ballroom.”

“I’ll be happy to teach you some ballroom,” Danika says. Her voice could grate cheese. “Benjamin, I think you’re done for today.” She walks forward and pokes a finger against his chest. “Leave this one alone or you will rue the day you ever stepped foot in here.”

Blitz holds his hands up. “I’m so sorry,” he says.

"Your school, your rules." His eyes meet mine only for a moment. "I'll be on my way."

He gives us a little bow and exits the room.

Danika turns to me. "I think maybe Blitz shouldn't work with your class on Tuesdays," she says. "If your father found out, it would jeopardize your ability to study here."

I'm ready to cry, or shout, or do something. I'm bubbling over with emotions that rush at me so fast I can't even name them. "I know," I say. "I know."

She wraps her arm around me. "You're special to us, Livia," she says. "I'm not going to let some womanizer wrap his talons around you."

The thing is, he already has.

## Chapter Eight

If Mom notices something different about me when I come home from the academy, she doesn't say anything about it. She generally doesn't grill me about things unless she thinks we need to shore ourselves up for the third degree from Dad.

I help Andy with his science and administer the test so Mom can do laundry. That only occupies an hour, so I head to my room to do some practice SAT reading.

But the lines blur on the page. I'm so full of Blitz, and so upset at Danika's interference. I know she's right. I know it. But I don't want to give Blitz up. It's the first time I've felt alive in four years, other than the moment when Gabriella arrived at Dreamcatcher Dance Academy.

And when I discovered where she was.

For a long time after the adoption, I had no idea what happened to her. I just knew one of the Catholic ministries had handled everything.

When I started volunteering at the church three years ago, I only got to do small tasks, such as resetting the hymnals and putting out the missalettes. I graduated to helping Irma open the offering envelopes and organizing the checks and cash. Then stuffing the mail-outs.

About two years ago, she let me into the locked cabinet where the church records were stored. There were many private files in there. Employment records for the priests and staff. Bundles of prayer requests. Tax documents.

I stumbled upon an adoption certificate. Then another. The file was small. Apparently the church had not been involved in many over the years. Until Gabriella, no baby born of a church member had been adopted through the larger umbrella organization since 1998.

But a copy of her birth certificate was there. And the contract sent by the agency, signed by me, my parents since I was a minor, and the new parents.

I had their names.

It took me months to find them. I didn't know Mindy yet, had no Internet access, and only vague awareness of social media like Facebook and LinkedIn. I did things the old-fashioned way, digging old phone books out of recycling bins and calling "information" from the church phone.

I got their address and phone number through that, but I didn't know what to do with it. They lived too far away to walk, and I couldn't just show up at their house anyway. I did call the number a few times from church and pretend to have dialed the wrong one when someone answered. Once, I heard a child singing in the background and my heart almost exploded. Was that my baby?

Then came Mindy. She was fourteen to my seventeen back then, but already more worldly and wise. And she had a cell phone. She showed me Facebook and how to use it, and then the laptop, which was newer then and often left out while Irma was in meetings.

Only once I was alone with the computer did I dare create a fake account on Facebook and start searching for Gwen. This was before the accident, when she and her husband were happily raising Gabriella as a three-year-old.

I won't forget the day I saw the status update about the crash. I didn't know until weeks after it happened, as I didn't get many chances to turn on the laptop with Irma in the office.

The pictures sent shock waves through me. Gabriella lay in a special bed, bandaged and immobilized. She missed her father's funeral. I so longed to have been there, holding her hand while everyone was at the service. Was she alone during those hours, with all the family gone? Surely someone stayed with her.

Those were dark days. I considered running away from home, or at least hitching a ride with a stranger to go to the hospital.

I fought with my father, resisted their rules. I stayed out late a few times, sitting in a local park. I really had no idea what to do to rebel. I had very few friends, and Mindy's family was as strict as mine on going places.

I hated my life, but I hated most of all what my letting Gabriella go had cost her. She was in that car because of me.

Stop.

I have to stop.

Once the blaming begins, there is no end to it.

I close the SAT prep book and go to my bedroom door. Generally, we are not allowed to close our doors except at night, but I angle it as far as I can get away with, only an inch gap, and sit on the floor by my bed. When I'm sure no one is in the hall, I bend down and push aside a plastic bin of old clothes. Behind it is another box.

I pull it out, then pause to listen again. All quiet.

The box is just a cardboard one that once held packages of ramen noodles. When I open it, the top is covered with old T-shirts from my former life. My elementary school logo, one from middle school, and a couple with irreverent expressions like "Don't blame me, I'm the cute one." Dad doesn't allow sass like that now. I set them aside.

Beneath them are the meager things I saved from my pregnancy and the hospital. One oversized shirt my mother gave me to wear, stretched to fit over my belly.

I hadn't had any actual pregnancy clothes, just a few Goodwill items in larger sizes. My family seemed to feel that if they weren't labeled maternity, I wasn't actually pregnant.

It didn't matter that I dressed like a bag lady. When I started showing, we moved from Houston to San Antonio. I wasn't allowed to go anywhere. Not school. Not the new church. Not even grocery stores. No movies or time at the park or even walking anywhere but our enclosed backyard.

They were so embarrassed. So shocked.

I accepted it. I had done this terrible thing. I deserved punishment.

In the box beneath the shirt is my hospital wristband. It has my name, Livia Mason. And the date I entered the hospital, Gabriella's birthday. May 12, 2012.

There is a hat with pink stripes. They put it on her head, but it must have fallen off when they took her, because I found it on the floor beneath my hospital bed as we were leaving. I stuffed it in my pants. I knew it was hers because it had a small pull near the crown, a quarter-inch of string that was loose. I noticed it the one and only time I held her.

A volunteer who hadn't realized the baby was leaving for adoption had given me a little card with her footprints. I stashed it as well, hidden from my parents, and it now lives in the box. The pink card with its smudged ink is easily my most prized possession.

That's it. A hat. A shirt. An ID band. And footprints.

If I could hook the laptop up to a printer, I would have made pictures of Gabriella to put in my box. I did learn to save them. If anyone dug around really hard on the old Dell, they'd find my secret folder of images, all named boring things like "Incomplete data save 1" or "Backup of system file." One of my goals has been to find a way to buy a thumb drive to save them on, in case the laptop ever dies or goes away.

But even small tasks like that are impossible when you never go anywhere other than church or dance. And you have no money. If I were a thief, I would sneak out at night and steal one, but I can't make myself do it.

I'm just grateful to have seen her grow up in the few pictures Gwen allows the public to see. I haven't dared try to friend her to get access to more, not even as the alias I am online.

Footsteps approach and I rapidly shove everything back in the box and push it under the bed. When Andy sticks his head in, I'm on the floor with the SAT book in my lap. "Dad incoming in five," he says.

"Thanks," I tell him.

He takes off, and my heart squeezes. He doesn't go to public school because of me. Mom came close to leaving Dad. And the boy. He had to go. I have no idea where he is now. He never even knew about Gabriella. No one could. Our lives became about the four of us, solitary and confined as my belly swelled.

So many lives changed in the wake of my actions. Sometimes it's more than I can bear.

I deserve to be kept away. I've earned my banishment. My judgment is poor. And Blitz is probably just one more thing I should be kept from.

## Chapter Nine

I have to suffer through a day without the dance academy on Thursday. I don't have class myself, no wheelchair ballet, and Danika would be displeased if I tried to see Blitz again, so I can't go practice. Mom would get suspicious too.

I don't know what to do. I try to study my SAT, but I can't concentrate. Andy gets frustrated with my lack of attention when I help him with math. Mom starts to notice.

I'm saved by Irma, who calls the house saying she just got a delivery of new pew cushions and she could really use my help. Mom sends me on my way with a sack lunch, which means I don't even have to keep myself straight in front of Dad.

When I get to the church, Irma is all aflutter.

"They are doing everything wrong!" she says. "Can you man the phones while I stay on top of this?"

"Where's Father Stephen?" I ask.

"Playing golf!" she says in exasperation. "It's some diocese thing. Today of all days!"

I want to point out that she could have had the cushions delivered some other day, but think better of it.

"Just handle the calls. If anything is something you can't answer, take a message and I'll call them back when this is done."

I nod and shoo her back to the sanctuary, where I can hear people dragging things around. I want to peek in, but then I spot the laptop sitting out and open. It's right beside her chair.

I sit before it, my fingers itching to search. Irma was in the process of ordering new prayer books. The website is up. I open a new tab and start a search for "Benjamin Castillo." Danika called Blitz that yesterday.

Wikipedia sends me to Blitz Craven, which I read the other day. But I want to know more about Benjamin, at least more than the facts about his show. I want to know everything.

I find what I'm looking for on the third page of results. A fan has created a site with all the pictures and information that's out there from interviews, school yearbooks, and social media.

Benjamin was a class clown, voted "Best sense of humor" by his senior class. When he was runner-up for Prom King, he kissed the Queen before the winner got a chance.

That figures. I can totally see Blitz doing that. I stare at his senior photo. His expression is serious at first glance, as if he's been told to look that way. But I can see the smile flirting with the corners of his mouth, and the laugh in his eyes. He's always been fun loving, that is obvious.

Everything I see there matches the Blitz I've seen up close.

I wish I had known him then, when there wasn't such an experience gap between us.

Irma comes into the room and I frantically kill the tab. When she sees me on the computer, she frowns, but I say, "I really like the cover with the doves. Does it come in purple?"

She relaxes. "Why don't you pick it, Livia?"

"Happy to," I say, eyes back on the screen.

A crash in the sanctuary makes her jump straight in the air. "Oh, those people!" she says.

I have to hold in my laugh. Irma is like one of those cartoon angry people whose curse words are always funny symbols. @%$#!

When she's gone, I have to start the search all over. This time I click on an interview with an entertainment magazine. The picture that accompanies the article is gorgeous, Blitz dancing solo on a dark stage with streaks of light behind him. I wish I could make a poster of it for my wall. God. My dad would freak.

Irma appears again, and I close the tab.

"The roses are in the lead now," I tell her.

She nods and hurries back to the storeroom. I sigh. If she's going to dash around, I'm not going to be able to look anymore. It doesn't matter. I have the real thing. And tomorrow I'm going to see him again.

I rest my chin on my hand and stare dreamily at the wall. I relive every moment I've had with him, from his arrival during my practice to the girls' ballet class to the dance lesson yesterday.

I have no frame of reference for how I'm feeling. I guess it would be a crush. A starstruck fantasy. For all I know, Blitz is acting this way with plenty of other women. When Mindy and I searched for girlfriends the other day, there was no shortage of recent love interests.

But he hasn't been in San Antonio long. Why did he come here anyway?

Irma passes by, holding a box fan by the handle. I wait for her to disappear through the door, then open the tab one more time. I go back to the Wikipedia entry. This time I notice a detail that I missed before.

Born 1990 in San Antonio, Texas.

When Blitz got in trouble, he came home.

## Chapter Ten

When I arrive at Dreamcatcher Friday afternoon, I know Blitz won't be with my class. Danika listed off the groups she'd given him. None of them are at the same time as my intermediate ballet class.

So he may have already come and gone.

But something told me he wouldn't leave. Advanced jazz ends just an hour before mine begins. I had told him in the storage room that I would be back on Friday afternoon. Maybe he had paid attention to that.

A girl can hope.

I'm a little early. Suze isn't at the desk. The foyer is empty except for a pair of moms talking quietly by a window.

Since it's after school, the studio hall is full of

parents. Every room is crowded with dancers. It's the busiest time of day.

I walk along, my string bag close to me, trying to avoid bumping into parents and siblings. Lots of ballet today and a hip-hop class. I pause by each window, looking inside. Maybe Blitz stayed to help in whatever room he was in earlier.

But he's nowhere. Just students and their regular instructors.

I try to avoid feeling crestfallen. When I get to the end of the hall, I open the door to the storage room. I might as well have a little reverie in there. Maybe try on the corset and the top hat Blitz wore. It's silly, but it's better than feeling totally down.

But when I get inside the darkened room, light spills through the open door on the side that leads to the stage.

My shoes squeak on the floor as I move toward it. Danika is probably in the recital hall again. I can at least make myself useful in the half hour until my class begins.

I step into the staging area, then onto the wings behind the side curtains. No one is on the actual stage. I feel timid about stepping out onto it since it's fully lit and the chairs are not, as if there is a performance about to start. I would hate to head out there only to discover there was a private exhibition happening that I didn't know about.

I peer into the seats, shading my eyes from the intense lights shining down, but I can't see farther back than the first few rows. There's a clipboard resting on a chair, but no people.

I duck into the wings and walk behind the back curtain over to the other side. Still nobody. Huh. Danika must have been here and then left. Or a prop vendor. She has to order the decor for the holiday show. Maybe someone was up here taking measurements.

I walk along the side curtain and take one step onto the stage.

"Hello?" I call out. "Danika? Did you need any help?"

My voice echoes in the empty space. Then all is silent again.

I move to the edge of the stage and sit down. It's wild being in here alone. Usually it's full of people. I picture an audience in the seats, the silence after the applause.

The air is heavy with expectation. I've done three recitals on this stage. I was totally nervous my first time, but now I'm used to it. Even my parents approved of the lovely grace of our performances, despite my father's anxious glances at my leotard.

I switch from the tennis shoes I walked in to my ballet slippers. I point my feet, imagining them in toe shoes. I've asked for a pair for Christmas, my only gift. I really want to be ready by then.

My leotard today isn't my best, but I couldn't repeat the light blue set again and I wore my yellow one Tuesday. So, I'm back in the pink set from the day I met Blitz. Maybe it will be good luck.

I've tied back my black hair with a pink ribbon, just away from my face, no ponytail. It's harder to dance that way, but I wanted it down for Blitz. I can still feel the tickle of it as he dipped me in the waltz, the way it swirled around my shoulders in a spin. I can always twist it up before class starts.

I stand, planning to pick up my bag and go back to the rooms to wait. But the stage calls to me, as if it's whispering in my ear to do just a little dance. Something small and simple.

I have no music, not even a cell phone to play a song. But I don't really need it. I run through the warm-up routine, neck stretch, Achilles, ankles, feet, then hips and thighs. When I feel good and warm, I take my first run across the stage. I spin and spin, reveling in the whoosh of air that is one of the best feelings in ballet.

When I've come out of the turns and am steady again, I dance-walk to one side and take a few running steps for a *grand jeté*. I know I'm not stellar at this move yet, but the extra space and knowing no one is watching makes me feel bold and free. When I land squarely, I head to the other corner to do it all again.

Then I see the shadowy figure in the aisle.

I halt instantly, breathing hard. I can't make it out, but it definitely isn't Danika. Too tall. Too solid.

He comes forward and the light hits him.

It's Blitz.

Today he's wearing knee-length spandex shorts and a form-fitting tank. Both are charcoal gray. There is no muscle or bulge that isn't perfectly delineated. My eyes glance where they shouldn't and dart away.

I tuck my hair behind my ear. "Oh, hey," I say.

"You look beautiful up there," he says.

Despite the strength and power I felt just a moment ago, I'm definitely melting now. "Thanks," I squeak.

"What is that leap you just did? I've seen it in a dozen ballets."

"A *grand jeté*."

He climbs up the steps to the stage. "How many steps do you take?"

"It depends on the dance leading up to the leap," I say. "And how strong you are. Some can do it with just a step. I need some lead time."

"Can you do it again?"

My face heats up from nervousness, but I say, "Of course." I'm tempted to add that my *grand jeté* is not perfect, but I swallow the words. Just let it be what it is.

I take a few steps back, then run lightly forward into the leap.

"That's fantastic!" he says. He imitates me, jumping into the air.

He is powerful and takes greater flight than I did.

When he is back on the ground, he turns to me. "Did I do it right?" he asks with the eagerness of a young child.

"Mostly," I say.

"Mostly!" He runs over to me and lifts me by the waist until my face is well above his head. "Mostly!" He expertly drops me sideways and catches my body, one hand beneath a knee and the other under my arm.

I'm breathless. He sweeps me out and sets me on my feet again.

"What was THAT called?" I ask.

"I have no idea!" he says. "I just felt like doing it. So tell me what I did wrong."

I extend my arms. "Arm position is very important in a *grand jeté*," I say, framing my face in the circle of my arms. "This is fifth position, but there are other popular arm extensions." I extend one arm to the side and one straight up. Then I place one arm straight in front and one straight back.

"What did I do with my arms?" Blitz asks.

"They were sort of all over the place." A laugh escapes.

"Amateur," he says. "I'm just a damn amateur."

"You're currently the most famous dancer there is. You have your own show."

"Used to have my own show." He shakes his head. "Maybe learning ballet is a good use of my time."

"We have a lot of good teachers here," I say.

He spins in circles around me. I turn to him as he makes his way around. He's amazing. His form. His energy. It's one thing to see recordings on a laptop screen. It's another one entirely to have him right in front of me.

"The whole world probably wishes they were me right now," I say.

This stops him. "Not exactly," he says. His face is serious. "I don't think there's a name I haven't been called in the past few weeks."

"Is that why you came home?"

He takes my hand and starts turning me in circles, roll out, roll in, away from him and back. Finally he says, "I couldn't trust anybody. Half of my staff quit and the other half is stabbing me in the back."

"So you wanted your family."

Blitz steps close and places my hand on his shoulder in what I recognize as waltz position. He grasps the other and we begin circling the stage floor. "Your favorite," he says.

"You didn't answer my question."

He spins me in a circle and lets go once I'm away. "You are my escape right now."

My heart threatens to stop. "Me?"

He nods. He runs a few feet, then leaps into another attempt at a *grand jeté*. He's full of nervous energy.

I decide to stop asking questions. If he needs escape, then I'll be it.

When he lands, he asks, "Better?"

"Yes. But I think for a man, you don't want the framed arms. I'd go with an extension."

He does it again. Each leap is higher than the last. He's a wonder. I can't believe Danika said a thousand dancers were as good as him. He has to be one in a million.

"I know there are basic ballet positions," he says. "But I don't know what they are."

"You want me to show you?"

"I'd love it."

"This is first position," I tell him, putting my heels together, toes out, and my arms in a circle in front of my chest.

"Like this?" he asks.

It's perfect, but I use this as an excuse to touch him, shifting his arms down the barest inch. His skin is warm, the muscles flexed and hard. Danika warned him away from me. I have to be careful.

But I can't stop myself.

"That's it," I say. "From there you go into second position, stepping your feet wide and extending your arms." I move into place.

He mimics me perfectly.

We go through all five positions.

"I love this," he says. "I guess if you've never danced with a partner, you don't know any ballet lifts."

I shake my head. "There aren't any male ballet instructors at Dreamcatcher, although I'm sure the other girls know some dancers."

"I might have to get some names." He places his hands on my waist and lifts me again. "I'm betting it's all very similar."

It's a little disconcerting how he keeps taking me airborne. He braces his legs with a lunge. Then his hands shift me so that my center of balance changes.

"Can you hold the position horizontally?" he asks. "It takes a lot of core strength."

I'm not sure, but as he tilts my body into a line, my legs stay in the air until I'm parallel with the floor. I remember my arms and hold them out, fingers in proper hand position.

"Now that's beautiful," Blitz says. "You ballet dancers really have pretty details in the hands and head."

He lowers me down. "You okay?" he asks. "Was that a strain?"

"Not at all," I say. And that part is true. But I'm so high, so outrageously overflowing with excitement in his presence, that it is almost painful. I can't tell him that.

"Too bad we don't have any music. I left my cell phone in my car." He notices my string bag. "Do you have yours?"

My face burns. "Not with me," I say.

"Good for you. Going off grid." He takes my hand and assumes the waltz position, but this time he leads me into another type of step, in a box. "I wish I could stop torturing myself with the Burn Blitz Burn hashtag."

"What's that?" I try to relax and follow Blitz's steps, but with no music or any idea what he'll do next, it's all I can do not to tromp all over him.

"It sounds like fun, which is why everybody keeps jumping in. They bash me pretty damn hard with it. Every time I think it's died down, it resurrects itself."

"Like Zombie Jesus," I say.

His laugh reverberates off the stage and walls of the recital hall. "Princess, where have you been all my life?"

Hiding under my father's iron rule, I think, but I simply continue to follow his step. He rolls me out, ducking me under his arm, then lifts my arm so he can turn beneath mine. We do this over and over again until I'm breathless and my arm aches. But it's fun, so fun. We're dancing almost as part of the conversation.

"So do you have class today?" he asks.

I let go of him. "Oh my gosh. What time is it?"

He flicks the round screen on his wristband. A watch face lights up. "Four-ten."

"Oh, no! I'm late!" I run for my bag, then stop. "Come with me," I say. "Betsy can teach you a few things!"

He hesitates.

"Do you have something better to do?" I ask. "Like reading nasty Burn Blitz Burn Tweets?"

"Touché," he says. "All right. But I'll have to keep my hands off you in there." We head off the side of the stage.

My heart revs up. "Why is that?"

"Your kindly boss Danika," he says. "I'm skating on thin ice after Wednesday."

Shoot. That's right. It was one thing to sneak a dance in an empty recital hall. Another thing to be together with an audience.

I stop walking. "Maybe we should go through the main entrance of the recital hall rather than just appearing from the storage room."

"I'll risk it if you will," he says. His smile is devilishly charming, and my heart immediately reacts with a jump in my pulse.

He takes my hand and we head into the staging area, where the door to the storage room still stands open.

My blood rushes in my ears. "Did you have some nefarious plan for in there?" I ask.

We dodge the costume racks. He pulls me behind one.

"Just this," he says.

He cradles my face in both of his hands, and before I can even think, his lips land on mine.

Kissing is everything I remember, and so much more. His breath caresses me, his mouth warm and welcoming. He takes it easy, nibbling across my lips, his thumb stroking my cheek.

When I lean in, the kiss grows more demanding. His body presses against mine. His tongue flicks against my mouth, and I open for him.

His arms come around me as he explores inside. He tastes like mint gum and smells like pine. I couldn't be more swept away.

Blitz's kiss is the key that unlocks the secret diary of my past, every suppressed need, every hidden desire.

The kiss goes on and on. His hands explore my back and neck, his fingers threading into my hair. I never want the moment to end. My body tingles, warming to all the old needs I once felt but shut away. I bring my arms around him too, hanging on to his strong muscled back.

He breaks the kiss and holds me close, pressing my head to his chest. He caresses my hair for long moments. I listen to his heartbeat, quick and sure. Finally, he lets me go.

"Ballet?" I ask.

He glances at the exit sign by a set of loading doors. They aren't entirely closed. Apparently whatever caused the stage to be in use involved a delivery.

"I think I'm going to jet this way, Princess," he says. "I'm afraid if we go out there the way we are feeling right now, everyone is going to see it." He gestures between us.

My heart feels ready to burst. So he feels something too!

"Besides," he says, "parts of me are more prominent than I'd like."

I glance down at his tights and my eyebrows shoot up.

"Oh!" I say.

"I know," he says. "I'm a damn teenager around you. But I'll be here next week."

I want to protest. That's a weekend away!

But he turns and heads through the double doors, leaping majestically off the loading dock.

I head over and watch him leave, moving across

the parking lot with easy grace. Then he turns the corner of the building, and I can't see him anymore.

I lean against the door frame. I'm in over my head. I don't care what a hashtag says, what the world thinks of him. This isn't the person they are talking about. It can't be.

Because he's the most amazing person I've ever met.

## Chapter Eleven

I don't even want to think about two days without Blitz.

On Saturday morning, I get up and throw myself into housecleaning with Mom. Dad and Andy take off for soccer practice. I'm relieved to be away from his constant supervision, as I'm afraid I'm wearing my obsession on my sleeve.

While Mom and I pick up knickknacks to dust beneath, I wish I could tell her what was happening. Ask her advice.

But it's not possible. I cannot cause her pain, can't get between her and my father again. She made her choice to stick by him even as he became this paranoid, punishing, unforgiving man.

The idea that I'm interested in a man like Blitz would no doubt cost me my freedom. She'd tell my father, and that would be it. No more ballet. No more Gabriella.

Not worth it.

I live and relive the kiss in the storage room like it's a favorite song I can play on infinite repeat. I'm still not sure how all this has happened. Why did he pick me out of all the girls in San Antonio?

Shortly after lunch, Mindy shows up to hang out. My father approves of our taking the short walk to the park two blocks down. I know he'll pass by every half hour or so to make sure we aren't talking to any boys, but that's fine. It's not like Blitz is going to show up, and I'm definitely not interested in anyone else.

When we're far enough away to talk, she asks me, "So what's happening with Blitz? I've been dying to know."

"He kissed me!" I say. I can't help it. I have to tell somebody.

"Oh my God!" she exclaims, then claps her hand over her mouth. "Now tell me every detail!"

I describe as best I can the encounter in the recital hall and then in the storage room, including his graceful exit.

"This is so romantic!" Mindy says. "My best friend is having a fling with a reality show star!"

"An ex-reality show star," I say.

"But isn't getting his show back the whole reason he's doing all this charity stuff?" Mindy asks.

"He is?" I ask.

"That's why he's at Dreamcatcher." Mindy pulls out her phone. "He's organized a fund-raiser and kissed a pig at a rodeo and —"

"He WHAT?" I try to picture Blitz and a pig and it so does not fit.

"Yeah, he went to some rodeo last weekend and kissed a pig. If they got so-and-so much money for some charity, he would do it in the arena."

"Show me."

Mindy taps on the screen. "Here's the video."

I look around, making sure my dad isn't taking a stroll right about now. I have to be visible when he walks by, but hidden enough that he can't see what we're doing.

I look around. "Let's sit on that bench," I say. Our backs will be to the sidewalk.

We head there and Mindy hands the phone over. The still shot is of Blitz in a cowboy hat and jeans. My pulse speeds up at the sight of him. He looks so different but still perfect.

Blitz stands on a stage with an announcer. It's not the big San Antonio rodeo, which isn't until February. It looks pretty small and informal. A teenager brings out a pig with a ribbon on its collar. Blitz gets down on his hands and knees to plant one on its pink snout.

I laugh. He's trying so hard. He'll do anything.

"If he gets his show back, he'll leave for LA again," I say, eyes still on the video.

"You'll just have to marry him and go!" Mindy says.

She's so crazy. And impractical. That's not how these things work. Even if I was his soul mate, he'd have to go back to his job. And his contestants. Women willing to strip naked for him in front of everyone.

His wife is supposed to come from *Dance Blitz*. It's part of the show.

The video ends and another one automatically begins. It's not a news station, but a celebrity gossip site.

A woman sits with a video in the background, like a newscaster. She says, "And Blitz Craven continues his wild nights deep in the heart of Texas. The dancing Romeo, who was recently the subject of a Twitter scandal when he posted a naked woman in his bed, is back in the saddle with socialite Avery Hines, daughter of tech mogul Michael Hines."

The video behind her shows Blitz, in jeans and a black jacket, escorting a woman in a slinky red dress to an open limo. His arm is on her back.

My stomach drops. "When was this?" I ask.

"Maybe that was last week," Mindy says. "Before he even met you."

But the woman goes on.

"The King of Dance has been seen with several prominent Texas women since he kissed a pig at a small local rodeo last weekend." Behind her flash several images of Blitz in various places around San Antonio, a different woman on his arm each time.

So he has been seeing other women all week. And unlike me, brushing off his kisses for days, these women probably do all the things he wants.

"You think any of those were last night?" I can barely ask the question, my mouth has gone so dry. "Do you think he went out with someone after he kissed me yesterday?" The words are physically painful, like barbs in my throat.

"No way," Mindy says. "You said the owner warned him away from you, right? That's probably what made him see other people. And now that he knows how he feels about you, he won't. There wasn't a date on that footage. It could have been a few days ago."

But I'm not sure about that. I close the video and look on her phone for Twitter. When I open the app, I type in #BurnBlitzBurn.

Page after page of Tweets appear. I read a few out loud to Mindy.

"Looks like the alphahole dancer is making moves

on Texas women. Maybe one of them will shoot him. #BurnBlitzBurn."

"Don't," Mindy says. "It'll make you crazy."

I find another one.

"Somebody tell the new girls to take his phone away before bedtime. #BurnBlitzBurn."

"Stop," Mindy says.

But I can't quit reading them, pausing on keywords. Jerk. Horrible. Worst kind of man. Shoot his balls off.

One of the Tweets has another hashtag. #Blitz-SightingTexas. I click on it and another set of messages fall in a line.

"Spotted on the Riverwalk draped over some chick. Wanted to push him in. #BurnBlitzBurn #BlitzSightingTexas."

The Tweet was last night.

*Last night.* The night after our kiss.

Some of the Tweets have pictures. I can't look.

I hand the phone back to Mindy.

She tries to hug me but I resist.

"He screwed up, Livia," she says. "He's trying to fix it. He kissed a pig!"

"He hasn't changed," I say, my voice dull. I feel numb now. "He's just a flirt. He probably kissed ten women yesterday."

And I was the stupidest one, I think silently. I

want to cry. He probably calls all of them Princess. What a stupid name, anyway.

But the weekend will be a lot easier now. I'm not waiting for Monday anymore. I'm waiting for him to be gone.

## Chapter Twelve

I drag myself to the wheelchair ballerina class on Tuesday, not sparked even by the chance to see Gabriella. Everything feels blunted and dull, like the world is drained of its color. I skipped Monday practice. It doesn't matter. Nothing matters. My dad is right. Boys make me stupid. I should stay away.

The girls come in, one by one. Marissa is better today, and I'm relieved to see it. Gwen is on time, Gabriella beautiful in a bright red leotard and sparkly tutu. "Where's Benjamin?" she asks as soon as she's in the room.

"He's with another group now," Janel says, starting the music.

Danika did say she was taking him out of my class. She was right all along. Maybe she had seen something I didn't. Flirting with Suze or some of the mothers, more than just accepting their attention. Maybe she'd even caught him with someone.

I picture him kissing one of the other instructors and I want to throw up.

"You okay, Livia?" Janel asks.

I shake myself out of it. "I'm fine," I say. I move forward to line up the girls.

About halfway through the class, the door opens and a woman enters.

I'm less necessary today, so I'm just standing in the corner watching the dance as she looks around the studio. She's definitely not from around here.

Her suit is red, tailored, and fits her like it was custom made. The skirt hits just above her knee. She's got killer red heels and her ash blond hair looks like she just came out of a magazine shoot. She's older, maybe fifty, but her skin is as radiant as a girl's. Her makeup is perfect, her lips the exact shade of her dress. She puts on a fake smile as she looks around.

Janel keeps the motions going to cue the girls. "Can I help you?"

"Where is Blitz?" the woman asks.

"He isn't in this class," Janel says. "Check with the front desk. They can help you."

"The front desk sent me here." Her eyes light up as she watches the girls. The song comes to an end. "Was Blitz here before?"

Gabriella turns her chair to her. "Do you mean Benjamin?"

The woman blinks for a second, then says, "Yes. Was he here?"

"Last week!" Daisy says. "He's a dreamboat."

Her wistful expression makes the woman laugh. "Did you all have fun with Benjamin?"

The girls chorus, "Yes! Yes!" and "Where is he?"

Daisy rolls forward. "Is he coming back?"

"Do you want him to?" the woman asks.

Another loud "Yes."

Janel and I glance at each other. A new song begins. Janel calls out, "Back to positions, girls. Livia, can you show the woman the front desk? Maybe Suze didn't know about the change. She can track down Danika."

Great. I don't know who this woman is, but I'm not pleased to meet yet another Blitz worshipper. She might be older, but who knows? He's probably into all ages.

I head toward her. When we're back in the hall, she says, "I haven't introduced myself. I'm Hannah Stanton, Blitz's manager."

At least I'm not having to escort one of his conquests. "I'm Livia," I say. "I'll help you find Danika. She owns the place and sets Blitz's schedule."

I head to the front, but Hannah doesn't follow. She lingers by the window, watching the girls work on arm movements. "They sure seemed taken with Blitz," she says.

Marissa's mom pops up her head. "Do you know where he is?" she asks. "Marissa was crushed when he wasn't here today."

"Are you one of the mothers?" Hannah asks.

I lean against the wall, my arms crossed. This woman seems slippery.

Marissa's mom stands and extends her hand. "Yes. Mine is the one in the middle."

"Beautiful girl," Hannah says. "Such gorgeous coloring." She looks at the mother. "Gets it from you."

The mom's smile is enormous.

So slick. I stand in awe of how she's working her.

Hannah looks around. "Any other mothers here?"

Gwen turns to them, and so does Daisy's mom. The others aren't in the hall, probably out running errands.

Hannah shakes their hands. "I'm so excited Blitz is here. He's very devoted to inspiring new dancers. Your girls are exquisite."

She watches them again for a moment through the window as if she's just getting an idea. "I would love, and I do mean *love*, to have your girls do a segment with Blitz for television. I think the world needs to see the incredible work your dancers are doing. It's so inspiring. Anyone can dance. They are proof."

She turns back to them. "They could be like little ambassadors, showing all the children that they can be anything they want to be."

I want to snort with derision, but I can see all the moms are totally buying into it.

"What would they have to do?" Gwen asks. She's skeptical, and I'm so happy about that I want to hug her.

"Just do their dance," Hannah says. "I can bring Blitz back. That will make them happy, right?"

The moms nod.

"I have a little waiver that just says you approve them being on the air. Naturally we won't say who they are, for their privacy." Hannah signs an invisible page in the air. "And we'll bring two, maybe three, cameramen to capture their beauty next week."

"What should they wear?" Marissa's mother asks.

"Just have them in their favorite outfit," Hannah says.

"We have their recital costumes already," Daisy's mom says. She turns to me. "Livia, is it okay if they wear them next week?"

"We're missing the hats," I say, but I can see that they don't really want to know what I think. It's practically a done deal. "But you can check with Janel."

Hannah claps her hands. "I'll speak to Blitz about

it. And the owner. It will be amazing." She passes out cards to the mothers. "I'll be in touch through the studio. Tell the other moms!"

She walks past me, her heels clicking on the floor. She doesn't seem to need my guidance or help, so I just let her go.

Seriously slick. So this is how Hollywood works.

The moms are abuzz, their heads together over their cards.

Gwen says, "Are we sure we want our girls on television?"

The urge to hug her strikes again. I'm glad she's hesitating. I don't want Gabriella to have anything to do with Blitz.

"I'm thrilled," Daisy's mom says. "I can't wait to tell everyone!"

They are going to push it through, I can tell. Their energetic chatter fills me with dread.

Janel is doing fine with the girls, so I head to the foyer to see where the manager shark has gone. When I get to the end of the hall, I peek around the corner to see if she is near the front desk.

Suze and Jacob are there, talking in hushed tones. They get quiet when they see me.

"Hey, Livia," Jacob says. "How are the ballerinas?"

"Good," I say. "Suze, I guess you figured out that Blitz isn't with our group anymore."

She nods and glances at Jacob. Something is up. I

give them a friendly wave and keep walking, past the desk to the other side where glass doors separate the studios from the recital hall.

I hear voices immediately. Danika's office is to the right. I scoot past the half-closed door and duck inside the auditorium, perching against the last row of chairs so I can still hear.

It's dark, but if I'm caught, I can easily say I was checking to see if anyone needed help with the stage setup for the recital.

I sit very still and listen.

First is that Hannah woman. "This is a brilliant opportunity! Those wheelchair girls are precious and it's good all around. Of course we want that one."

"Blitz is not welcome in that class," Danika says.

"Nonsense," Hannah says. "They love him. They were heartbroken that he wasn't there."

When Blitz speaks, I nearly jump out of my skin. I had no idea he was even here! "Hannah, there are plenty of classes we can use for the video."

Hannah's voice takes on an edge. "The dancing elderly will be good for a laugh, but let me assure you, those ballerinas are what you need to get back in the producer's good graces."

Nobody talks for a moment. It's a stalemate. My fingers squeeze the back of the cushioned chair. This is all my fault. If Blitz and I had just stayed apart, he could have had his video and nobody would be fighting right now.

I push down the seat and plop into it, sinking down low. Maybe I am the one who should leave.

But Gabriella! I can't. I just can't.

Tears threaten. I'll tell Danika I will skip next week. They can do their video. I wasn't going to be in it anyway. I won't see Blitz again. It's not like I really want to. I was just one of a half-dozen San Antonio conquests. His most naive and pathetic. The others were so glamorous, so sure of themselves.

The stage is dark other than a few safety lights along the edge. It has a hallowed glow to it, as if it is illuminated by ghosts.

The voices in the office drop down, talking in quiet tones. I wonder why, but my curiosity isn't strong enough to get closer to hear. I just sit in the chair and feel sorry for myself. I won't regret that kiss. And remembering how we danced onstage is a choice. There isn't any reason to make it an ugly memory.

For a little while, I got to teach ballet to the most famous dancer in the world. That was something. Really something.

I sit up. Time to go. Class is probably about over and I might as well hug the girls good-bye before I head home.

But the shadow of a figure crosses the pale light onstage.

Blitz.

He's come inside and gone up the stairs in the dark without my even noticing. I hunker down in the seat, wondering what he's up to.

He takes a few leaps, turning, legs scissoring. His form is lean and true, striking and powerful. He drops to the floor and pops back again in a back flip, so unexpected that I almost gasp out loud.

Then he runs and attempts a *grand jeté*. It's not bad. His arms still aren't quite right, but then, I'm not really an instructor. Just a two-year ballet student with a crush. He really should get Betsy to fix his form. I picture him doing one on *Dance Blitz* when he returns and my heart glows. It's a little bit of me he will take with him.

He does another *grand jeté* but when he gets to the floor, he drops to one knee, head down. It's like he's broken, struck by grief.

Without thinking, I jump from my chair. "Blitz! Are you okay?" My feet carry me up the aisle to the stage.

He quickly stands, resuming his easy posture. "Livia?" he asks.

I hurry up the stairs. "Yes. Why are you dancing in the dark?"

"Why are you sitting in it?"

I want to run up to him and throw my arms around him. But I stop short, the image of all those women, all those nights, running through my head.

Blitz moves forward to reach for me, but I take a step back. He drops his arms. "What's wrong?" he asks.

I don't want to ask about the other girls or admit I cyberstalked him. But it isn't really in me to lie to him. And I have no explanation for my behavior today compared to Friday if I don't say it.

"How is Avery Hines?" I ask.

He lets out a long rush of air. "Nicer than people give her credit for," he says. "And madly in love with another girl. She just won't go public yet."

My legs wobble, so I plop down on the stage. "Really?"

Blitz sits next to me. We both look out to the shadowy seats, the entrance, how close Danika and his manager are right now. But we're just two people sitting on a stage.

He must feel the same, because he kicks his legs out in front of him and leans on his hands like this is any ordinary conversation. "I'm guessing if you saw one, you saw them all." He doesn't wait for a confirmation, but goes on. "Jenna is someone I knew from high school. She's about to get married, but after those pictures came out, her fiancé is not speaking to her. I really screwed that up. I'm hoping she can fix it."

"Oh, no."

Blitz stares up into the dark canopy above the stage, the mass of stage lights and curtains invisible in the blackness. "Yep. And then there were two women with the network. I'm pretty sure one was testing to see if I would act like a man-whore to justify them killing my contract without even paying me."

He shakes his head. "The other was just — God, I don't know. Bitter, I guess. It was a difficult dinner to force myself through. There were two other men with us but of course the photos cut them out."

Somewhere deep in my chest, a tiny glow of hope starts to light up around my heart. I want it to go away, to take me back to the safe place where I knew it was over. But it refuses.

"I guess it was pretty tough seeing all that," Blitz says. "I didn't go anywhere this weekend, though. I turned everything down. Just spent time with my parents."

His eyes shine in the low light. He's watching me earnestly.

My chest rises and falls with each breath. I refused to wear the light blue leotard, so it's the white and yellow today, glowing in the dark. I pull my knees up to my chest. "It was definitely hard," I manage to say. "But I didn't do a Burn Blitz Burn Tweet."

His laugh rings in the silent hall. "Oh my God, Livia, this was the longest weekend of my life." He shifts close to me and pulls me into his arms. "All I could think about was my princess. Even my mother noticed."

My face snaps around to his. "Really?"

"Really. She asked why I acted like I was walking on a cloud."

He shifts me onto his lap. I sit sideways on him, my head on his shoulder. It's frighteningly intimate, closer than we've been before. My heart thuds wildly.

His fingers trail along the nape of my neck, my back, my shoulders. "I don't think I've ever gotten so worked up over a kiss before," he says. His breath tickles my jaw.

I turn my face to his and our lips meet. The kiss is tender, conciliatory, a reconnection. His hand moves to the back of my head. His mouth covers mine, increasing the urgency, his tongue seeking entrance.

I taste him, no mint gum today, but a hint of coffee and cream. My body is less hesitant, more eager to move in close, to feel his muscular body tight against mine.

I shift to face him, my legs straddling his waist. His dance tights are form fitting and sleek. I move against him, feeling our bodies connect. It's slippery and smooth, so easy to shift into place.

His hands grasp my ribs. His thumb slides up, flirting with the underside of my breast.

I suck in a breath against his mouth. Fire licks through me. It's way beyond what I felt in the storage room. It's needy and unquenched. I break away, my breathing rapid.

"We should probably be careful," Blitz says.

I nod and shift away from him. I don't want to, but my brain is buzzing. So many reversals in the past few minutes. Hating him, feeling despair, then hope, and now fire.

"Why is Danika against us?" Blitz asks. "I mean, I know I have a horrible reputation, which I totally deserve." He stands up and reaches for my hand to help me rise as well. "But she's the owner, and you're a student. Is she a close friend of your family?"

I shake my head no. I don't want him to know my situation, how sheltered I've been, how abnormal.

"Then let's see each other away from here," Blitz says. "We can go anywhere. Will you do that?" His eyes implore mine, flashing in the dark. "Tonight? Tomorrow? I can't wait any longer than that."

I think about my time, how to get away, searching for possibilities. I could lie again, say I'm coming here, say Danika has a work session and lunch planned for the staff. I'll make it work. I can always just walk away. Dad won't be home. Mom can't exactly lock me in my room.

"Yes," I say. "Tomorrow. Away from here." I think frantically. "I'll meet you at the park on this street, a few blocks down. By the swings."

"That's adorable," he says. "And a date. When?"

"When do you have a class here?" I ask.

"Ten. Done at eleven. Tappin' Grandmas, remember?"

Right. "Okay, eleven-fifteen at the park."

He pulls me to him fiercely. "It's a date, Princess."

We scurry off the stage and go separately out of the hall.

Class is long over, so I don't talk to anyone, but just head outside and into the bright fall day. I'm halfway home when it hits me, and I *grand jeté* on the sidewalk.

I have a date with Blitz!

## Chapter Thirteen

I dress carefully the next day in a loose T-shirt and baggy cropped sweatpants, like I'm going to be doing hard physical work. Beneath them, I have on my favorite red shirt, casual but with a little shine to it, and a simple black skirt. I've carefully folded it flat against my belly and hips so it won't be too crumpled when I change out of the pants.

I sling a clearly almost-empty dance bag on my shoulder. I need it to put the old clothes in, but I couldn't risk a change of nice things in there in case Mom checked. It only holds a pair of flats so I don't have to wear my work sneakers with my skirt later. She should assume my ballet slippers are in there.

This has to work. If she says no, I have to walk out anyway. My heart is pounding fiercely in my chest. I'm going to lie. Big-time lie. I haven't lied since the time before, when I got pregnant.

But I don't feel guilty. This is too important. I'm nineteen. I should be allowed to date. I can't live with my parents forever. I can't be punished all my life.

Mom folds towels on the living room sofa. Andy is having recess time in the backyard. Good. I don't want any witnesses, and Andy has an uncanny ability to notice when I'm trying to get away with something.

"Your hair sure looks pretty," Mom says, and I lift my hand to it self-consciously. I've plaited a single braid around my crown. The rest flows black and shiny to my shoulders.

"Thanks. Just trying something new."

"What's the bag for?"

"Today is the day at Dreamcatcher when all the staff and helpers unearth all the holiday decorations from the storage room. It's a big job and Danika will have lunch for us brought in."

Mom frowns. "I don't remember this from last year," she says.

I'm ready for this. "I wasn't assisting with the wheelchair class last year."

She nods. "Well, I guess that is okay." She glances out the back window at Andy digging in the sandbox. "He'll miss you today."

"He'll be fine," I say. "Have you thought about enrolling him in school? I think he's lonely."

She shakes her head. "I'm not ready to let him go yet."

I don't get why. He's only eight. And it's not like he can get pregnant. But now is not the time to get into this argument.

"I'll see you later this afternoon. I'll be home way before Dad."

"Make sure of it," she says.

I wave and head for the front door. As soon as I'm a block away, I want to start skipping. I'm out! I'm going on a date!

It's only 10:45. I'm early so I can duck into the public bathroom to shed the outer layer of my clothes and change shoes. I have a panicky moment, picturing myself going home and forgetting to put the sweatpants back on. But I can't make that mistake. I won't.

When I get to the park, it's mostly empty, just a few moms and small children. It's not a popular place, rundown and in dire need of new equipment.

The trees shed leaves on my path as I head toward the bathroom. The weather still hasn't broken for autumn yet, although it's cooler than the ninety degrees of summer. The walk is bright and pleasant, the sort of day when anything seems possible.

The inside of this outdoor bathroom is about as

romantic as a sewer tank. I wrinkle my nose and quickly remove the sweatpants and T-shirt, carefully rolling them so they won't look oddly scrunched when I wear them later.

Then I switch shoes. There's no mirror here, but I doubt I look any different than I did at home. Simple, a little plain, no makeup, but with a pretty hairstyle, like a princess. He calls me that. I have no idea why. I should hate it. A lot of people would find it condescending.

But I can't. It makes me think of us dancing across a ballroom, him in a uniform and me in a ball gown, finding that happily ever after.

I'm such a wreck! Reality, Livia!

My bag is packed. I check my watch as I exit the bathroom. Straight-up eleven. He'll be here before long, however much time it takes him to extricate himself from the grandmas and put his shirt back on.

The thought makes me laugh. At times like this, I still struggle to align the man I've gotten to know with the larger-than-life personality of his show. It's as if there are two people — Blitz from television, and Benjamin the charmer.

I walk along the path to a bench near the street, so he can spot me easily.

I know intellectually that Blitz and Benjamin are the same person. And in the footage I saw with Mindy over the weekend, him with all those different sophisticated women on his arm, the two versions definitely collided.

But none of that is what he is like at the dance academy. He shies away from the women who come on too strong. He delights in the children.

He worries about me. *Me.* A plain naive girl who can barely *pirouette* and hasn't earned her toe shoes.

But maybe I am more than that. There's this power in me now, the strength and determination I once felt, before my family hid me in shame. I am a survivor. I can be brave. I can reach for what I want.

I can love someone again.

The crunch of leaves makes my head pop up expectantly. It's just an elderly man walking his dog. He nods at me.

I sit on the bench, looking up the sidewalk. There is a car coming down the street. The fanciest car I've seen in my life. Cherry red. Sleek. The hood is low and long. It looks like it could scoop you up and sweep you away all on its own.

This is a pretty poor part of town, mostly families. We don't see cars like that around here. There is only one person who could be driving that car.

Blitz.

I squint at the windshield, but I can't see inside. There's a glare from the sun and the rolling reflection of leaves from the trees overhead.

So I wait, sitting primly on the bench. The car slows down as it nears and sidles up next to the curb.

And stops.

The driver-side door opens, and a familiar black head of hair pops above the roof. He's wearing sunglasses that obscure his eyes, but I'd know him anywhere.

"I think I'm having a dream," he calls out. "About rescuing a princess from a dystopian land."

I glance around. It's true. The park is mostly broken concrete and the paint on the bench is peeling. The grass hasn't survived the summer.

"Are you a white knight or a black one?" I call out.

"The blackest," he says as he comes around the car. "But I'll scrub myself clean for you."

Then he's in front of me, tall and strong. He's changed into jeans and a loose button-down shirt, pale yellow and expensive looking.

"Well, I guess I'll take my chances," I say and lift my hand.

He pulls me up from the bench, then brings my fingers to his lips. "At least my chariot is fancy."

We turn to it.

"I'm afraid of getting it dirty," I say. "Should I take my shoes off?"

He opens the passenger door. "Uh, you haven't seen the inside yet."

I peer in. "Oh!" I exclaim. The interior is fancy,

black leather and a dash that looks like an airplane cockpit. But, wow! There are cups and papers and crumpled clothes and wrappers everywhere.

I sit down and try to make room for my feet. "You need an intervention," I say. "Or a maid."

He bends down and peers in. "It's really bad, isn't it? I should have stopped somewhere to have it cleared out."

His face is very close to mine. I could turn my head and kiss his cheek.

"I guess you need to have some sort of flaw," I say.

This makes him laugh. "Oh, I have plenty," he says. He stands up and closes the door. A moment later, he appears on the other side and slides in.

"So where are we going?" I ask.

"My private helicopter to fly to Mexico for lunch," he says.

My heart hammers. "What?"

He laughs again. "I'm kidding. I'm not that crazy." He fastens his seat belt. "I was thinking the San José Mission. I haven't seen it in years. It was my favorite."

"It's my favorite too," I say. My father had us visit all the missions, including the Alamo, as part of our homeschooling.

"There's a little hole-in-the-wall restaurant nearby, owned by the most amazing lady. She's a friend of my family."

The car zooms forward, and I resist the urge to clutch the door handle. "That sounds good," I say.

We drive toward the freeway. I glance around at the debris in the car, trying to get a feel for what Blitz likes.

"How do you stay fit eating McDonald's all the time?" I ask.

He glances down at the cups and bags. "Busted," he says. "That was mostly on the drive from LA."

"You drove?"

"Yeah. I avoid airports and other places with tons of people," he says. "I think you underestimate how hated I am right now."

"But you kissed a pig!"

He laughs again. "I'm going to have to do a lot more to get past this." He signals and speeds up to enter the highway.

I screw up my courage and ask, "So why did you do it?"

"Do what?" he asks.

"The terrible thing," I say. I really don't want to say it out loud.

He sighs. "It wasn't supposed to be a Tweet. I was tired. And sick of that girl. She was making my life hell. How that was supposed to make me pick her as the winner, I don't know. She wanted to go somewhere off camera, so I took her to a hotel."

His expression is dark. It's as hard for him to say

this as it is for me to hear about this girl he slept with.

"Are there usually cameras around?" I ask.

"Yes and no. The show makes it appear that they follow us everywhere, but they don't really. Now, my house in LA is definitely rigged. You never know when they are going to activate something or where one might have been moved that you don't know about."

"That's a crazy life," I say.

"Yeah, well, we were avoiding it. I've been under some pressure since I didn't pick anyone last season. The producers said I had to choose a girl this time, even if I didn't propose." He glances over at me. "I have no plans to propose, by the way. I might have danced with one of them for a while. They were all good. But there was no real love affair happening."

I figure he has to say that. He's on a date with me, after all.

"So you posted the picture without paying attention where it went?"

"That's the thing. I just sent the picture to my friend Duke. It was a joke between us. A terrible, horrible joke. But meant to be private."

"Still, sending a picture of a girl like that."

He nods. "I know. I freely admit to being a bastard. I guess I just sent it to the wrong account. And screwed myself. I was going to throw this deal at some point anyway. Nobody could get through that lifestyle unscathed."

My stomach sinks. What am I doing here? It's so hard to talk to him. He looks like Benjamin. Acts like Benjamin. But this discussion is all about Blitz. That decadent life. And even if he didn't mean to share that picture with the world, he still took it. And said what he said. Even if it was just to a friend.

I look at his car. His life as Blitz is just like this. Fancy on the outside. Trash on the inside.

"You think you'll get your show back?" I ask. "Will kissing a pig and dancing with girls in wheelchairs really do it?"

"I adore those girls," he says. "Don't think for a minute I don't."

"Okay," I say. I'm not sure I believe him right now, but I'll go along.

"I'd rather leave them out of it, but it looks like we're filming them on Tuesday."

"I gathered."

"I don't know about the show. I'm not sure I even want it back at this point." He reaches over and takes my hand. "I had forgotten what normal life was like."

His fingers are warm and strong. I feel that glow again. I'm running hot and cold. I don't know what is real and what is acting. It's so confusing.

I glance around the car. "Did they put cameras in here too?"

He shakes his head. "No. This car is brand new. I bought it on my way out of town."

"But your old one had them?"

"Yes. And I didn't feel confident that they weren't still turning them on even after the show was suspended. Some of the camera work was done remotely, and footage of me is easy to sell to tabloids and gossip shows."

"Wow. That's quite a life."

"It is no life at all."

We're already near the exit that leads to the mission. It's a beautiful day to go, warm and breezy. And midday during the week with school in session means it should be quiet.

"Do people recognize you around town?" I ask.

"Not as much as you'd think," he says. "Generally I can walk around fine until somebody does spot me. If they start taking pictures, others figure there must be a reason, and before I know it, I'm mobbed."

We drive down Southcross. The houses here are large and historic looking with wide flat lawns. The trees grow more numerous. I feel happy about my city, full of pride that I live here, and that Blitz was born here. I aim to have a good time today. Nobody's giving him a chance anymore. But I will.

We park in the near-empty lot. In the distance, the round-topped church and the stone tower are visible. It's always breathtaking to see the old buildings after the modern drive on a highway surrounded by cars. I feel settled here, like I'm walking a path that has been paved by people braver than I am.

"I love this view," he says. "It's like nowhere else."

We peer out the window, then seem to simultaneously realize how silly that is when we could be walking around. Within seconds, we're out of the car and flying down the path toward the mission.

Entering through the stone arch is like walking into another world. The mission grounds are large and surrounded by a stone wall. The modern city is erased, invisible from inside.

"I've forgotten how peaceful it is here," Blitz says. He takes my hand, and I let him. We've escaped everything that plagues us in our lives. His Blitz Burns. My overbearing father. We're not affected by those people right now.

We wander down a path, heading toward the towering church with its round roof. The tiny cross on top seems almost an afterthought. Only a few other people wander the grass, which is still green, even if patchy with dirt.

Instead of aiming for the church doors, though, Blitz leads us up to the long row of double archways, two stories that were supposed to be reconstructed but never were.

We duck inside the roofless enclosure. It's one of

the most beautiful places I've ever been, just as breathtaking as the first time I saw it.

But now, with me feeling so happy with Blitz, it's beyond beauty and into the magical. The light and shadows of a dozen arches cast patterns across the ground.

"Fit for a princess," Blitz says, and his hand position changes on mine. I recognize it, and without him having to cue me at all, I twirl into him until I rest against his body, chest to chest.

He whirls me out again, and soon we're waltzing, one-two-three, music not necessary, just the beats of our hearts. My shoes slide along the rough floor, keeping time with him.

Blitz brings me back to him and we cross through one of the archways in big sweeping steps. Then we're inside again, through the next arch, turning as we go. The light flashes bright and dark, and the stone walls rush past.

He turns me again, and this time when he reels me back, he holds me close, leaning me back on his arm.

I'm breathing hard, staring up into his face. His eyes are on me, happy, light. I wait, expectant, so happy, for his kiss.

When it comes, I feel sparks, honest-to-goodness fireworks all throughout my body. The breeze rushes through the arches and tousles my hair. His lips are warm and seeking.

I open for him, drawing him in. He breathes into me, and it's like life itself has caught hold of me. I'm so alive, feeling everything. The heaviness and misery fall away. I release his hand and bring my arm up around his neck.

My fingers memorize his skin. The muscles that lead up to his head. The bristle of the short hairs behind his ear. I want to know everything, touch it all.

The ground crunches as someone else enters the archways. I hear "Did you know this used to be a convent?"

Then an abrupt stop and a startled "Oh!"

Blitz smiles against my mouth and breaks this kiss. "It doesn't feel like a convent right now," he says against my ear.

He stands me upright and we dash away from the tourist couple with their cameras and information book. We run along the path, past the stone water well and the spartan trees. We fly to the farthest corner of the mission, away from anything interesting enough to draw probing eyes.

And he kisses me again, thirsty, hungry, longing. He leans against the stone, drawing me against him, our bodies pressed tightly together.

I never want this moment to end. The warm air,

the cool stone, his lean muscled body against mine. His hands roam my back and waist and shoulders. I long for more privacy, to release myself into his possession. But I know I can't do that. I'm glad we're here, this beautiful place, but also public, and outdoors. We can't be tempted.

My traitorous stomach rumbles against his. He breaks the kiss and his mouth nibbles along my jaw. "Hungry?" he asks.

I want to shout, "No!" but I can't deny the noises of my belly. When it happens again, he laughs.

"Come on, then, let's eat something." He takes my hand.

We walk slowly along the path. The world is so bright, green and blue and beautiful. I can't remember feeling quite this high, even in the time before. Maybe because I was young then. Maybe because we were so wrong.

Today feels right. I've lied to get here. I've taken risks. But walking here with Blitz is absolutely worth whatever the cost.

## Chapter Fourteen

The restaurant Blitz chooses is definitely a hole in the wall. The outside is white stucco with a dark brown door. The roof is tin.

But the gravel parking lot is packed with cars and pickup trucks. When we go inside, a couple gruff-looking men with bushy beards are ahead of us for a table.

A stout Hispanic woman in a white ruffled blouse and brightly striped skirt whisks one of the men to a booth. Blitz stands patiently by a window, drawing me close to him, his chin on my shoulder and his arms around my waist.

When the woman returns, she notices him and her eyes light up. "Benjamin! Is that you?" She fans herself with a menu. "*¡Dios mio!*"

A few customers notice her surprise, and she

immediately straightens her expression. She motions him forward. "Come this way."

We walk toward her, and she gives him an enveloping hug. "How is your mama, *hijo*?"

"She's good," he says. "Glad I'm home for a bit."

"You not cause her any trouble, no?" The woman's face is stern.

"No, no," he says.

The woman turns to me. "And who is this? She is lovely, but not Mexican!" She fingers my black hair.

I have no idea how to act. I just stand there, trying not to look panicked.

"No, Lito, I'm seeing a white girl." Blitz can barely contain his laughter as Lito clucks.

"Well, I'm sure we'll like her anyway." She smiles at me. "You don't put up with any nonsense from this one, okay?"

I nod.

Another table leaves and she waves for one of the men in line to go take it. "You wait right here, Benjamin. I'll seat you somewhere no one will look and see who you are."

"Thanks, Lito," Blitz says. He takes my hand and pulls me closer to the side wall, behind the little podium where Lito keeps the menus.

When she has settled the other man and motioned for a waitress to attend to him, she returns to us. "I'll take you to the family table, of course," she says. She picks up a couple of menus and looks me over. "You could use a few tacos, little one," she says to me.

"She's a dancer," Blitz says as we walk along the wall that borders the kitchen. I can hear the sizzle of fajitas and smell something in a fryer. My stomach rumbles again.

"Ah, so she has to stay skinny," Lito says. "A pity."

A half wall in the back corner separates a long table from the rest of the restaurant. The chairs are empty, although the space is littered with cups and newspapers and books.

"Everybody works the lunch rush," Lito says. "You will have your secret space." She winks at him. She is about to pass us the menus, then thinks better of it and tucks them under her arm. "Never mind these. I will bring you what you need." She takes off to go into the kitchen.

"She really is like family," I say.

Blitz holds a chair out for me. "Lito is a very pushy friend of my mother's."

"She doesn't want you dating a *gringa*, then?"

He laughs. "She is just seeing how you will react. It doesn't matter. Nobody cares."

When we sit down, Blitz takes my hand and kisses each finger, one at a time. The food smells divine, and I try to relax. I'm in another world, and it's good to be out among new people, even if it's scary.

"So who is your best friend in the world?" I ask him.

He presses his lips against my knuckles and scrunches his eyebrows. Finally he says, "Well, up until the scandal, I would say it was Duke. We grew up together, and I moved him to LA to be a bodyguard of sorts. But we haven't talked since everything went down."

"Hasn't that been a while?"

"Almost a month now. I stuck around a couple weeks, hoping it would blow over. But I swear every day there was some new women's group ready to express their outrage."

"Have you talked to the girl?"

He closes his eyes as if the thought of it is painful. "My lawyer has advised against it."

"I'm sorry I keep bringing this up," I say. "I really didn't know anything about this until I met you."

"It's okay," he says. "I wouldn't go out with me either without the third degree."

"I don't even have a Twitter account," I say. "So at least I can't jump on the Burn Blitz Burn hashtag."

He smiles, kissing my hand again. "I'm hoping I never make you feel like you should."

My heart flips. This is intense. I lay my cheek against his hand, wrapped around mine. I want this moment to last, every moment to last. But I don't even know how often I can see him, or how long he'll be here.

Lito returns with a pitcher of tea and two glasses. "It's got sugar," she says. "You can burn it off later." She plops them on the table. Behind her, a short man sets down a basket of chips and an enormous bowl of queso.

Blitz and I look at each other and laugh.

"What?" Lito says. "Your girl will blow away otherwise. You too!" She throws her hands up in the air. "Humans are supposed to eat! And don't tell me you want vegetarian *frijoles*! They aren't any good without lard!" She takes off again, followed by the server.

"My LA friends would run screaming from this place," Blitz says, dunking a tortilla chip deep into the melted cheese. "But Lito's right. We can burn it off." His eyes dance with mischief. "One way or another."

My chest constricts. I look away, picking up a chip and nibbling on the corner.

"Come on," he says. "Dunk it good. Don't make me eat all this cheese alone!" He picks up another chip and buries it in the queso, then lifts it to my mouth.

I bite it, feeling the queso drip. Blitz catches it with his finger, then brings it to his lips. "You cannot take the San Antonio out of this LA boy."

"You think you'll go back?"

"I haven't succeeded in convincing them to let me yet. I'll have a decision then." He picks up another chip and taps it on the edge of the bowl. "I really don't know what to do."

The thought of him leaving just as I get to know him, to pick out a dance partner on live television, is just too much.

At least it isn't a wife.

Or so he says.

Lito returns with a steaming platter and a tortilla warmer. She plops them down. The metal plate, nestled on a wooden base, is filled with shrimp and chicken, peppers, and onions.

"Flour tortillas," she says with a huff and makes the sign of the cross. "Because you've gone as white as the belly of a whale."

"Lito, you are so cruel to me," Blitz says. "Come give me a kiss."

Lito rolls her eyes, but leans down and presses her lips to Blitz's forehead as if he is a child.

"You know you love me," he says.

"I do." She laughs and shakes her finger at him. "Bring your mama around. I haven't seen her in too long."

"Will do."

The other server comes up and sets down more

plates. A bowl of pale orange rice. A plate of refried black beans. Then a pile of something green, flat, and somewhat squishy looking.

I don't want to ask what it is in front of Lito. She looks over the plates that have been placed on the table and nods in approval. "Let me know if you need anything else," she says.

"It looks great," Blitz says. "Thank you."

Lito waves her hands at him as she leaves, the server trailing in her wake.

When she is gone, I poke at the green things. "What are these?"

"*Nopales*."

When I look at him quizzically, he adds, "Cactus."

"Oh!"

"It's really good when done correctly," Blitz says. He adds one to my plate. "And Lito really knows how to prepare them."

I poke at it tentatively. "I'm game to try anything."

"Really?" His fork halts in the middle of spearing a piece of shrimp. His smile is positively devilish. "How are you with handcuffs?"

My face blossoms with heat. I scoop a spoonful of beans and plop them on my plate.

"Too cliché," he says. "I knew it."

When I still don't look at him, he places his hand

over mine. "I'm sorry. I forget sometimes that you're real, not part of a studio audience."

I can't look him in the eye. It's not that I'm offended by him mentioning handcuffs. It's just how casually he treats sex, like it's something you do with anyone, like sharing a pair of headphones to listen to a song. Or passing over a cup so someone else can sample your peppermint coffee.

I almost want to bring up the paternity suits. If there were fifteen of them, there had to be a lot of women. Like a ridiculous amount. But instead, I open the tortilla warmer and pull out a fluffy warm tortilla, flour, just like Lito said.

Blitz sits back in his chair. "I've wrecked things," he says. "I'm really sorry."

He sounds so contrite that I take pity on him.

"It's okay," I say. "I'm probably more uptight than you're used to."

I want to tell him that I'm not really prudish. I'm more passionate than he can imagine. I can ignore anything, even the red sirens going off that tell me I'm wrong, so wrong, because I am buried in such bliss.

But I don't say it. I'm not sure it's even true anymore.

"I don't believe that," he says. "I've danced with you."

Our smile at that is genuine and the tension falls away.

We dig into the meal. Lito checks on us, opening the tortilla warmer and squinting at the dishes to make sure we are eating to her satisfaction.

It's delicious. There's some sort of spice on the shrimp that builds with every bite, but the fat in the refried beans cuts the heat so that I can keep going. The food starts to make sense, like culinary chemistry. It's so much better than the plain meat and potatoes that serve as the base of most of our meals at home.

I want to keep the mood light, so I lean over to Blitz and say, "So if you do choose a wife from your show, are you going to make sure she knows how to cook like this?"

His smile spreads slowly. "Are you interested in the position?"

I sit back. I hadn't expected that. "I can cook. Give me a recipe and I'll try anything."

I can tell he wants to make another innuendo out of that, but he resists, folding his cloth napkin and setting it beside his plate. "Can I have you for the whole day? Can we just keep going all afternoon and into the evening and until it's a new day?"

If only. I check my watch. It's already been three hours. I can spare maybe one more.

"I'm sort of a daytime Cinderella," I say. "I'm supposed to be back to scrubbing floors at three."

He sighs. His hand reaches across the table for mine. "Tomorrow, then? I didn't see you last Thursday."

I wonder if I can get away with dancing tomorrow. Maybe, since I didn't today. I can remind Mom that I'm working for my toe shoes and need the practice. Three times a week minimum, Betsy has said.

"When are you at the academy?" I ask him.

"After school," he says. "It's hip-hop day."

"Come early," I tell him. "Like at two. We can dance." This will also create a deadline. When it's time for the hip-hop class, he'll have to go and I can run home.

"I'll be there," he says. He lifts my fingers to his lips. I'm so used to this gesture now that it's almost like our private code. I refuse to think about him kissing anyone else like this. I'll assume it's a Benjamin thing, too old-fashioned for the fast lane with Blitz Craven.

Lito comes out. "I hope you liked it all. You know you aren't paying for it."

Blitz nods. "I wouldn't dare offend you like that."

She kisses his cheek and turns to me. "You will be good for this ne'er-do-well," she says. "I think you have him by the tail."

What does she mean by that? I look at Blitz, who shrugs. "Probably so."

We head back to Blitz's car. A couple of guys are standing by it, taking pictures.

I hang back. "Do you think they know who you are?" I ask.

"Nah," he says. "The Ferrari always draws a crowd." The car chirps as he approaches and the boys back away.

"Sick ride," one says.

"Thanks," Blitz calls back.

They look at me, and one elbows the other. He says, "I bet she is too."

Before I can even process what is happening, Blitz has rushed the guy and punched him in the face.

"Blitz!" I say. "Stop!"

The guy is sprawled out on the asphalt.

"Don't talk that way about her," Blitz says.

"What the hell?" the guy says, holding his jaw.

"Please get in the car," I say. "It's okay." My hands are shaking. I'm scared to death. I'm so afraid they'll make a scene, that there will be a big fight. Blitz could get hurt, the police could come, someone could video us. I could be discovered. It's all blowing through my mind like a horror film.

Blitz stands there a moment, staring the guys down, daring them to do or say anything else. But they walk away, shaking their heads.

Finally, he turns to the passenger door and holds it open for me. I slide into the seat. He walks around the front and sits as well, but he doesn't start the car.

"You okay?" I ask him. "Did you hurt your hand?"

"No."

Now that we are safely in the car, I'm less freaked out and more worried about him. "Let me see."

He grips his steering wheel, so I reach for his hand myself, pulling it toward me. Then I do what he has so often done for me, bringing his red angry knuckles to my lips to kiss each one.

He comes down from his anger. I can feel it dropping, degree by degree. When his breathing is back to normal, I hold his hand to my chest. "You better now?"

He nods. His voice is strangled when he says, "I'm sorry."

"Is this common, taking punches at people who insult your women?"

Blitz laughs a little. "Actually, no. I've been in the tabloids for a lot of things, but never for hitting someone."

"Good to know," I say. I wonder why this time was different. "Do people usually not dare to insult your dates?"

He shakes his head. "No, it's been done. I've just never felt quite so..." he falters. "Protective. And angry. He really pissed me off. Nobody should disrespect you like that."

I don't point out that sending a naked picture of someone isn't exactly respectful. But maybe he's learned his lesson. Maybe these hard knocks are what he needed to realize he couldn't keep living his life the way he had been.

"Well, thank you," I say. "For defending my honor."

He starts the car with a low rumble of the engine. "You're welcome," he says.

We head back to my part of town. It's been an interesting afternoon, full of reversals and revelations. My time with Blitz is always like this. He's not like anyone I've ever met.

And since I don't know how long it will last, I have to hold on to every moment.

## Chapter Fifteen

I'm back in the light blue leotard, the one Blitz likes, on Thursday. I'm skating on thin ice at home because Mom is unhappy I'm going to the academy in the afternoon instead of the morning.

But I performed beautifully at lunch for Dad, being extra useful with Andy's studies and showing him my latest practice test results for my SAT.

It was only afterward, when I came out in my leotard, that Mom tried to put her foot down.

"You're going up there every day now," she says. "Your father won't like it."

I admit to being a little flip with her, saying, "You act as though he is the only one in this family who can have an opinion!"

My heart doesn't slow down until I'm well along the path to the academy. I've never given my parents pushback about how they limit my activities. I let my shame control me, assuming I deserved what happened. I had taken a fall. A big one. With exactly the wrong person.

But I feel differently now. I'm awake again, fully alive. And I don't want to live their way. I want to choose my own.

Danika is in the foyer when I arrive, dressed for a meeting in a suit and heels, not dance clothes. She pauses when she sees me. "This isn't your usual day."

"I want those toe shoes!" I tell her.

She nods and passes a set of keys to Suze. "I'll be back tomorrow," she says to her. "Lock everything up for me tonight."

I'm relieved she'll be gone. That means she can't catch me with Blitz. Hopefully I've beaten him here so she doesn't even have to worry.

"What's open?" I ask Suze.

"Two, three, and four," she says. "It's quiet back there until the after-school classes begin at three."

"Awesome," I say, practically skipping as I head to the studio hall.

The corridor is quiet. In Studio 1, Betsy is doing a private lesson. All the toddlers are napping at home, and all the school-aged kids are in class. So there isn't much going on.

I head into Studio 4, the one with the Dance of the Shades, because it is officially my favorite. I met

Blitz here for the first time, and it's also where he taught me to waltz.

I sit on a stack of mats and change out my tennis shoes for ballet slippers. I wish I had ballroom shoes, but I can't possibly ask for a pair. Tipping my father off to my dancing with a man would definitely put my ballet work at risk.

Blitz has to know I don't have much money. It's obvious in the leotards that I wear over and over again and my worn shoes. This doesn't seem to matter to him. Maybe it's even a point in my favor.

I go to the barre and begin a warm-up routine. I really do want to try and get some ballet in before Blitz arrives. The thought that he might get to watch my first *relevé* on toe shoes is a powerful motivation.

Not that he'll be there that long. As I run through my *pliés*, I picture the day he drives off in his cluttered red Ferrari, back to LA. My eyes burn, and I flick the back of my hand across my face. I have to stop that.

Blitz is a happy space for me. A temporary reprieve. I can't think of him as anything else. I'll go crazy.

"What has the princess so sad?"

I pop up out of my *plié*. Blitz is here, standing by the door!

"Oh!" I say. "Nothing important."

He walks up to me and is about to kiss me, when

I point at the two-way mirror. "Everyone out there can see us."

"There's nobody out there right now," he says, and presses his lips to mine.

I accept the kiss, but my anxiety is still high. Blitz feels it and pulls away. "Did you know you can defeat a two-way mirror?"

"How?" I ask.

"Well, it only works because it's so bright in here." He gestures to the room. "And dimmer out there." He points to the mirror that is a window to the hall.

"Really?"

He walks over to the light switch. "All you have to do is make it dimmer in here than out there." He flips off half the lights. "And now it's equal."

I can see in the hall now, the mirror turning to glass. "Why did I not know that?" I ask.

"You've never had to be sneaky." He pulls me to the corner, where it is dark and we're not easily spotted in the wall mirrors on the opposite side, and kisses me again.

This definitely feels forbidden. Sneaking in the academy gives me a thrill I haven't known for a long time. I'm anxious at first, but as his tongue slides against mine and I taste him, feel him against me, I'm lost.

It's safe here, things can only go so far. A surge of boldness courses through me and I lift one leg to wrap around his hip. He grabs my outer thighs and pulls both legs around him so that I straddle his waist. He presses me against the wall, his kiss heated and urgent. When my ankles are locked behind his back, he frees up one of his hands and goes straight to my breast.

I gasp, shock waves blasting through me. I can feel him now, erect against me, our dance clothes hiding nothing. For a moment, I'm weightless, floating in a void where there is no academy, no studio, no window, no world. Just Blitz's hands and mouth and body.

Outside the window, the lights flicker. A transition is starting. There's no one to move about the hall, but some may come if there is a class in the next session.

Blitz groans and releases me. "We have got to stop doing this here," he says. "I can't take it."

My body is pliant and warm. "Agreed."

"Can I see you tonight? I want darkness and cover and just you." His eyes are pleading.

I can't think of any way to make that happen. My parents. Dinner. Bedtime. Check-ins. My house is a prison.

"My parents are very strict," I say. "I'll have to think of something."

Something flickers across his face. "How old are you, Livia?" he asks. I can tell he's picturing another scandal, statutory rape or some underage sting operation.

"Nineteen," I tell him. "Nothing to worry about."

He releases a rush of air. "Thank God."

A couple figures pass the window, and Blitz pauses by the light switch, waiting for them to enter Studio 3 across the hall. When the corridor is clear, he turns on the lights. "Being alone with you is bad for my self-control," he says.

I have nothing to say to that, so I return to the barre, holding on with one hand as I stretch the muscles that are critical to toe work, calves and feet and ankles.

"I could watch you all day," Blitz says. "I wish I'd done ballet first." He comes to the barre and mimics my movements.

"You're doing pretty well without it," I say. "Pretty much every dancer wants to be you."

"Not lately," he says.

He's very good at matching my poses. I'm sure he learns choreography very fast. "What happened to all the staff people on the show?"

"They had contracts," he says. "They should be okay. But many of them will have moved on, so even if we get to do the finale back, I'll probably only have half the staff."

"Wasn't that one going to be live?"

"Yes," he says with a sigh. "I'm not sure we can

risk that without the team. But again, they haven't exactly agreed to do it. I haven't made a lot of headway."

"Kissing a pig didn't help?" I tease.

"It made for some funny Tweets," he says. "There's a meme going around where they caption the image. My favorite was 'He ate him like bacon.'"

I shift away from the barre and hop in place, warming my legs. Blitz continues to copy everything I do.

"Is the charity work embarrassing for you?" I ask. "You seem okay with it."

"It's all by design," he says. "Hannah set up the embarrassing stuff to give everyone a chance to purge their feelings. But it also keeps my name out there. The worst thing in Hollywood isn't to be hated or ridiculed. It's being forgotten."

I run through the five basic positions as I think about what Blitz said. If I were going through all the hate that Blitz is, I would want to be forgotten fast. But then, I've always shied away from the spotlight.

"And now she thinks the ballet class will help?"

Blitz holds fifth position. "Hannah thinks so. Nobody's talking about the scandal anymore, just the pig. She'll keep the social media manager feeding them topics to shift their attention."

I begin to practice my turns. Blitz should know as

well as anybody how long the public's memory can be. But I do hope their plan works.

Or do I?

"If you don't get the show back, will you stay here?" I ask.

He stops his spin and grins at me. "I'm starting to see some reasons why I might."

In three quick steps, he's crossed the space between us and taken my hand. "Would you like to try a lift?" he asks.

"Okay," I say.

He drags a mat to the center of the room and unfolds it. "I've never dropped anyone, but we usually have spotters," he says. "We'll do something easy."

"I've seen some of the dancers practice on the floor to start," I say.

"I remember doing that in the early days," he says with a smile. He kneels down. "The dancers on the first season of my show weren't as experienced as this last group. I had to start some of them from scratch."

"Like me," I say.

"There's nobody like you," he says.

My body warms over. "So show me what I don't know," I say.

"Come here." He motions me close. "Now sit on my shoulder."

I turn around and prop myself against him. One

of his hands steadies me at my rib cage and the other goes beneath my thigh.

With a powerful movement, he moves to standing. I'm high in the air, trying to keep myself from gripping his head.

"Now act as though you are going to lie facedown, straightening your body while letting your head fall in front of me."

It's hard to do, sort of like choosing to fall off a shelf, but I follow his instructions.

The hand on my ribs slides forward to encircle me and the other grasps my leg. I tumble down in a roll, but when I'm facing out again, Blitz has caught me with a hand on my thigh. I'm head down, legs angled up and away, like a swan dive. We're facing the mirror, and it's beautiful. I quickly arrange my arms so that they are not just hanging there.

"Nice," he says. With a quick shift of my weight, I'm back on my feet. "The whole concept is that when I go low, you go high."

He stands directly beside me and bends over at the waist. "Now lean over me but keep your body straight as a board."

I do as he says, and soon I'm lying across his back. He stands up partway. "Arms down," he says. "To the floor and cartwheel out of it."

I drop my hands and bring my legs around. When I'm upright, he says, "See? Easy!"

We do that move a few more times.

"Now we'll combine," he says, back on one knee. "On my shoulder, roll across my back, and come out with the cartwheel."

I'm panicked about trying this, but I turn my back to him.

His hand pushes me as we go up. I lie flat on my back as he stands, and cartwheel out.

"Wow!" I say. "This is fun!"

"It is when it works," he says. "And nobody lands on their head."

"Does that happen?" I ask.

"Yes, when a pair isn't a good fit." He places his hands on my waist. "Jump when I squeeze."

We move across the room, me jumping with his guidance. To the mirror, it appears that he is lifting me across the room, but really it is a coordinated effort.

"Now spin in my hands," he says, his hands lightly around my waist.

I turn, feeling his touch telling me when to go faster and when to stop, communicating just as we had in the waltz.

When we finish the turn, I ask, "What makes a couple a bad fit?"

"Height, body style, strengths and weaknesses," he says. "But more than that, it's the power struggle.

Some dancers want to be in control no matter what. It can be hard for some to give up the lead."

I spin again, paying attention to the pressure, then jump, and suddenly I'm up on his shoulder, rolling across his back, and cartwheeling down.

"Oh!" I say. "You just told me how to do that without talking!"

He grins at me. "That's what good partners are made of."

The door to the room opens. Suze pops her head in. "I hate to be the dance police, but this room is about to be for hip-hop." She looks at the two of us, and I can see her biting her lip. She wants to say more, but she doesn't.

"Thanks," Blitz says.

Suze nods. She backs out, but leaves the door open.

"We should have a couple minutes," Blitz says. He bends down and snatches up my string bag. "Come with me."

I don't ask questions, just follow him out. The hall is starting to get busy for the afternoon classes. We've been dancing for over an hour. I should feel tired, but I'm exhilarated, like I could do anything.

He heads to the back of the hall and the doors to the storage room. My pulse leaps when I see where he is going.

Blitz glances back to see who is noticing us, then opens the door. We duck inside, blinking in the dark.

The door is barely closed when he pulls me to him. “God, I want you alone,” he says, then his mouth is on mine.

His hands lift me, pulling my thighs around his waist again. We take a few steps through the room, then he presses me against an empty wall. His hands immediately go to my breasts, cupping them and thumbing the nipple.

His erection is instant. I feel it against my body and everything wakes up, all the need and emotion I’ve stuffed down for four years. I want him, desperately. I’m willing to do anything he asks, to get alone, be together, all the way.

I don’t hesitate, but give back every kiss, nibble, and bite. I run my hands down his neck and back, rocking against him, creating friction that makes him groan.

His kiss is deep and long and demanding. But the leotard is impossible, everything connected and layered. He can only touch me through the fabric.

I’m not as hindered. His shirt is open on bottom, so I lift it to run my fingers across his skin. He breaks the kiss, burying his face into my neck. “Please say I can come get you tonight,” he says. “I can’t beg any harder.”

I think about the evening. My parents go to bed

at ten. Could I get away, sneak out my window? Dare I do it?

"I'm not sure I can," I say. "I can try."

"What is your phone number?" he asks.

I'm trying to think of a way to explain about my lack of phone when the storage room door opens.

Jacob, the jazz instructor, comes in and heads for the wall of props.

I quickly drop my legs to the floor. All he has to do is turn and he'll see us.

Noise filters in from the busy hall. Blitz holds his finger to his lips and motions for me to move behind one of the costume racks.

But when I try to move, my elbow bumps a box of egg shakers, and it falls to the floor.

The noisy eggs roll everywhere. Jacob jumps straight in the air and whips around.

"Blitz? Livia? What are you two doing lurking in the dark?" He looks from one to the other, then says, "Oh."

My face flames. God, if he talks to Danika, we're doomed. Blitz will be out of here. I think fast. "Blitz was teaching me lifts and we thought we might need to double up the mats."

"Is that why the mat was out in my room?" Jacob asks.

"Yes," Blitz says. "Livia is a very quick learner. Sorry if it's in your way."

Jacob waves his concern away. "I'll have the boys move it. Are you helping with our class today?"

"Yes," Blitz says. "That's why I was here. I saw Livia practicing and thought—"

"It's all good," Jacob says. "Say no more. Just watch out for the boss lady. If she thinks you're going to take advantage of sweet Livia, she'll cut off your balls." He picks up a box. "And I do not mean figuratively."

He heads out. Blitz hesitates, looking back at me, but I scurry out behind Jacob. As much as I want to figure out a way to be alone with Blitz, I have to think this through.

If there is a way, I'll find it.

## Chapter Sixteen

On Friday, I have to rush through the academy to get to class and can't ask anyone where Blitz is.

I wasn't able to come early. My mother gave me a thousand chores to do, still angry about my insistence on dancing yesterday.

The other girls are already at the barre as I jerk off my sneakers and slide on my ballet slippers. Betsy nods at me and gestures for me to get my place on the barre as she calls out commands for the warm-up.

I join in, wishing I could see into the hall. I can only hope he'll wait.

Last night, I planned and plotted for a way to escape and see him. On Saturdays, my parents always go see a movie and leave me to watch Andy. Afterward, though, they generally go to their room early and don't come out again. If I can convince Andy to go to bed early, or at least stay in his room, I can sneak out at a relatively decent hour, ten or so. For someone like Blitz, that probably isn't late.

As long as they don't discover I'm gone, I can be out most of the night.

I'm distracted by these thoughts, and Betsy reprimands me repeatedly for my sloppiness and lack of form. I focus back in, pretending Blitz is at the window watching me, and get back on track.

She's more pleased with me after that.

Class still drags. When we're finally done, I snatch up my string bag and race out of the room.

The hall is mobbed with parents and dancers. I can't stand to search through the crowd, so I jump onto one of the benches so I can see over everyone's heads.

He's not there.

I hop down, feeling low. Surely he waited.

Jacob is in Studio 2, so I pop in as he picks up mats.

"Was Blitz here for Advanced Jazz?" I ask.

"Nope," he says. "Big ol' no-show."

My belly sinks. He wasn't here at all. Why?

"Thanks," I tell Jacob. I wonder who would know what happened. I curse my lack of a phone. I have no way to get in touch with Blitz. And he can't talk to me either.

Even though I know it's pointless, I wander through the academy, down the aisle of the dark recital hall, across the stage, and into the storage room. He isn't anywhere.

When I get back to the front, I head out. No use getting in trouble for lingering if there's no reason for it.

I head home to a dismal weekend without Blitz.

## Chapter Seventeen

The weekend is horribly long. I take Andy on walks past the academy, but I never spot the red Ferrari. I'm not surprised. I don't think he's there for any of the weekend classes.

But I know he's still in town, because at church on Sunday, Mindy and I hole up in the girls' bathroom reading Tweets about Blitz sightings.

Unlike the previous weekend, however, there are no date pictures. Just Blitz with his parents, eating at restaurants or shopping. The mentions are slowing down and almost none of them have anything mean to say. There's one or two "Go home to Mama" messages, but overall it's just general excitement to see a celebrity.

He is, however, doing another charity event Sunday evening. We find a link to a Holiday Giving kickoff for Any Baby Can. Seeing that he's doing a fund-raiser for children makes my heart squeeze.

Knowing that he's avoiding anything that even looks like a date gives me hope.

On Monday, I decide not to go up to the academy and risk him not being there again. I want to save up my escapes for when I can actually see him. So I plod on to Tuesday. It's a good plan, because Mom has calmed down about all my time at the academy last week. She doesn't even look up when I wave bye for the scheduled class with the wheelchair ballerinas. Hopefully she won't be upset if I'm not back right on time.

Since Blitz didn't see me in the light blue leotard on Friday, I carefully wash it to wear again. I'm anxious about this class, because Hannah the shark manager has told the mothers we're going to be filming the video with Blitz.

As I approach the academy, I see it must be true. There are two vans in the parking lot, both for some production company. A couple men are hanging out behind the open doors of one of them.

When I get inside, the foyer is pandemonium. The girls are getting made up by actual makeup artists under bright lights. Two women are modifying their recital costumes, making sure every strap is perfect.

All the parents who aren't involved in our class are

standing around too. Dancers who should be in class are whining and begging to stay and watch rather than attend their own practice.

Danika weaves through the chaos, trying to move people along and maintain order. Her spiky blue hair is easy to follow in the crowd.

Despite being anxious to find Blitz, I look for Gabriella first. She's waiting near the makeup table, her eyes bright with excitement. A woman approaches from behind and talks to Gwen, who nods. The two of them swiftly remove the sequin scrunchie and start braiding her long black hair.

She looks so pretty. As they twist her hair into an updo, I realize she closely resembles an image of me hanging in our hallway at home. Anyone who knew Gabriella would see that image and think it was her.

My heart hammers. I can't imagine a scenario where Blitz or Janel or Danika would be in my house, but I have to make sure it never happens. I never did answer Blitz when he asked if Gabriella was my sister, but it hasn't come up again. I'm sure he knows I would have mentioned it by now if she were. The truth might scare him. It isn't time to reveal it.

I head up to the girls and hug them. "You all look so beautiful!" I say.

Janel hovers nearby, looking perturbed. "Did you sign a waiver?" she asks me.

I shake my head. "I can't. My parents would never allow it."

"You're over eighteen," she says. "You can do whatever you want."

"Not worth it," I say. "I have to live with them."

Plus, Blitz will be in the video. God, I have to hope they never see it and realize he was here. This whole thing is so hard. I have to protect my dance.

A woman with a clipboard approaches me. "Are you Livia Mason?" she asks.

"Yes," I say.

Janel slaps her hand on the clipboard. "She's not signing, so back off." She's more forceful than I'm used to her being.

The woman takes a step back. "She can't be in the video unless she signs."

"I don't want to be," I say. "I'll stay out of the way."

The woman frowns. "We have the right to remove you from the room if you don't sign."

"Back off, shark attack, she assists the dancers," Janel says. When the woman finally moves on, Janel turns to me. "They are super pushy. That's why I was up in her face."

"Thanks," I say.

Danika spots us and heads over. "This is more than I bargained for," she says. "I guess it always is."

"You want some help clearing the foyer?" I ask.

"Good luck with that," Danika says. "I already tried to herd them. We'll just have to muscle through." She glances at her watch. "I probably should have moved this to a quiet time, not the regular slot," she says. "I thought it would be safe enough on a Tuesday morning without any school-aged kids."

"It's the homeschool day," I remind her.

"Yes, it is. So a lot more kids and parents, all with open time." Danika looks around. "We'll get it done. The day's probably a wash anyway." She sees someone behind me and looks surprised. "What is Bennett doing here?" She excuses herself and heads toward the door.

A tall man in a perfectly fitting charcoal suit stands just inside, looking over the chaos. Danika approaches him and gives him a long, tight hug.

I've never seen Bennett Claremont before, but I know he's important. He built Dreamcatcher Dance Academy for Danika, his mother-in-law. He married her daughter Juliet, a professional ballerina who sometimes comes in between tours to give the girls a pep talk.

He's the reason I can take ballet, I know, funding the academy so that it doesn't have to turn a profit to stay open.

His handsome friendliness makes me think of Blitz. I'm not tall enough to see clearly through the crowd, but I don't think he's there. All the attention is on our ballerinas, and I suspect that if he was in the foyer, a lot of faces would be turned to him.

Surely he'll be here, though. They can't do the video without him. Maybe I can get a moment to ask Suze if she knows what happened to him Friday, and if he was here yesterday. I hate being unable to communicate with anybody. I had no idea today would be this crazy either.

Maybe I'll volunteer a second day up at the church just to get more access to a phone.

Jacob comes up behind me and squeezes my arm. We're officially in the transition now, and the foyer gets even more mobbed as dancers come out of the studios, joining the ones who were waiting for their class.

He leans in. "He's already in Studio 3," he whispers.

"Thanks," I say. It's nice to have an ally in this. I want to hug him.

Danika is still with Bennett, and I don't think she'll go to the studio until the girls do. They are absorbed with makeup, so I take one more look at Gabriella and then push my way to the dance rooms.

It's crowded here too, everyone buzzing about what is happening. I make my way to the back and peer through the window of Studio 3.

Blitz is in there. He's got a makeup girl of his

own, an older woman who is applying gel to his hair. The manager is there too, in a plum suit today, looking just as put together as last week. She's talking into a phone while simultaneously pointing at a man who is moving a light pole around.

A couple other crew members are in there, but I don't see any reason why I can't go in.

As soon as I'm through the door, Blitz pulls away from the makeup woman and heads straight for me.

"Princess!" he says. "I have got to get your number! Nobody here would give it up and I had no way to find you. I even hung out at your dystopian park this weekend."

He did? "We'll figure that out," I tell him. "What happened?"

"She happened," he points at Hannah. "Had me going a mile a minute. I missed Friday and you didn't come yesterday."

Oh! I could have seen him.

"Let me program in your number." He reaches in his pocket and comes up empty. "They took my dang phone," he says. "They are always doing that."

Hannah approaches, clicking her own phone off. "Blitz, I'm not sure about that outfit." She tugs on the pants over his hips in a familiar way that makes my cheeks blaze. "I do not want a hint of sexy. Not even the suggestion."

"Should I wear something baggy?" he asks. "I have sleeping sweatpants in the car." He laughs.

"Blitz, this is not funny," she says, but this makes him laugh harder. "The last thing we want are ugly jokes about you and young girls."

"Hannah, relax," he says. "Let's just make a good video. Don't let anybody take a crotch shot."

She ignores him and tugs at his fitted black short-sleeved T-shirt. "This is just right," she says. "I'm just not sold on the pants." She waves at a girl standing near the door. "Abigail, run to the car where we keep Blitz's wardrobe bag. I swear we have the pants from episode three in there. Black, loose, a little shiny."

The girl runs out.

Blitz shakes his head and pulls me away again. "Give me your number. I'll commit it to memory forever."

Before I can tell him I don't have a cell phone, we have to move aside for a camera man pushing a black stand on wheels.

"Finally!" Hannah says. "I was wondering if we were going to get a lighting test anytime today!"

The camera operators bring in more lights and argue about placement with all the mirrors in the room.

Blitz takes my arm as if to lead me out of the room, but Hannah catches him. "Oh, no, you don't," she says. "You're staying right here."

His expression is pained. "I'm just trying to get you alone," he whispers in my ear. He pulls me up against him, his arm around my waist.

Abigail rushes back in with another pair of pants. Blitz slings them over his arm, then grabs my hand to leave the room to put them on.

Hannah stops him. "There's a bathroom in the corner." She avoids looking at me. I can't tell if she cares that he's paying so much attention to me or not.

Blitz gets an evil gleam in his eye. "You just got promoted to wardrobe manager," he says to me. He leads us toward the side wall, where a corner is taken up by a tiny bathroom and the shelves that hold the sound system.

He pulls me inside and shuts the door. "Alone at last," he says, lifting me up to sit on the counter, what little there is surrounding the sink.

He doesn't waste a moment, but pulls me into a kiss. His mouth is gentle and seeking.

My heart is beating fast, and I wonder what everyone out there thinks we're doing. Blitz pulls away and trails his thumb across my cheek. "This is a lot, isn't it? The crew and Hannah?" he asks.

I nod. "I rather like the pants."

He laughs. "I would fight her on it, but I have bigger battles. She generally has good taste. Other than taking me on as a client, maybe."

He steps back and kicks off his jazz shoes. They are new and gleaming. Then he pulls down the pants.

My face burns. His legs are muscled, only moderately hairy. He wears skin-colored underwear, smooth and fitted, same as a leotard. I drag my gaze away.

"You are adorable, Livia," he says as he steps into the new pants.

"What makes you say that?" I ask.

"You are just so genuine. And sweet." He straightens the shirt and moves close to me again. "So girl next door. I feel like I should be asking your father for your hand in marriage before I kiss you anymore."

"You're crazy," I say. I want to breathe him in. His clothes smell new and expensive.

His hands separate my knees so he can step in closer. The movement sends a rush of heat through me. I want more from him. I want to get lost in it. He will take care of things. We won't be stupid like I was before. Although there is the matter of the fifteen paternity suits.

"Why do all those women think their babies are yours?" I ask suddenly.

He sinks back a little. "That's one heck of a segue," he says. "You think your father would ask? Because when I was trying to get your address or number or anything to get in touch with you, everybody said your dad would kill me."

"I don't know," I say. "It's just that if all these girls think their babies are yours, then you couldn't have been very..." I hesitate. "Protected."

"So your mind is going there." He leans in, his fingers sliding around my neck. "Only one of the fifteen was even someone I slept with," he says. "The others were just opportunists who thought I would buy them off. It's a common thing, especially when you have a reputation like mine."

"What about the one, then?"

"Her boyfriend saw the lawsuit and had a cow. He spoke up that the baby was his. The timing was all wrong from when I was with her anyway. It was dismissed."

"Was she a contestant?"

"No, she didn't make it that far. But she did audition. I met her before season one began, when I was still naive enough to think girls liked me for who I was."

It hadn't even occurred to me that Blitz would be the one to feel used.

He leans in, touching our foreheads together. "I'll answer any questions you have. I know I'm up against my own horrible reputation."

"Are you trying to leave all that behind?" I ask.

He says, "I already have." And his lips brush mine.

From outside the door, we hear "I have a key and I'm going to use it!"

Blitz breaks away. "Lovely woman, my manager. I guess our time is up."

As he turns to the door, I stop him. "Blitz, I don't have a cell phone. My father keeps me on a very short leash. He has his reasons. It's very hard for me to get away and see you. But I want to. I do."

His eyes flicker with anger for a moment, but he controls it. "Then we'll make our own way to keep in touch."

He opens the door. Hannah is outside. His voice is firm when he says, "I need a second cell phone, before the end of the shoot."

Hannah tries to open her mouth, but Blitz stops her. "I mean it. I won't sign off on this video without it."

"You're such a diva," Hannah says, but she waves to the same girl who got the pants. "Go see Roberto for the car keys and the credit card. Pick up another cell phone, whatever is close. Get it activated and ready to go and come back."

The girl nods.

"Good enough?" she asks Blitz.

He nods. "Thank you." He kisses her cheek. "This is why you're my main girl."

Hannah rolls her eyes. "Scoot! All of you!"

Blitz heads toward the camera, and I scurry out of the way, next to a couple guys holding big silver disks.

Class should have already begun, but the girls still

aren't here. Hannah says to the makeup woman, "Go check on the dancers. We'll need lighting tests. And bring me the instructor. We need to review the shot list."

"I'll go get Janel," I say. Blitz is busy with the cameraman, who is doing footage of him dancing. Another man, presumably the director, is consulting a clipboard and calling out commands like "Long shot. Get something establishing. Now go tight. B-roll on the feet."

I hurry out of the room. The hall is quieter and the classes seem to have finally gotten underway. The fourth years are working with Betsy. Jacob has his class. The toddlers are with Aurora.

In the foyer, a few mothers and their kids murmur near the front desk.

The class is still together. A cameraman is out here too, getting shots of their faces and the women adjusting their hair.

Danika turns to me. "We're about to come down. Were you there?"

"They're filming Blitz," I say.

"Okay, hopefully we'll get this going. I'll have to move Janel's next class to the recital hall, I bet. Can you help with them if they still need Janel for the shoot?"

I really want to stay with Blitz, but I say, "Of course."

Daisy rolls up to me, and the camera follows her. When she gets close, though, the clipboard girl jumps forward. "Not the one in blue! She wouldn't sign." She glares at me.

Danika laughs. "This is ridiculous."

The cameraman heads back to the table.

"What's up, Daisy?" I say.

"Am I going to be a star?" she asks.

I kneel close to her. "You already are," I tell her.

The assistant says something to the cameraman. "All right!" he says. "Time to head to the dance." He hustles ahead to film them coming up the hall. Unlike the fancy lights in the studio, his is a little grid over his camera.

I hang back to make sure I stay out of his frame. Each girl gives me a high five as she passes. The excitement is infectious. The moms follow the line of girls, holding dance bags and glowing themselves. It's a big day.

All of us are benefiting from the arrival of Blitz Craven.

## Chapter Eighteen

The majority of the shooting is pretty mundane. The girls turn. The cameramen glide around, catching different angles. The director stops them, has the lights rearranged, and they do it again.

"How long is this video going to be?" I ask Danika. We're in the corner with the other unnecessary crew.

"Three minutes," a lighting guy says.

"An hour of shooting on two cameras to get three minutes?" I ask.

"That's how it works," he says. "This is a short one. I've had thirty-second commercials take twelve hours."

The director motions to us. "I'd like the girls in a half circle around Blitz!" he calls.

The dancers who can power themselves or have

motorized wheelchairs move forward. I can see Marissa is a little fatigued. When she doesn't move, I jump forward to push her into the circle.

I figure someone will yell at me to stay out of camera range, but no one does. Blitz kneels before them, taking Gabriella's hand. I'm so touched, seeing it, that my eyes instantly tear up.

The cameraman comes beside me to catch Blitz's face. He's smiling up at Gabriella, but when he glances a little higher, he sees me. His expression softens. His face is radiant, full of understanding and emotion upon seeing mine.

"You really love this, don't you, Princess?" he asks me.

I nod, afraid to speak out loud since they are filming. I slowly back away so they can get the shot with Blitz and the girls.

"I know I love it!" Gabriella says.

"Me too!" the other girls chorus.

"And I have loved spending this day with you," Blitz says.

He goes around the circle, hugging each girl. They seem to know it's over and some of them start crying. I know how they feel. There is a definite crash after the high of being a part of Blitz's world.

"That's a wrap," the director says. "Thank you all, young ladies. This was beautiful."

The moms come inside the room to collect their

girls. The crew is a whirl, breaking things down quickly and loading up bags. I stay out of the way in the corner.

Blitz speaks with the director for a few moments, nodding and listening. He catches my eye a few times and smiles.

I'm perfectly content to stand outside his limelight and watch the craziness. I can't imagine living this sort of life all the time. But that was what he had to do on the show. Cameras in his car. His home. During his practices and his dates. Why had he done it? The Blitz I've gotten to know does not seem to seek the spotlight. I'll have to ask him how it all happened.

He breaks away from the director and heads over to our corner. Hannah, who has been on the phone, hangs up abruptly and hugs him. "You were brilliant, as always," she says.

"Thanks." He turns away from her to talk to me. "Can you break away from here for a little while?"

I hesitate. On Tuesdays, I head home for lunch and then go do my work at the church. But I have an idea.

"I'm doing a lunch thing," I say. "But after that I could make some time."

Blitz turns to Hannah. "What're my obligations?"

"I don't need you until tomorrow night," Hannah says. "The auction." She looks around. "Honestly, I think now that we have this, you're done here. I don't see a point in two charity dance videos."

My stomach sinks. "You're done with Dreamcatcher?" I ask.

"I'll finish out the week," he says. "It was never meant to be a long gig."

I feel flushed with panic. "I won't see you."

He turns to Hannah. "Did you get that phone for me?"

"She's on her way back," Hannah says. "Actually, there she is."

They wave to the girl, who holds a box. Blitz takes my arm and heads over to her.

"Here," she says. "It's prepaid for a year."

"Perfect," he tells her. "Thank you." He takes the box and glances around. I think I know who he's looking for.

"Danika left before the shooting ended," I say.

"Awesome," he says.

We open the door and peer out into the hall just as the lights blink for the transition.

"Time to blow!" he says, grabbing my hand. We run for the storage room door.

When we're on the other side, he laughs. "Princess, I swear you turn me into a high school boy every time we're together. Sneaking around like the teacher is going to catch us."

"But she is!" I laugh too and Blitz sets down the

box so he can pick me up and twirl me in a circle. We spin between the storage racks and the door until I'm dizzy and breathless.

"I'm never going to feel the same way about a closet," he says.

I don't get a chance to respond, because his lips are on mine, hungry and demanding. I melt into him, our bodies separated by so little that I can feel each muscle, his hip bone. And before long, him erect between us.

"You make me so crazy," he says, his hands tangled into my hair. "And you're always in all this spandex."

I laugh against his jaw. "I won't be this afternoon."

"Please tell me you'll wear a skirt with no panties."

I suck in a breath, shocked and excited by his sudden drop in gentlemanly manners. "Blitz!"

"Sorry, I didn't mean to offend you."

"No, no, it's okay. I mean, it's just funny."

He holds me tightly against him. "I'm going insane for you. Did you say you could see me this afternoon or did I dream it?"

"I think so," I say. "I have some volunteer work, but I could leave early." God, this has to work. I have so little time away.

"Tell me when and where and I'm there." His hands run along my back and side, across my shoulder blades, as if he's memorizing the terrain of my body.

It's distracting and makes it hard for me to breathe or think.

"Two o'clock," I say, "at our dystopian park."

"I'll be there," he says. Then, in a whisper, "And I expect no panties."

He lets go of me and hands me the box. "I'll text you on this so you have my number."

My jaw drops. "Wait. You got this for me?"

"Who did you think it was for?" he says. "Open it up."

My hands shake as I lift the lid. It's a shiny gray phone. I press the side button and the screen flickers on.

"Let me put my number in it," he says. He opens the contacts and types in his numbers. In the name he puts "Love slave."

"Blitz!"

He laughs. "Text me right away so I'll have the number for it. Promise?"

"I promise." My eyes smart with tears for the second time today. "Thank you."

He kisses the top of my head. "Go to your lunch. I'll see you in a few."

We head out the door. The hallway is mostly quiet. One of the cameramen is pushing an equipment crate out of Studio 3.

He heads back into the room where Hannah waits. I wave and head on down the corridor, glad not to have been spotted by Danika. I shove the phone box in my string bag. I'll have to ditch the packaging in the trash in the park on the way home, as Mom will notice that. And make sure it's silenced.

The foyer is quiet. The makeup girls are packing their table and chairs and mirrors and boxes.

I push through the doors. When I'm past the parking lot, I pull out the phone and locate the texting feature. It's a couple blocks of walking before I figure out what my first text to Blitz will be. My courage surges and my body feels hot as I type it.

*Park. Check.*

*Skirt. Check.*

*Secret date. Check.*

*Panties? You'll have to find out for yourself.*

## Chapter Nineteen

At home I change into a long skirt and a sweater. I can't leave the panties off. I try twice, but only get as far as the hallway when I turn around and put them back on again.

I'm just not Blitz's speed on that.

Dad comes home for lunch, and I have to fight to keep my expression calm. When we're all seated at the table, he passes an envelope to me.

"What's this?" I ask. I pretty much never know if something from my father will be good or bad.

"Read it," he says.

I open the envelope. It's a confirmation of my testing date for the SAT. It's in three weeks.

"Your last practice score was pretty good," he says. "I figure if you knuckle down for the next few weeks, you'll be ready."

"That's wonderful!" Mom says. "You're going to do great."

"Once I take it, I have to start applying, or the score will expire," I say. My future whizzes before me. Classes in an actual school again. New people. Girls. Boys. Teachers.

"One step at a time," Dad says. "I hear there are lots of good online colleges these days."

My excitement wilts. Right. He's still planning to keep me here.

"Thank you for signing me up," I say. It costs money to take the test, and we don't have a lot. I know that's a big deal.

"I'm really proud of you, Livia. I think extending your learning will really do you good." He reaches for a bowl of mashed potatoes and loads some onto his plate. "Of course, you may have to drop some of your dancing. College takes a lot of time."

My heart falls to my knees. He can't mean that. Attending class is free and only once a week!

But I know better than to argue. I just focus on my plate. Less than an hour until I head up to the church, and then I'll make an excuse to leave early. I won't have as much time as I did last week, but it's something.

I already plan to escape one night after dark. That's even riskier, because my father might go so far as to call the cops or try to have Blitz arrested. I don't think it would work, because I am nineteen, but he could try. The press would be bad.

No, actually, maybe I won't try.

I swirl my fork through the potatoes and keep quiet until lunch is over.

My exhilaration isn't quite as high heading to the church. My list of sins involving it is growing — using the phone to call Gabriella's adoptive mother, sneaking looks at Blitz footage, and now I'm straight-up lying about being there.

Not only that, I unplugged the phone at my house so that it wouldn't ring if the church secretary decided to call my mom about my leaving early. I don't think she'd do it, but then, Mindy showed up when I was there alone that time. My parents may have made some sort of agreement with Irma to be notified if anything unusual happens.

So, yes, I'm being terrible. Liar. Sneak.

Just like four years ago.

I circle the building and go in the side.

Irma is at her desk as always. Usual messy twist. Today's paisley print dress is pale blue.

"Don't you look pretty!" she says. "Your hair is a crown!"

I touch the braid encircling my head, the long strands falling from it. "Mom taught me how to do it when I was young."

"It's a beautiful look. You tell her I said so."

"I will."

Irma waves her hand to the back room. "There's a ton of mail to sort. Lots of junk. Just don't toss any bills."

"On it," I say. Then I take a deep breath so I can speak the lie. "I'm only here for an hour today. Mom needs me at home."

"Okay," Irma says. "Plenty of time to get the mail sorted."

"Yes, I can do it."

And it's done. The lie is out.

I set my string bag on a shelf, tugging it open so I can easily pull the phone out to check. It's on silent, and Blitz hasn't returned my text. No telling what has him tied up after something as big as a video shoot.

The box of mail waits on the counter. I sit on the floor with it. But I've only sorted three envelopes when I stand up and move my string bag closer. I'm jittery, as anxious as I've ever felt. What if he can't meet? I've already told Irma I'm leaving.

My hands shake as I toss advertisements for coffee companies and religious tract printing in the trash. I'm glad the work is fairly mindless. I can't concentrate on anything.

I hear a buzzing sound. What is that? It makes the floor vibrate a little.

I pick up my bag. It's the phone. I thought it was on silent! Maybe the buzz is what silent means. I have to find a way to turn that off too. It's very loud in the quiet.

But Blitz has texted me back.

*Princess, I'm officially your slave.*

I smile.

Then another comes through.

*I can already picture my hand sliding up your thigh.*

A rush of heat blossoms down low. I glance wildly around, wondering if the prayer books are going to come crashing down on my head for reading this in a church.

*When it reaches its destination, I'm going to make you scream.*

I suck in a breath, and a piece of hair catches in my mouth. I inhale it, sputtering and coughing and making a terrible racket.

Irma pops her head in. "You okay, Livia?"

I shove the phone under my skirt. "Just swallowed wrong!"

She nods and heads back to her desk just as another buzz comes. Then another.

God, I nearly got caught. I frantically push all the icons until I find the settings. It takes several eternal moments to locate the vibration setting. I finally find it and now the phone is truly silent.

By the time I look at my texts again, there are a line of them.

*I want to taste the inside of your knee.*

*I bite ankles, is that okay?*

He seems to get nervous that I'm not replying, so he asks,

*Am I going too fast? Because I can back off. I just can't seem to tick off the minutes until I see you any other way.*

I'm not sure what to say. I did start it with my panties text.

Finally, I write him.

*You don't scare me. Not anymore.*

His response is instant.

*But I did?*

*At first.*

*I never want you to feel a second of fear. Not ever.*

*I won't.*

*Is it time yet?*

*I have to finish my work!*

*Okay, I'll just sit here and pine for you at the postapocalyptic park.*

He's already there!

I quickly tap out:

*Be there as soon as I can.*

And sort the mail literally as fast as my fingers will fly.

Within minutes, I've created a stack for Irma and hand it to her.

"See you next week," I say. "Unless you need me before."

"We'll get by," she says. "Tell your mother hello."

My feet can't move quickly enough as I hurry down the street. I don't want to cross in front of my own house, as it's too risky, so I duck down a block, then come back up to get to the park.

The red Ferrari sticks out, sitting against the curb like a shiny Christmas ornament. I walk up to it, but Blitz isn't inside. He must be in the park.

I shade my eyes from the afternoon sun and walk up the path. There are box hedges that obscure parts of the playground.

Children shout on the swings. I walk that direction, planning to take a quick circle of the park and then text if I don't spot him. He can't be too far away, since his car is here.

As I approach the playscape, I spot an empty wheelchair. Then Daisy's mom, holding a toddler squirming in her arms. She's talking to another mom.

When I see Blitz, my heart swells like it might burst.

He's pushing Daisy on a swing.

Her mother sees me. "Livia!" she says. "Imagine finding you here! We saw Blitz already. He's playing with Daisy."

The toddler kicks her way to the ground. The other mother scoops her up.

I'm speechless for a moment. For one, to see Blitz

hanging out with children. And also, because we've been seen by a parent who could mention it to Danika.

"Livia!" Daisy shouts. "Look who is here!"

Blitz spots me and waves, continuing to push Daisy. He's in jeans and a long-sleeved fitted shirt. He's like a billboard for fatherhood, good looking and hands-on. I would imprint the image on my brain if I weren't so panicked about seeing people we know.

Daisy says something to him and he nods, carefully stopping the swing. He lifts her out and sets her in the chair. Soon she's speeding across the dead grass to us.

"Did you come to see Blitz?" Daisy asks. "He was sitting all alone when we got here!"

Her mom snaps her head around at that, as if considering whether or not this is a coincidence.

Blitz saves me. "Livia told me about the park," he says smoothly. "It's nice to have a place to chill out near the academy."

He leans down to give Daisy a squeeze. "I've got to get going." He pulls his keys from his jeans pocket. "See you all at the academy!"

I follow his lead. "Bye, Blitz."

He pulls his phone out and holds it up. I know he's telling me that he'll text me where to meet instead. I'm terribly relieved that he understands the situation, and I'm so glad I told him about my parents already.

I give Daisy a hug and wave to her mom. "I was just cutting through. I live close by. See you next week!"

And I continue on through the park to the next street.

As soon as I'm out of sight of Daisy, I pull out the phone. I've forgotten the phone is on silent, and I already have two messages from Blitz asking where to meet me.

I give him the name of the two streets at the corner and wait at a bus stop bench. I hear the roar of his Ferrari before I see it. He pulls up in front of me and rolls down the passenger window. "Pretty lady need a ride?" he says. "I've got candy."

I walk up to the car and lean in the window. "I only take candy from strangers."

"Then pretend we've never met," he says, laughter in his eyes.

I open the door and hop into the seat.

And I can see the floor!

"Hey, you cleaned up," I say.

"See, you're already good for me," Blitz says. He pulls away from the curb. "How much time do we have before the clock strikes twelve?"

It's so much easier to navigate this with Blitz understanding my situation. "A couple hours."

"Is there a movie theater around here?"

"Sure. It's kind of old and dumpy, though."

"All the better. Tell me where."

He steers through the streets as I give him directions. I've only gone to the theater a couple times. It usually offers second-run movies and old black-and-white features. My parents let me see *Singin' in the Rain* and *The Wizard of Oz* there when they played them for special occasions.

"What will we see?" I ask as he parks in the lot, almost empty on a weekday afternoon.

"Whatever is about to start," he says. "You've never done that before? Just gone potluck on a movie?"

I shake my head. I don't want to tell him I'm not allowed at modern movies, at least not anymore. I got to go plenty when I was a kid. Now Dad says they promote loose morals. Same as pop music and television. I'm too susceptible to ideas.

It's probably true. But I can't stay sheltered forever. And this is probably his worst nightmare, getting tickets to an unapproved movie with one of the sexiest, wildest men on TV.

It makes me want to laugh. My dad would probably spontaneously combust if he saw us.

"I like seeing you happy," Blitz says as we get out of the car. "Let's go find out what we're watching."

He wraps his arm around my waist as we walk. We

could be any couple walking to a movie theater. It feels so good.

"Besides, I want to get you in the dark," he says.

My heart thumps against my sweater. "And no Danika or Hannah to interrupt."

"Exactly."

We walk up to the box office, where a girl is leaning her cheek on her hand. She doesn't recognize Blitz. "Can I help you?"

Blitz scans the marquee. "Two to whatever starts next."

She rolls her eyes and prints out tickets. Blitz passes a twenty under the Plexiglas window.

We go inside. "Hungry?" Blitz asks. "You're bad for my fitness regimen, but then, my trainer quit."

"Really?"

"Yeah, she said she wasn't going to work with anyone who had so little respect for women." He walks up to the counter. "Can't blame her."

I squeeze his hand. "I'm sorry all this happened."

"My own fault. I was out of control. The network wanted a hot-and-bothered guy who didn't take no for an answer, and I delivered."

"But it wasn't really you?"

"I don't know anymore. I played the role so long, it sort of became me."

"But you're not like that right now."

He looks down at me. "Not with you."

We stop at the empty concession counter.

"You know how to work a popcorn machine?" he asks.

"I'm game to try."

The same teen from the box office comes around the counter. "Can I help you?" she asks in the same bored voice.

"Do you run the projector too?" Blitz asks.

She shakes her head.

"Okay. Big popcorn. Like, big as your face. And..." he looks at me. "Should we be good with bottled water or go for the teeth-rotting soda?"

"Teeth are overrated," I say.

"Two giant Cherry Cokes."

The girl fetches them. Blitz takes my hand and within seconds, I'm turning in circles, following his cues.

How does he do that?

We dance around the empty foyer of the theater while the girl assembles our order. My skirt billows out a little, but it's long, so nothing shows but my knees. I remember the panties and wonder if I can go to the bathroom to take them off. The very idea makes my face burn hot.

"You're blushing," he says, twirling me into him. "What's on my sweet princess's mind?"

I wish I were bold and flirty and could say things

like "Wouldn't you like to know?" But I'm tongue-tied.

Fortunately, the girl plops our drinks on the counter, making them fizz though the top.

"Now that's service!" Blitz says merrily. He lets me go to hand her money and pass me one of the drinks.

"You can go on back," she says. "Theater 2 on your right."

"Has anyone else bought tickets?" he asks.

"Not to that show," she says.

Blitz picks up his drink and the popcorn, and we head to the hallway.

The previews are flashing onscreen as we pass through the doors. I peer into the seats. She's right. There's nobody here.

I hesitate in the aisle, not sure where Blitz wants to sit. He heads straight up the stairs to the back row. Of course.

My head buzzes with nervous energy as I follow him. What will happen here? Technically, we're in public. Realistically, we'll probably be alone the whole time.

Blitz plunks down in the center seat and props his sneakers up on the seat back in front of him. "Still a surprise, but the previews will give us a hint."

"I'm going to laugh if it's a kid movie," I say.

Blitz picks up a piece of popcorn and presses it to my lips. I open for him and accept it.

It's salty and warm and Blitz's fingers linger after I've closed my mouth. My body wakes up, vibrating and on edge. I think again on the panties and wish I had been more daring.

But the movie will probably distract us. Something with lots of action and violence, or maybe a comedy.

I glance back at the screen and Blitz picks up his drink.

The preview is dark and moody, an art film. So is the next. There is a flash of skin, a sensual instrumental setting a mood.

So definitely not a kid movie. Or an action blockbuster. I remember those from the time before, *Percy Jackson and the Olympians*. The *Karate Kid* remake. The last movie I saw before my parents locked me away was *Tangled*. I can still see that girl in the boat, looking at the lights after escaping the tower and feeling that finally her life had begun. Fitting.

The previews end and the company logos for the feature begin. I guess they really do expect you to know what movie you're seeing, because this one just sort of begins.

It's in Japanese with subtitles. I glance over at Blitz, and he shrugs. He leans in. "All the better to make out."

He sets the popcorn in the seat beside him and

takes my hand. He lifts it to his lips. "Mmm, buttery," he says and takes one of my fingers in his mouth.

My body flames so suddenly and so hot that I suck in a breath. His eyes watch me as he takes in each finger, his expression mischievous and bright.

I wish the seat arm wasn't between us, but I lean in as close as I can. He lowers my hand and kisses my mouth instead. He keeps it easy, light feathery movements that steady my hammering heart.

His hand moves to my waist, flirting with the underside of my breast. Then his thumb slides up, crossing the nipple. I suck in another breath, everything flashing hot.

Blitz leans in even closer, his mouth seeking me now. We're barely into the movie and things are moving fast. But I want them to. I want to take this as far as we can go. I want to remember all the things I've forgotten and pushed aside.

And learn more. Who better than Blitz to show me, remind me, teach me?

I reach for him, placing a tentative hand on his thigh. He places his hand on me more fully, capturing the entire breast in his palm. I'm on fire now, wanting more, to feel skin on skin. I want to burn the panties away, wondering if he'll feel disappointment when he encounters them, or if things will even progress that far.

A sudden noise onscreen startles us and we turn

to it. Then gape. A maid is giving another woman a bath in an old-fashioned tub, and the scene is intensely erotic.

"Perfect," Blitz says in my ear, then his mouth moves to my neck, kissing along my collarbone. His hand moves to the bottom of my sweater, and then I get what I want, his fingers brushing my skin.

An electric charge bolts through me. I want to moan with the pleasure of it, but try to stay calm and quiet. I have to keep some sort of control, although thinking back, that was never my strong suit. I was impulsive once. Passionate. I let emotion carry me way beyond society's boundaries.

His fingers travel up along my ribs and rest at the base of the bra. I don't require much, and there is no underwire or thick cups for him to wrangle with. He doesn't hesitate, but slips his thumb beneath the fabric and touches me without hindrance.

Now I can't stop from groaning near his ear. His mouth returns to mine, taking my tongue in deeply. I fall into the kiss, his touch, my own hand gripping his leg in the jeans.

My body arches toward him. I wish we weren't here, in these seats, separated by the silly armrest. I want fully against him, so close. Everything is flooding back, every feeling, every need. I don't care that I've only known Blitz two weeks. I understand him. I see what nobody else does. How he can really be.

I break the kiss and look around the theater. No one is here. We're well into the movie. Nobody is going to come.

Summoning every bit of daring I possess, I stand up and turn to Blitz.

He looks up at me in surprise, probably wondering if he's taken things too far and I'm going to leave.

But I slip my knees on either side of his thighs and slide forward, straddling him as best I can with seats on either side. My skirt gets trapped between us, so I jerk it free and let it fall across my thighs.

His hands go to my legs beneath it, caressing the skin.

"No dance tights," he says.

"Finally," I say.

I wrap my arms around his neck. I'm slightly taller than him in this position. I could lift up and my chest would be at face level for him. I think of doing it, but his hands slide up my thighs and the buzzing is so intense that I stop thinking.

He'll encounter the panties soon. My heart threatens to falter. I hold my breath. He whispers, "Your skin is perfect," then his lips find mine again.

Blitz doesn't push, just trailing his fingers along my inner thigh.

Then his thumb brushes between my legs, and I'm jolted into the next level of need, wanting the touch harder, more intense. I kiss him with more fervor, letting him know that this is okay, that I want it.

His hand presses against me, molding the cotton fabric to my body. A finger finds its mark, pushing as far as the panties will allow.

I can't kiss anymore, too lost in the roar of sensation overwhelming me. I want him inside, need him inside. I'm desperate and rock my hips to press harder against his hand.

"I love this," he says. "God, you're so hot and wet."

I hang on to him, my arms around his head, my face pressed into his hair. I take in the smell of his shampoo, the texture of his sideburn stubble on my cheek.

Then he takes it further, slipping a finger inside my panties. I can't stop myself from softly crying out. It's what I've been longing for, desperate for.

He slides one finger inside me, then two. I cling to him, moving with him, pleasure blasting through me. He knows exactly what to do and how to move, where to put the pressure.

When I was young and playing around before, it was thrilling and forbidden, but this is pure gluttony by a practiced hand. I've never felt so consumed.

His free hand slips back inside my sweater, up beneath the bra. He rolls a nipple just as he shifts his fingers inside my body. I've lost all sense of anything around me but his touch, and the need for him has become agonizing and fierce. I don't think I can take it anymore. It's too much, too intense, I can't back away, can't retreat.

Then everything just lets go. My body pulses around his fingers and I gasp, half-crying, gulping air. I've never felt anything like it. It's like my body turned inside-out and released a thousand petals that are now descending like feathers brushing against my skin.

I grip his head. "What did you just do?" I ask, then immediately feel silly. I know about orgasm. And I thought I'd felt it before. But I hadn't. Not if this is the real thing. That was nothing. That was just the beginning. I hadn't known.

Blitz withdraws his hands and wraps his arms around me. "My sweet, sweet Livia," he says. "I'm going to fall so hard for you."

I drop my head to his shoulder, eyes wide. Will he? What happens now? I want to do more with him, explore him, learn his body. But he just holds me tightly and still.

Behind us, the movie goes on, inexplicable in its foreign language. It doesn't matter. I don't even want to see it. I just want Blitz to hold me like he is, forever, and for nothing to change.

But I know that can't happen. The video will come out. Everyone will see that Blitz is more than his mistake. That he is making amends. That he is sweet and kind and children love him.

Then he'll be gone.

## Chapter Twenty

Wednesday morning I plan to dress for the academy and see Blitz, but my mother has other ideas.

She comes into my room far earlier than usual. "Your father has signed you up for an all-day study class for the SAT," she says. "I'm going to go with you. Andy is staying with the Wallers." Mindy's family.

I want to refuse to do it, to say no. I want to see Blitz. He's only going to be at the academy another week.

But after yesterday, surely he won't leave. Surely he wants to learn me too.

"Hop in the shower," Mom says. "We leave in half an hour."

I was up half the night texting Blitz, so I'm definitely off schedule. As soon as she leaves the room, I race to the desk drawer where I've hidden the phone. In order to charge it, I've kept the drawer out a little, placed the phone behind it, and plugged it in directly behind the back panel, so nothing can be seen.

There are several messages this morning. He's heading up to see the Tappin' Grandmas soon. Hannah has made the video team work all night on the video and there should be a rough cut to view this afternoon. He hopes I can come up and see it with him.

No no no no. I won't be able to do any of that!

I let him know about the class and that my mom is staying with me all day. I want to weep, pretend I'm sick, jump out the window. No no no no!

I have zero interest in showering, dressing, or eating breakfast. I'm doing my best to keep a poker face as Mom drives us to Mindy's house to drop off Andy, but I can barely hold it together.

Mindy comes out to the car while Mom walks Andy in, and it's everything I can do not to tell her everything right there and risk getting overheard. I do show her the phone and when her eyes get big, I just say, "Blitz."

This is enough to make her jump up and down. I give her the number and now she can text me too. Little by little, I'm back in the world.

I ask Blitz to let me know how he's doing

throughout the day. I'll do whatever I have to do, pretend to have a weak bladder and take a bathroom break every hour, whatever. I can't think about anything else and going to an SAT class is going to be pointless.

Even so, once I'm in the room with other people, Mom taking up a corner to make sure I don't jump anyone's bones, I guess, the studiousness of the others infects me. I'm out in the world. I'm moving forward. Maybe I can apply for other schools anyway. I don't need my parents' permission for that.

As we work on critical-reading passages, I find I'm able to shove the rest of my life out of my mind and really dig into how to dissect the sentences to answer the multiple-choice questions. To my surprise, I'm actually doing better at this than anybody else in the class.

Of course, maybe that's why they are here, because they aren't doing well.

For lunch, Mom takes me to a small cafe in the same strip mall as the class. A few of the other students also go, and two girls strike up a conversation with me in line. I think I might get to sit with real people my age, but unfortunately, before we can order, a boy joins them at their table.

Mom steers us to the other side of the room.

I have to get out of here.

In the bathroom, I dig the phone out of the bottom of my bag and scroll through Blitz's messages.

*Back at home. Mom is making enchiladas. Probably won't fit in my costumes even if I do get the show back.*

*Hope your prep class isn't too boring. Don't think about my hand up your skirt while you're solving equations.*

*Hannah says the sample video will be ready to view mid-afternoon. Wish you were in it. I don't even have a picture of you. We'll have to fix that.*

I hug the phone to my chest. I just want to read the messages over and over, but I know Mom is waiting. So I quickly tap out a reply.

*Love your messages. Thank you. Prep okay. I'm doing better than I thought. If I bomb, it will be your fault!*

*P.S. Wearing a shorter skirt today.*

I power the phone all the way off and stick it back in the bottom of my bag. I'm going to sneak out tonight, I've decided. And if we get the chance, if it feels right, I'm going to move forward with Blitz. I want to. I want him. It's been so long.

I'll be careful this time. I will guard myself. No risk taking.

The main thing I'm putting on the line this time is my heart.

## Chapter Twenty-One

When the interminable full-day SAT prep is finally over, Mom declares she is too tired to cook.

Mindy's mom insists that Andy and I stay for dinner so that Mom can relax a bit with Dad without us around.

We all jump at the chance for this. I wonder wildly if I can say I'm spending the night, then leave for home and end up having an entire night with Blitz!

But watching Mindy and her mom work together in the kitchen to make dinner for all of us, I can't do it. She's just sixteen and I can't get her in trouble on my account.

Her mom sees how anxious we are to talk and waves us off to Mindy's room. She doesn't have a rule about keeping her door open, so as soon as we're alone in there, Mindy pulls out her phone.

"It's out, Livia. You have to see it."

"What's out?"

"The video."

Oh my God. I dig my phone out of my bag and power it back on. There are a slew of messages from Blitz. He's seen the video. He loves it. He's given the green light. Can I come over and watch it with him?

If only I could. Maybe I'll sneak out after I get home. Maybe I'll just run away!

"Play it play it play it," I tell Mindy.

She holds out her phone. The video already has a couple hundred thousand views and it's only been up for three hours.

The title is "Blitz Craven's precious new dance partners."

It opens with a few seconds of the girls prepping, powder on faces, hair getting braided. Then the mirror of Studio 3 and an empty room. The girls come in, the images carefully close up to show only their faces. Then Blitz holds his arms out to greet them.

He goes down the line, straightening their arms and adjusting their chins. They move together, arms in fifth position, framing their faces.

Then Blitz turns in a circle, the view pans out, and you see the wheelchairs.

It's very powerful.

There are a few more seconds of dancing and turns, the middle section of their recital piece, and then they do the half circle around Blitz.

I know I'm behind Marissa in this shot, as I've moved her chair. The camera closes in on Daisy, then Gabriella. My Gabriella!

Then he looks up, and his face is just as I remember in the moment, so full of emotion. My heart catches.

"I think I just fell in love," Mindy says.

The video fades out with the words "Any dancer can be a star."

"That is wow," I say.

"Look at the comments." Mindy scrolls down. Other than one or two who still call Blitz evil and horrid, most are swooning over the video and how he treated the dancers. One says, "He had me at minute 2:17." A bunch of others agree.

We go back up to the video. Sure enough, it's that look he gives the camera, raw, naked, vulnerable.

The look he gave me.

I pull out my phone. I'm not even sure what to say. That it's going to work? That I love it? And maybe him? That I want to spend the night with him? That I'm the luckiest girl on the planet?

I tap out something simple instead.

*The video was incredibly beautiful. I am so proud to have been there. You are perfect.*

I can feel the smile in his response and picture his happy expression.

*The thing that made it work was you.*

And then another.

*You make me a better man.*

I show it to Mindy. She falls back on her bed. "This is the most romantic thing, like, ever."

Then she rolls on her side. "You think he'll get his show back?"

I don't want to think about that. "Let's watch it again," I say.

And we do, over and over, reading new comments, until Mindy's mother calls us to dinner.

I'm afraid it is the beginning of the end.

## Chapter Twenty-Two

By the time I get home, I'm determined to escape. I'll take any risk, do anything.

But Mom and Dad don't go to bed at their normal time. They've had a good evening together, and they dawdle on everything, insisting Andy and I watch a classic movie with them until Andy falls asleep.

It's almost midnight before I even get a chance to text Blitz, and that's only because I hole up in the bathroom.

*Where are you now?* I ask him.

*Hannah has us all in her hotel suite, reviewing social media activity and having a strategy team react.*

*Are other people Tweeting for you now?*

*Hell yeah. Hannah says she'd rather have Donald Trump handle my Twitter account than me.*

I don't want to pull him away. It's obviously an

important night. I hear footsteps in the hall and quickly flush the toilet. While I run water to pretend to wash my hands, I text him one more time before I have to stop until my parents are asleep.

*I'm so happy it has gone well. Can't wait to see it with you in person.*

He doesn't respond right away. I picture him in a room with a dozen people, trying to find moments to look at his phone. It's okay. I know this is bigger than me. It will always be bigger than any girl, especially a shy homeschooled girl who hasn't gone anywhere near a television studio.

I tuck the phone in my bra and hurry to my room, afraid that someone might notice the bulge. I can't imagine anything more devastating than losing this phone right now.

I finally go to sleep in the wee hours. I'm going up to the academy tomorrow whether Mom likes it or not. I won't go another day without Blitz. I'm not sure I have many left.

WHEN I MAKE IT TO THE ACADEMY THE NEXT afternoon, everyone is talking about Blitz.

Moms have their phones out, playing the video.

Danika runs around, pushing dancers into their classes.

I know Blitz isn't here yet, because I asked him. He is coming early before the hip-hop group, though, and we'll dance together before class.

I'm wearing pink today, a ribbon woven into my elaborate braids. If I owned makeup, I'd sure as heck be wearing it. But this is how Blitz knows me. I can't change anything. I'm not going to compete with those sexy dancers on his show by trying to beat them at their own game. I have to stay the same, no matter how much panic I feel that he's slipping away.

"You doing okay, Livia?" Suze asks me as I approach the desk.

"Sure," I say. "Why wouldn't I be?"

She steals a glance over at Danika before she says, "You know about Blitz, right?"

My stomach falls. He didn't tell me anything had changed. "He said he'd be here for hip-hop."

At this point, Danika comes forward and takes my arm. "Let's go for a little walk, Livia."

"He's on his way," I tell Suze. "Can you let him know where I am?" I know it's desperate, but I want to establish that he comes for me. That we're more than just a couple people who flirt in dance class. That I really do know more than she does about Blitz.

Danika leads me to her office. "Sit down, Livia,"

she says, dropping into her oversized chair behind her desk. Her blue hair is electric against the dark brown leather. Her voice is kind, but it puts me on guard. I feel like she's going to warn me off Blitz now. She has no idea how far things have already gone. No one does.

I sit in a cushioned chair opposite her, warm with my secret. I'm old hat at forbidden romance. There is nothing she can do to change how I feel or what I want.

"Livia, Blitz is not coming up here today."

I sit up in the chair. "Yes, he is. I just spoke to him."

"Within the past fifteen minutes?" Her voice is still kind, like she's having to give me a talking-to but doesn't want to come off as an authoritarian.

Still, I rebel. "Before I walked over here."

"I just asked him not to come. He's going back to LA tonight, and I felt a protracted good-bye could do more harm than good."

My whole body freezes. Tonight? Already? Why hadn't he told me?

"We just shot the video two days ago!" I exclaim.

"And he's all over the media already. He's getting bookings on morning shows, late-night shows, press in every direction. I'm calling a meeting with all the girls' parents this evening to discuss how to maintain their privacy during this."

I sit back. "You think they'll be in danger?" I picture photographers stalking Gwen and Gabriella and my panic rises.

"Mostly an annoyance," she says, waving her hand to dismiss the idea. "But I want to make sure they are using common sense and that even if some of them want to talk about their experience with Blitz to the media, they don't compromise the privacy of any of the other girls."

"Gwen won't," I say, then realize I'm giving myself away. "Probably only Daisy's mother would be interested."

"I agree," Danika says. She looks at me pointedly. "So what is your situation with Blitz?"

I don't know what to tell her. It isn't really any of her business, is it? "Why is that important?" I ask.

She runs her fingers across the back shaved part of her hair. "I'm responsible for you when you're here. Your parents were very insistent that we watch over you or else your ability to attend dance here would end."

"Well, it doesn't matter now," I say. "He's leaving tonight and I won't see him again."

I'm proud to have said that with strength and confidence, rather than falling apart like I want to do on the inside. I'm desperate to check my phone, realizing I might have texts there that explain everything

Danika is saying. The phone is totally silenced, so I wouldn't have heard them on the way.

He might even want to try and get together before he goes.

"You two seemed very close during the filming," Danika says. "Are you okay?"

Her concern chips away at my bravado. "I just need to check my messages so I can see what's going on."

"You can do that," Danika says. "I just worry about you. I know you can't speak to your parents about this ... relationship you've gotten mixed up in. I feel very responsible."

"Nothing has happened," I say, hoping she can't hear the tears in my voice. "It was just some harmless flirting."

"It doesn't look harmless based on your expression right now."

I want to be alone to look at the messages. "I'm a big girl," I say. "No matter what you or the other instructors or my parents think."

"I know that," Danika says. "I've encountered parents like yours before. It's just gone on a lot longer than it should. You're well over eighteen, right?"

"Nineteen," I say. "I graduated but I'm homeschooled. I'm taking my SAT soon."

"Will you go away to college?"

I look away, staring at framed portraits of Danika's daughter Juliet dancing.

"I take that as a no," Danika says. She stands up and comes around the desk to perch on the corner. "Livia, would you like some help? We can get someone to advise you on college applications, how to get financial aid and on-campus housing. You seem like a smart girl. I bet you can go anywhere you want to go."

"I like it here," I say.

What I can't say is that if I go away, I don't get to see Gabriella. And this is Blitz's hometown. Even if he returns to LA, he has to visit his family. Thanksgiving is next week, and then Christmas. That's two chances to see him. I'll do anything.

"You can go to UTSA right here in town and still stay on campus. If you want to stick with your Catholic heritage, there is St. Mary's."

I know about these places. They seem like pipe dreams. "Dad thinks I should do online college."

Danika leans in, her blue hair bright on the tips from the lights overhead. "I know Blitz seems like an easy out. Like he can rescue you. But he's leaving tonight for LA. He's going on a talk show tour. And if the groundwork he's laid here at the academy and around the city works out, he'll be back on his show. There will be no place for a young, impressionable dancer who has very little experience in the world."

Her words are gentle, but they still cut through

me. “We’re different,” I say. “He’s a different person with me.”

“I believe you,” she says. “He’s been good here. The best he has to offer. But when he’s back in that world, he’ll be back in that role.”

I can’t take any more. “I’m going to go now,” I tell her. “I’ll be here for Betsy’s class tomorrow.”

She stands up, but as I get up to go, she stops me. “There is something else.”

What now?

“I spoke to Betsy. You’ve completed your two years in ballet and you’ve done a heck of a lot of extra dancing the past few weeks.” She turns to the back corner of her office. “She expects you are about to earn these.”

She passes me a small pink bag from one of the dance supply stores that the instructors use. I’ve seen the logo a dozen times.

I accept the bag, my hand shaking. Too many reversals again. My life has been so complicated since Blitz arrived. I know what I’ll see inside, but I still take in a breath when I see them.

Toe shoes, perfect and gleaming in pink satin.

“We based these on your ballet slippers, but we can exchange them for a better size,” she says. “Bring them when you do your assessment and Betsy will check to make sure they are a good fit for you, and we’ll go from there. This was mainly a gesture from me to let you know that I have absolute confidence in you."

I press the shoes to my chest. "Thank you," I say. My eyes smart. "When will she do my assessment?"

"The week after Thanksgiving. Do lots of stretching and strengthening at home to make sure you don't lose any ground over the holiday."

"I will." I place the shoes back in the bag.

As I head out of the academy, my feelings are a jumble. I pull out the phone and start walking down the street. There are a pile of texts from Blitz.

*Hey, Danika has asked me not to come today.*

*I want to see you. Can we meet at the park?*

*Let me know if you can get away.*

*I'm flying to LA tonight. I really want to see you.*

*Please text me as soon as you get these.*

I don't know what to say exactly. I'm about to write him to come to the park when I hear Andy's excited "Livia!"

I look up and see him running ahead of Mom. I guess they are going to the park for recess today.

I shove the phone in my string bag. I don't think she's seen. My heart hammers ninety to nothing.

Andy crashes into me with a hug. "Race you to the swings!"

I let him go without running. I need to face Mom first.

Her face is drawn with concern. "What are you

doing at the park? You're supposed to be at dance."

"There wasn't any studio space available today," I say. "Everyone is practicing for the recital." I hold up the bag. "But guess what! I get to be assessed for my toe shoes right after Thanksgiving! Danika gave me a pair!"

"Really?" My mom sits on the bench and holds out her arms for the bag.

I pass it to her and sit down.

She pulls out the perfect pink shoes. "They are beautiful, Livia." She hugs me with one arm. "I am so proud you've stuck with this. Will you get to dance in them at the recital?"

"I don't think so. It will be too new. But the spring one for sure."

"We were going to get you a pair for Christmas, but now we can spend the money on something else," she says. "You'll have to let us know what you need. A new leotard, maybe?"

My freedom, I think, but I don't say it. "Might need to save it. Sounds like college tuition is coming," I say. "I know Dad talked about online classes, but there is St. Mary's. It's Catholic."

She carefully places the shoes back in the bag. "Livia, you know your father. He won't allow it."

"I'm a legal adult," I say. "If I get accepted and get financial aid, I can go without his permission."

She bites her lip. "Do not speak that way, Livia.

We have taken care of you all these years, despite your terrible wicked actions. You tore this family apart. We had to move."

"It wasn't my secret," I say.

"But you exposed it." Her voice is hard.

I stand up. I have to get away. "I'm going home," I tell her.

Out of the corner of my eye, I see a shiny red car coming up the street. Oh no no no. It can't be Blitz.

I'm so torn. If I wave him down, I can just get in his car, and be gone. Never come back. Would he do that? Would he take me, no matter what the consequences? If I called the police myself, told them I had left home and was not in danger, would that prevent any trouble when my father found out?

I take the bag from my stony-faced mother and hurry along the sidewalk.

I'm halfway down the block, then the red car turns the wrong direction, away from the park, and I see it's some other sports car, not a Ferrari.

I slow down, realizing how rash I was being. Not thinking. Not planning. Not being smart.

My time with Blitz is done. I have to face it. When Mom can't see me, I pull out the phone and text one quick line. Then I turn it off for good.

*I've had a wonderful dance with you, Blitz. Enjoy your limelight again. I hope you find the perfect partner on your show.*

## Chapter Twenty-Three

I make it through most of Thanksgiving week without turning on the phone. I'm like a pendulum, and the moment in the park when I thought about running away was the upswing. Now I'm all the way back on the other side, being a dutiful daughter, working hard to earn my toe shoes, and volunteering like a good Catholic.

But after dinner on Thanksgiving Day, Dad leaves to watch football with some friends, an activity he won't do at home due to the salacious commercials. Mom starts pulling out the Christmas decorations and gets totally absorbed in it with Andy.

So I'm alone in my room, supposedly studying for the SAT, which is now only two weeks away. I want to do well, be eligible for as many scholarships as possible. I want to learn, excel, be better. I won't live here forever, and I need options.

I avoid all thoughts of Blitz.

But in this alone time, I can't help but wonder if he's in town, eating with his family. At church last Sunday, Mindy tried to tell me what was going on with him and the show, but I stopped her. I don't want to know.

The phone lost its charge days ago. I did take it out once in a moment of weakness, and the dead battery helped me pull myself together.

But it calls to me, hidden in a drawer. The charger is still behind the desk.

I can't do it. I shouldn't.

I roll to the edge of the bed. What if he's here? What if the show hasn't worked out? What if he's been rejected and needs me?

Idle hands are the devil's playground. It was something that was drilled into me in the weeks after my pregnancy was discovered. It's happening now. I should go out into the living room and sort the ornaments. I'm the only one who likes tinsel.

But I don't. I kneel by my desk, blocking the view of the drawers with my body so no one passing by my door will see. And I dig out the phone and plug it into the charger.

It's dead enough that nothing happens for a moment. Then the screen flashes on. Once it's past the opening logo, notification after notification scrolls up. Many are from Blitz. A few are from Mindy, links to news sites before I saw her and asked her not to tell me anything.

It's been seven days since I sent my last text to Blitz. I feel sick now thinking of all the unanswered messages. When did he give up? Did it take a day or two? Or is he trying still?

I have to know.

The phone is cold in my fingers. I bring it closer, stretching the power cord to its limit. If anyone comes, I can just drop it in the drawer. I can't decide if I should go back to the first missed message, or read the most recent one.

It doesn't matter. My eyes fall on the newest, sent just an hour ago.

*Happy Thanksgiving, sweet Livia. I wish I were in San Antonio today, close to you. I'd be happy just sitting in our dystopian park, hoping for you to walk by.*

A tear plops on the surface of the phone, and I wipe my eyes, a little shocked at how quickly my body has reacted.

He hasn't given up.

Now that I know this, my finger swipes through all the new messages to go back to the first one, after I told him I hoped he found the perfect partner.

*I don't have the show back yet. And I still have to accept the conditions even if they offer. My lawyer says I have a case for not returning even if they ask. Please let me know if you'll take me instead.*

I almost drop the phone.

God. I never answered that. What had he thought?

I want to respond now, to say YES, but my eye falls on the first message from Mindy, a day later.

*Saw Blitz on clips from the late-night show. You were right to ditch him. I'm sorry, Livia. He's an asshole.*

There's a link to the clip.

I hesitate. Those are strong words from her. What did she see?

The divide between the Blitz I know and the one he is in LA is greater than ever. Maybe I shouldn't look. Just accept the Blitz who wants to wait for me in the park and forget the other.

Except I can't. They are both him.

I click on the link. The title says "Blitz gets his banana back."

My face flames. I remember the bad Tweet he sent out was something about the girl eating him like a banana. I don't know the expression, but I can guess.

I press play on the clip. Blitz sits next to a desk with another man. They are laughing as it begins. The other man asks, "So you've kissed a pig, raised a quarter of a million dollars for women's charities, and danced with girls in wheelchairs. You think that's it? Will the girl you shamed take you back?"

Blitz looks devastatingly handsome. His hair is glossier, bright black in the stage light. He wears black pants, a charcoal shirt, and a black leather vest. His sleeves are rolled up and when I see his fingers, my body quivers.

I know him. I know him so well.

"I'm not sure," he says. "But I'm doing the best I can."

"Why don't we ask her?" the man says. "Can we bring out Giselle?"

Blitz and the man both stand, Blitz looking anxious, as a woman in a glittery dance outfit struts onstage. She whips and whirls, does a leap, and the audience cheers.

"This is Giselle Andreas, one of the final three contestants of *Dance Blitz*," the man says. "Give it up for Giselle as she lets Blitz know if she's forgiven him for his viral Tweet about her!"

The music swells, and she dances around Blitz, climbing up on the chair, then back around. She pulls on the side of her dress, and in a flash, it's off and a tiny outfit, red glittering stripes that fall in just the right places, is revealed.

And she holds a banana.

She dances around him as the music matches her tone, peeling one section at a time.

It's bawdy, and the audience is screaming, and finally she tosses the banana peel away. When she kneels in front of Blitz and places the banana near his crotch, I stop the video.

I put the phone back in the drawer and close it, breathing hard.

I sit on the edge of the bed, trying to pull my thoughts together. This was last week, the day after he left.

And he's still writing me.

He has to know I've seen these things.

Did he try to explain them? Did he think I wouldn't notice? Or care?

I have to know what he said about it. Maybe he was upset, blindsided by what happened. Maybe he was told to behave a certain way or he'd be fired.

I want to believe anything, anything but that he enjoyed it, wanted it, sought this meeting out.

I open the drawer again and go back to his messages. I read through them quickly.

*I'm guessing you know by now I'm not in San Antonio. I will come back, Livia. I know we've barely gotten started but I can't let you go.*

*Headed to the studio for the first talk show. I hope it goes well.*

*Just got out of rehearsal for the show. It should go easy. Just some chatter and a few clips from the video. It's going well. Miss you already.*

Then a few hours later.

*Shit, shit, shit, Livia. Don't watch the show. It was horrible. They got me. They pulled one of their stupid ratings-seeking pranks and had Giselle on the show. It was insane. Please believe that I didn't know anything about it.*

I take in a deep breath. I believe him. He's too upset for it not to be true.

*I'm so angry about this, Livia. The producers have a whole set of appearances for me, and I fear everyone wants Blitz back. Old Blitz. I'm good for ratings. Apparently assholes sell. We have a contract meeting on Monday.*

There is a day gap after that.

*I don't know what to say, Livia. I got to rehearsal for the second show, and they wanted a dance number from season two. It's like the bad stuff never happened. I thought we'd talk about the Dreamcatcher dancers, your girls. But nobody cares about that. They just care if I still have a show, and if I still act crazy enough to garner lots of views.*

Then hours later.

*The show is recorded. The dance number is good, but it's all so crazy. I have two more to do. I don't mind the dancing. All the girls are really talented. It's just the rest of it.*

My heart feels stabbed. Of course those girls are good.

The next one is over the weekend.

*Gotten through the scheduled shows. I've asked for a break. The meeting is Monday. I want to try and come home for Thanksgiving Day. I don't know if you're getting the messages, or if your father has taken the phone. I'll try calling Dreamcatcher Monday and talk to Danika. If she won't give you a message, I'll try Jacob. Then the Tappin' Grandmas. They'll do it!*

This makes me smile. He's trying hard. He sounds tired.

I wonder how those other dance numbers went. Until last Sunday, I hadn't told Mindy not to tell me about Blitz. So she probably sent more links before I stopped her.

Should I look at them, or keep reading Blitz? I want the whole picture. And to see these "talented girls."

I switch over to Mindy's messages.

*This one isn't as bad as the last one, but they are definitely making him into his old self. Did you touch those abs? Because, wow.*

This makes me click. It's another show, and it begins with a dance number of just Blitz. He's wearing a white suit with a matching old-fashioned hat. There's a park bench, and he dances on and around it until a girl appears. She's wearing a flapper-style dress.

Then another comes, and another. He's trying to decide who to dance with.

One takes off his jacket, then another his vest. The girls get more frenzied, and the dancing whirls faster. He spins one after another after another until one tears off his shirt.

I see the abs moment. I swallow. I should have touched them. I was just so frightened all the time. I hadn't wanted to lose control, and by the time I was ready, it was too late.

The other shows are a mix of talking and dancing. One of them, a super-tame morning show, actually does show a clip from the wheelchair girls.

But the Giselle girl appears again in the last one. And the other two contestants. The host convinces them to have a kissing contest and the studio audience judges the hotness level.

I watch him kiss only one of the girls, and I have to stop the video. Too much. Thankfully, it's the last of the clips. There are no more to torture myself with.

But the frozen still shows me something I had started to notice. Blitz is smiling. His honest-to-goodness, happy grin. He's enjoying himself now. And he wasn't fighting that kiss. He was into it. Giving it all to the camera.

He belongs there. The role has become him again.

I want to switch back to his thread, feel some reassurance, see if he did call Dreamcatcher. We didn't have class this week due to the holiday. But I know what the texts will say. That he misses me. That he wants to see me.

But it's become clear that he wants it all. The

show. The fame. The talented dancers. And me too, the quiet reminder of his private life. That piece of him that he is afraid to let go of.

The thing is, I want more for myself than he is going to be able to give. And just knowing him, sneaking around when he's so popular again, with Blitz sightings all over, puts my privacy in danger. If I got caught with him, and my family overreacted, then I would lose my ability to see my daughter.

So instead of responding to anything, I pull the power cord from the phone and bury it in the drawer once more.

## Chapter Twenty-Four

After church on the Sunday after Thanksgiving, Mindy immediately pulls me away from my family, saying we're needed to organize the avalanche of holiday decorations Irma has pulled from storage. Her mother has packed a lunch for us to eat in the office, and I'm surprised to see how well she planned to get me away from home.

My parents, who have seen me cooped up in my room for an entire week, actually think it's good for once for me to get out. So soon I'm left in the church sanctuary with Mindy and a dozen boxes of Christmas decor.

Irma pops in to say she has her weekly ladies' lunch, but that Father Stephen will be in and out.

As soon as we're alone and have enough garlands

and white Chrismons around us to be respectable, Mindy pulls out her phone.

I hold up my hand. "I'm not sure I want to see anything," I say. "Those clips you sent before were plenty."

She sets it down. "But he got his show back."

I open a new box and start untangling a string of lights. "During the contract meeting on Monday?" I ask.

"So he has been writing you!" She shoves at me. "Why haven't you written me back?"

"I took the phone out one time to check on him. Once I saw the clips, I had to stop."

Mindy frowns. "Well, the live finale is scheduled for December. He is choosing the winner during it."

I shrug. I figured that would be the case. "He didn't think he would propose," I say. "Just be a dance partner."

"So there's still a chance for you two?"

I shake my head. "He's in LA now. I am here. It's done."

Mindy sets her phone down. "Are you okay, Livia? This is tough stuff."

"We didn't get anywhere," I tell her. When she looks crushed, I manage a smile. "I'll never be able to find out if they sleep with him because of who he is or if he's any good."

Mindy opens a box and pulls out a plastic Baby

Jesus. She holds him up and shakes him as if he is talking when she says, "Good thing, since I was watching the whole time!"

I pull out the Virgin Mary. "Go to sleep, Baby Jesus! It's past your bedtime."

We dissolve into laughter.

And just like that, we're back to who we used to be. Two sheltered girls being silly, trying to make the best of our situation.

Blitz is in the past.

I HEAD UP TO THE ACADEMY EARLY ON TUESDAY SO I can get in some ballet practice before Gabriella's class. Danika said my assessment would be sometime this week. I've done stretches and strengthening at home, but now I need to be at the barre.

It's a little surreal walking into Dreamcatcher, almost as if Blitz could be here somewhere. He became such a fixture in the weeks he was here. I can't help myself, but instead of going directly to dance, I pass the empty studios and head into the storage room.

The ghostly racks and supply shelves are no different. I pick up the top hat he wore and place it on my head. I run my hand down the wall where he kissed me. This is hard. As hard as anything I've done other than letting go of Gabriella.

But I still have her. She's here. And she's why I won't go away to college. Why I'll stay.

I set the hat back on the shelf and head to a studio. If there is anything that can get me out of my melancholy, it's dance.

I avoid Studio 4 where I always met Blitz and choose Studio 2 instead. The room is bright and colorful. I run through my exercises and imagine what it will feel like to *relevé* in a toe shoe, extending higher than I ever have before.

Danika pops in and gives me a few pointers, lifting my back leg and squeezing along my calves. We roll my feet over and over, and she leaves me to do it more, as that will be the first motion I take in the new shoes, if I pass.

She leaves the door open, so I hear the rumble of students arriving before the lights even flicker for the transition. I pick up my string bag and head to Studio 3 for our class.

The girls are chatty and excited, seeing each other for the first time since the video came out. They circle around each other.

"Where's Benjamin?" Daisy asks when I enter.

I don't have the heart to tell them he's gone for good, so I leave it to Janel to break the news. They sit glumly for a while, so Janel passes out the ribbon sticks, a tactic that gets any group of kids excited and happy.

We circle the room in a conga line, me helping push the girls who can't easily move with only one hand. It's funny and awkward with me and Janel racing between chairs, and before long the girls are cheerful and ready to work.

If only I could soak in some of their joy.

I roll up the ribbon sticks while they run through the recital, remembering when I did this with Blitz, the day he taught me to waltz. I'm having the worst time today, unable to think about anything but him. The hardest part is knowing I can relent. I can pick up the phone he gave me and text him. I'd still be in his life. It's just so little. And he has so much going on. All those women.

At some point in my life I want to have more than just scraps.

The class finally ends and the girls head out with their mothers. I watch Gabriella with Gwen. If my baby had to have another mother, I'm glad it is her. She cares. She is careful. She pays attention.

Apparently a cold front has blown in while we were in class, so the moms wrap the girls in jackets and blankets, anything they have in the car. It will be a cold walk home for me in my leotard. Maybe I'll run.

I change shoes and cross the foyer. Every space

has an image of Blitz associated with it. I decide that I'll write him one last time, after my assessment when I earn my toe shoes. He'll be happy about that. Contacting him will be my reward.

Thinking about this gives me a bit of joy to hold on to as the frigid air hits me outside the academy. The temperature has dropped at least twenty degrees and the wind feels icy.

I hurry along the sidewalk, my arms wrapped tightly around my body. Good Lord, it's cold.

By the time I get to the park, my nose is running. I pray I don't get sick. We'll have to delay my *pointe* assessment if I do.

My head is down, so I don't notice the red car until I'm right beside it.

I stop short.

It's a Ferrari.

I peer in the window. The inside is empty.

A heavy wool coat comes around me, and I whirl around.

It's Blitz.

I'm so happy to see him that I almost lose the coat as I throw my arms around him. He draws it around both of us, holding me tightly against his warm body.

"Just like a princess to run around expecting people to bring you a coat," he says.

I can't even speak. I just press my face into his

shoulder, trying not to weep. He's here. He's here. He's here. Everything I've just promised myself about not settling dissolves in the light of his actual presence.

"Let's get you in the car," he says. "Can you spare a little time without getting in trouble?"

I nod. We walk together to the car and he opens the door. "Keep the coat on," he says. "Texas weather sure does change on a dime."

The car is still clean. There's a fresh McDonald's cup in the console, which makes me smile.

Blitz gets in. He's wearing jeans and a deep green sweater that makes his hair seem black as night. I can't do anything more than take him in.

"I knew you'd be walking this way after the dance class," he says. "I could only hope you hadn't gotten so stuck that your parents didn't allow you to go anymore. Did they take your phone? I've been writing you and writing you."

I don't know what to say. That I got the messages and didn't respond? That it was pointless?

A woman and her dog pass by, and I startle, petrified it will be my mother trying to bring me a coat. It could happen. "Let's get away from here," I say. I've gotten good at lying again. I'll figure a way out of it if she goes to Dreamcatcher and I'm not there.

He starts the car with a low rumble of the engine. In seconds, we're far enough away that I don't have to worry about being seen. "Pull over here," I say, pointing to the parking lot of a bank. It's hidden by a tall hedge.

Blitz parks the car in the corner and reaches over to unbuckle my belt. He takes me in his arms again, holding me tightly, as if he can't believe I'm really there.

I understand the feeling. "You came back," I say.

"Of course I did," he says. "I didn't even get to say good-bye."

My stomach falls. "Are you now?"

He pulls away a little so he can look into my eyes. His are deep, dark brown, and full of concern. "Of course not. I flew back to find you again. I've been so worried. That you got caught. That your parents flipped out."

I shake my head. "They don't know about you still."

"Do you still have your phone?"

I nod slowly. "I just couldn't answer. I saw the video with that girl. Giselle."

"God," he says. "That was so screwed up."

"I know," I tell him. "And I know that wasn't your doing. But then I saw some of the others. And you were so happy."

He stiffens, and I press my palm to his cheek. "You were!" I say. "I saw it myself. You are back in your world. It's what you wanted."

"No," he says, his voice low and hard. "I don't want it at the cost of you."

My heart sings at this, but I'm not sure I can believe it. It seems impossible.

"Blitz," I say. "We've known each other, what, three weeks?"

"Are you saying you don't feel this?" His voice catches at the end, and my heart squeezes.

"I do, Blitz, I really do." I don't know what I'm saying anymore. "I just see that you love that life. And I can't do it with you."

He closes his eyes, a muscle ticking in his jaw. "What would you like me to do? Meet your parents? Whisk you away to LA? Break my contract and quit the show?"

I hesitate. Something must be really wrong for him to want to throw everything away. "None of those," I say. "Let's just be for a minute."

He pulls me back against him and I sink into the feeling of his arms around me, the smell of his hair, the soft tickle of the bristle on his cheek against my forehead.

A cold splat of rain hits the windshield, then another. Soon it's pelting down, bits of ice mixed in. My mother will panic and try to come for me. I know it.

"I have to go home," I say to him. "Meet me back

at the park tonight. I'll text you. Probably after ten, maybe eleven."

He kisses my hair. "Okay. I'll be there. Can you write to me in the meantime?"

"Yes," I say. "I'll charge the phone."

He pulls away from me and starts the car. We drive through the deluge. I have him drop me off as close to home as I dare and make a run for the door.

Inside, Mom is just putting her coat on to come fetch me. She's pulled out some towels. I let her dry my hair, thinking, plotting, wondering what I'll do to get away tonight to see Blitz.

## Chapter Twenty-Five

Part one of my escape plot is to feed my family into sleep oblivion. Chicken pot pie is everyone's favorite, and they will all eat it until they can't move. I volunteer for kitchen duty and slice celery and onion, chicken and potatoes, adding peas and carrots, and putting the monstrous pie in the oven.

For dessert I make chocolate cake from scratch with a thick creamy layer of frosting.

I texted Blitz the moment I changed clothes from the rain, and throughout the day I've caught up on all the messages he sent while I wasn't checking. I can see his mixed emotions in them, ranging from elation to regret. I guess even reality TV stars are allowed to have moments of doubt.

At dinner, I encourage seconds and large helpings. I handle the dishes afterward too, keeping everyone sluggish. I make coffee, but it's decaf, and by the time Andy goes to bed at eight, my parents are making comments about an early night as well.

I stretch and agree, heading to the bathroom to change into pajamas.

I pick up a novel, a parent-approved story about a Quaker family, and say good night to everyone. I turn out the overhead light and keep on only a small lamp.

And listen.

Water running. Doors closing. Murmurs. Then quiet.

The phone is charged so I keep it tucked under a pillow. Wherever Blitz is, he's obviously not distracted as he responds to every message within seconds.

Around ten, I carefully crack open my door. The house is dark. I close it again and change clothes. I know what I want tonight from Blitz. I slide on a sweater without a bra. And a skirt. No panties. The feel of the rough fabric against my skin is sensual and I shiver. I send him a quick text that I'm heading out.

I hold my shoes in my hand. My hair isn't fancy, just up in a ponytail. I'll pull it down at the last minute. I grab my puffy red coat off the back of a chair. I tuck the phone in a pocket.

The hall is dark and silent. I close my door and creep to the living room. I'm afraid the front door is too close to my parents' bedroom wall, so I head to the kitchen and go out the back. We don't have a garage, just a covered carport that holds Mom's sagging minivan and Dad's rusting old Pontiac.

The cold hits me in an icy blow. I still manage to turn and close the door carefully. At this point I just have to run. If I've been heard, I want to at least get away.

I shove my shoes on my frozen feet and take off across the yard. God, it's cold. We don't get weather like this very often in San Antonio.

The street is quiet as I run down the sidewalk to the park. At least it isn't raining anymore.

I haven't gone far when I see the red Ferrari slowly inching down the street. I pull out the ponytail holder and shove it in my pocket. My hair streams behind me. By the time I reach the car, Blitz has opened the side door for me.

"Oh, Princess, it's way too cold for royalty to be out in this weather," he says.

I slam the door closed, sucking in a breath. "I'm fine," I say, my teeth chattering from both the chill and the anxiety of my escape.

Blitz cranks the heater and it blows fiery bliss onto my feet.

"Is it okay if we go to my hotel, or is that too much?" he asks.

"That sounds perfect," I say. I had hoped that

would be the case, not his family's house or some public place. I'm done with that.

I finally warm up enough to take in where I am and what I've done. Blitz peers out onto the street as we take off. The fog makes visibility low. The lamps over each intersection have a hazy glow. You can't see much past each traffic light.

"Spooky," I say.

"It's like we're driving into oblivion," he says.

Maybe we are.

He reaches over for my hand. "I'm very close, just at the interstate. I didn't want to be far from you."

My heart hammers. "Does your family know you're in town?"

"I didn't tell them, but I think my mom follows the Blitz sightings hashtag. She says it's nice to know where her boy is."

"Have you been spotted here?"

"Not that I can tell."

"If she follows you, then she saw the Tweet?"

His lips pinch together. "Yeah. Hers was the only call I took the next day."

"What did she say?"

"That I would get through this."

"And your dad?"

He laughs, a bitter sound that startles me. I've never heard Blitz sound that way. "He thought it was a riot. He's never been fond of my dancing. He's one of those 'men should be men' sort of fathers."

"I remember you saying he didn't allow you to take ballet."

"Yep. Good ol' Dad. I swear half the time I say something disgusting on the show, it's a phrase I learned from him."

"But he's proud of you now, right?"

We pause at a red light. "I guess. He definitely approves of my carousing. He always asks ridiculous questions about..." He falters. "Stuff he doesn't need to know."

I can imagine. "Well, you could tell him my bra size, but I'm not currently wearing one."

He sucks in a breath. "Princess, you're tempting me sorely, and my intentions are strictly honorable tonight."

They are? I press my knees together. Why is it I wear panties when we're being crazy, and I skip them when he's being a gentleman? I need an instruction manual for torrid relationships.

For the uninitiated, Blitz Craven is a crash course in sexy.

We pull up in front of a towering hotel. A man in a uniform dashes out and opens my door. "Come inside, Miss," he says.

Another man heads around to the driver's seat.

I'm escorted into a posh lobby, warm and cozy,

the lights dimmed for evening. The man heads back to the doors as Blitz makes it inside. I can finally take him in, the long gray wool coat he wrapped me in earlier, black jeans, a thick corded sweater in steel blue.

He takes my hand as we cross the lobby to the elevator bank.

"Just so you know, I didn't book the room we're about to go to," he says. "I tried to pick something ordinary, but the staff upgraded me anyway. For my privacy, allegedly. Probably they are worried I'll throw a party."

He takes me to an elevator away from the grouping in the center. Blitz extracts a card from his pocket and passes it in front of a sensor. The elevator doors open smoothly.

"You need a special pass to ride this one?" I ask. I haven't been in a hotel in years, since the time before. And even then, they were always motels with stairs on the outside of the building.

"Keeps out the riffraff," Blitz says as we go inside. "Or perhaps in my case, prevents access to the riffraff."

There are no buttons, and a display screen reads "Good evening, Mr. Craven."

"How does it know?" I ask. I'm like a child in a toy store, looking around. The back of the elevator is glass and provides a view of the atrium.

"The card tells it," he says. "So it knows what room to send you to."

"What if you want to go somewhere else?" I ask.

He laughs. "I don't know, actually. Maybe nobody ever does."

I punch at the screen. A menu comes up. One of the choices is "Override destination." I hit it. The elevator smoothly glides to a stop.

"There you go," Blitz says.

A list of rooms comes up, all with names like Presidential Suite, Executive Retreat, and The Ambassador. Then the other floors of the hotel.

I click on The Ambassador. A message pops up. "Your card is not authorized for this floor. To request access, please contact the executive desk."

"Bummer," I say.

Blitz laughs. "We're in the Presidential."

I click on that one instead. The elevator resumes its steady climb.

The doors open to a small lobby area with red velvet sofas and a bar. A man is behind the counter. "Hello, Mr. Craven," he says. "Would you or your young lady like anything from the bar?"

Blitz looks at me.

I lean in. "I'm underage," I say.

"Nothing right now, thank you," Blitz says.

The man nods and resumes drying a glass. His

eyes return to a television mounted on the wall, its volume low.

Blitz leads us to the right. There aren't many doors in the hall. A gold plate with the words "Presidential Suite" announces which room is ours. Blitz waves the card by the handle, and it pops the door.

When we step inside, my breath catches. It's unlike any place I've ever been. A pure-white sofa rests in front of a fireplace with several logs already burning. There's a piano in the corner by huge windows, open wide to look out on the city. Thankfully we're facing away from the highway, so you can see across San Antonio, the circular Tower of the Americas visible in the distance.

"Wow," I say.

"Fit for a princess," he says. He sets the card on a counter in front of a small kitchenette and bar. He shrugs off his coat and reaches for mine.

I slide it off my shoulders and pass it to him. I walk over to the windows. It's amazing. We're on top of the world. I press my fingers against the cool glass.

Blitz comes up behind me and sweeps my hair off my shoulder. "You okay with getting away?"

I shiver from his light touch on my neck. Now that I'm here, I'm not sure. I still have to get back in my house. Or maybe I just don't go back. I don't know. I lean my forehead against the glass.

"Come sit with me," he says, taking my hand and leading me over to the sofa.

We stay close together, his arm around my waist, as we settle on the cushions. He draws my head against his shoulder. "This is so much better than the insanity I've been through the past two weeks," he says.

"You want to tell me about it?"

So he does, lulling me with his voice as he describes the sets, the dances, the green rooms, the people behind the talk shows. The meetings with executives, how Hannah being a shark was in his favor this time. How most of the staff were eager to return, only his trainer and a few other minor players had held out. Hannah was working on replacing them before the finale.

"So you have to do it?" I ask. "Choose a winner?"

"I could break the contract," he says. "I'd go bankrupt from the fines, but there are worse things. I'd never work in Hollywood again, but maybe I don't want to."

"That seems terribly extreme," I say.

"It's extreme either way," he says. "The lifestyle, the scrutiny, having to live up to everyone's expectations."

"How did this happen?" I ask. "I saw some of your early stuff. It wasn't all naked women and acting crazy."

"In the beginning, it's always about the dance," he says. "Then something happens, and it gets attention, and you're driven to do more of the same. In my case, it was acting like a jerk."

"I don't understand why that is so popular. You'd think girls would want a gentleman."

"Gentlemen don't make for compelling television," Blitz says. He picks up my hand and kisses each finger. "You'd be bored with me in a week."

"Not if we dance," I say.

"True. We do have that."

I lean my head on his shoulder. "Blitz," I ask. "Why am I here?"

He holds my hand against his cheek. "Because I can't *not* have you here."

"But why? You've got so many choices." My cheeks burn a little. I'm embarrassed to ask these things, but I have to know. I'm risking everything for this.

"All those women audition for my show to get their brush with fame. Not for me."

"But you're supposed to pick a wife from it."

"I didn't design the show. And my contract specifically says I don't have to marry anyone. I wasn't that crazy."

"But you still have to choose."

"I choose this." He squeezes my hand.

"Well, it's really inconvenient right now."

This makes Blitz laugh. "Princess, I was miserable without you." He turns my cheek so that his mouth can reach mine.

He's said enough for me. Even though I'm not sure I believe that we have anything that can last, I still want it. But my life can't just revolve around him. I have to protect the most important things. And Gabriella is still more important.

But tonight doesn't change any of that. I can do this. I can be what Blitz Craven needs right now. And he can be what I want.

His lips nibble along mine until I part for him. Then he deepens the kiss, pulling me in close.

Our bodies collide. He runs his hands along my back and down my arms. I reach up to thread my fingers through his hair. I'm ready to get lost again. Every muscle in my body feels warm and pliant.

Even if he's going to go back to LA for good, and even if I'm just a blip in a sea of women, I'm ready for one perfect night with Blitz Craven. If I end up stuck with online college and more years under my father's rule, it might have to sustain me for a long time.

He presses forward until I'm lying back on the sofa and he is propped above me. His lips leave mine and trail down my jaw to my neck.

I literally feel pinpricks in parts of my body, as if it's waking up from a long slumber. Everything his lips touch jolts awake, and my pulse is wild and erratic. I remember how quickly he affected me in the movie theater and my heart jumps again. I want this so much. So much.

His fingers flirt with the bottom of my sweater, brushing against the skin of my belly. I suck in a breath and he smiles against my collarbone. “Sensitive, Princess?” he asks.

I can’t answer as he moves more of the sweater out of his way. When he lifts it high enough, a low throaty moan escapes. “You made it easy for me. God, that is hot.”

His mouth drops to my breast and my body arches toward him. Heat floods through me, and I feel on fire from the need of him.

He lifts the sweater higher and pulls it over my head, dropping it over the back of the sofa. He moves from one nipple to the other, caressing them both.

I slide my legs apart so he fits more solidly against me. He’s low, his chest over my stomach as his mouth and hands mold me.

I clutch his head and the glossy black hair. He moves down, dipping his tongue into my belly button. “What else am I going to find?” he asks.

I’m so glad I didn’t wear panties. I want to delight him. He lifts himself away from me to nudge the hem of my skirt with his nose. His mouth finds the sensitive skin inside my knee and begins to work its way up.

The fire I felt earlier is nothing compared to the eruption going through me now. I want him to arrive where he's headed. I need him there.

He takes his time, nibbling along my inner thigh. When the skirt is high, covering my bare stomach, he lets out another groan. "You're perfect," he says, and I can feel the words as he breathes them so close to my most tender places.

I'm dying. I want him to taste me, to work his magic. He slides a finger inside and my body rises right to him. And he's there, his tongue delving inside.

The intensity I felt in the movie theater is nothing compared to this. The world is down to just these sensations, his warm mouth, the pressure of his hand, the buzz building deep inside me as he works.

I'm lost, so lost. I move with him, gripping his hair, the only sound the gentle snap of the fire logs. The frenzy inside me accelerates, and the pleasure of it ratchets up into more than I can manage. I need it to go over the top, to release out, to free me.

"Blitz, please," I manage to say.

And he knows just what I need, increasing the pressure, diving in more deeply. And it happens, my muscles clamping down for the orgasm, lightning shooting through my body, sparked where we are joined. I hear myself crying out Blitz's name and fat tears squeeze out of my eyes.

He brings me down easy, withdrawing slowly and gently, his kisses flowing back down my leg. I lie on the sofa with my arms crossed over my face. I'm not sure how he'll feel about me crying.

Blitz leans back over and kisses the length of my forearm. When he sees the wetness, he gathers me up against him. "You okay, Princess?"

I nod against his chest. I'm not sure what it is about, maybe the bliss after so many years with little to hold on to. Returning to that emotional space I had to let go of when they took Gabriella away.

"Hey," he says, sitting us up. "Talk to me."

I'm ruining this moment, I know it. I shake my head. "Just old stuff."

He goes still. "Did somebody hurt you once?"

"No," I say quickly. "Never. No. It's just been a long time."

He cradles me against him. "That's all right. We don't have to do anything else."

But I want to. I do. I shove all the old thoughts away and shift in his arms. "I think we do," I say.

My hands go to his cheeks and I kiss him this time, hard and deep.

I don't have to say that twice. Before I can figure out what's happening, he's swept me into his arms. He crosses the living room and heads through a doorway on the far side.

It's dim, lit only by the light coming from the

bathroom. The bed is enormous, four poster, and silks cascade down from it. "It's a princess bed!" I say.

"I couldn't have chosen it better myself," he says. He nudges the sheer fabric aside and lays me on its surface. "Now I'm going to really look at you."

Blitz tugs on the skirt until it's down. He stands to toss it across a chair.

Then he's back, sitting on the edge of the bed, his hands running down my body, tracing every curve.

I'm surprisingly unembarrassed as he takes me in, eyes lighting on each part of me. Then he stands up, pulling his sweater over his head, and the shirt beneath.

I've seen him shirtless before, on the day with the Tappin' Grandmas. He's strong, muscled but not overly so, lean like a dancer should be.

Blitz kicks off his shoes and pulls his belt from his jeans. It jingles as it hits the floor.

I watch him quietly. It's so different from seeing the pictures of him on the laptop with Mindy. He's here, his body shifting in the light, revealing himself to me.

My eyes threaten to tear up again. He's really beautiful. I almost want to dance like this, skin to skin, and once the idea gets in my head, I can't let it go.

I sit up. "Can we dance?" I ask. The room is

outrageously large. We can do it easily around the bed.

He kicks off the rest of his clothes. "A naked waltz. Now that's an idea."

Blitz takes my hand and pulls me to him. Every place our body touches is like a caress, stirring and intimate.

He squeezes my hand, and we're off, crossing the rug, then onto the surrounding hardwood floor. The steps are simple, just a few turns. My hair falls down my back, a gentle tickle, until he spins me out and sends it flying.

The air on my body is erotic and stimulating. When I turn back into him and our skin makes contact again, he holds me close. "You are so beautiful," he says. "This is the most perfect moment I could have imagined."

His mouth is warm on mine, the kiss full of tenderness and wonder. I hold on to his neck, and his hands grasp my thighs, pulling my legs up and around his hips.

He's hard and pressing against me, and I feel almost dizzy as the need of him bolts through me. He walks us back to the bed and lays me back down on the cool sheets.

"Condom work for you?" he whispers against my ear.

I nod.

He disappears for a moment, and when he returns, leans down for a kiss as he crawls across the bed to me.

My body is on fire. When he touches my breast, I lurch upward. He smiles against my mouth. "I've wanted you for so long. It feels like years."

He parts my knees, pressing his palm against me. My body responds again, desperate for him, so full of need.

Blitz shifts his hand away and he's there, moving against me, slipping gently inside.

I cry out, my body so ready for him, so willing to take him in. He presses his lips against my neck, easing himself out and back in.

My hands flatten against his lower back, clutching him. I'm breathless and eager. Everything is new again, the sensations, the emotional flood.

Blitz quickens his rhythm, reaching between us to add to my sensation. I've never felt this before, and I rise to him, spiraling up again. It seems impossible after the moment on the sofa, but I feel it, burgeoning inside me, the tension and the desire.

"My sweet Livia," he says. "How I have pined for you."

His finger moves more swiftly, and his pace increases to match. I can't think of anything other than this man, his touch, his body shifting over mine.

The frenzy builds, and I can feel the moment

arriving. I open my eyes and see Blitz watching me, attentive and so very close.

The look there is nothing I've seen before, not in all the pictures or all the clips, not even in person in all the moments we've shared. It's adoration and tenderness, beauty and care. It sends me over the top, crying out, falling into bliss.

His body tenses and his strokes move into me with more force. Then I feel it, the subtle contractions of him inside me as he holds still, reveling in the moment.

I hang on to him until he relaxes, and we come down together, his face next to mine, his body still pressed against me. I touch his skin, his back, his waist, the textures of him. I want to know him, memorize all the parts that make his whole.

After a moment, he shifts next to me and draws me close. We breathe together, content and happy. There is no outside, no world that demands things from us. Just our bed, the silk drapes around it, and the air we take in.

We're calm and relaxed, but there's no way I can sleep. I trail my finger along his sideburn, down his neck, along the strong shoulder just where I hold it when we waltz.

"Tell me something about Blitz Craven that I can't read on the Internet," I say.

He picks up my hand and kisses my fingers. "That

the kids in my elementary school thought I was a dork and used to sing, 'Bennie, Bennie, not worth a penny.'"

"Oh!" I say. "I bet they don't think that now."

He rolls on his back. The glow from the bathroom light highlights every indentation of his abs. I could stare at him all night.

"That is one of the perks of the gig," he says. "Making my enemies mad with envy."

"Do you have a lot of them?" I ask. "Enemies?"

"I didn't used to," he says. "But when you get to this level of the game, you rack them up pretty fast."

I lay my head on his chest, listening to the steady thump thump of his heart. "Your character is rather larger than life. I'm sure it's intimidating."

"One day it will be gone. Poof. Show over."

"Then what for Blitz Craven?"

He twirls a piece of my hair. "Watch old movies in a rundown theater with a girl who sometimes doesn't wear panties."

I roll my face into his chest to hide my blush, which is silly given that I'm lying here naked with him now.

"So tell me, Princess Livia, what is something I don't know about you?"

My throat constricts. I immediately think of Gabriella. Can I tell him? I'm not sure. Despite everything, this night, him returning for me, the phone — I could still just be a fling.

"I'm not very interesting," I say.

"How about you tell me how you got involved with the wheelchair ballerinas? I read an interview with Danika about it that said she had a young dancer who brought the idea to her. I'm guessing that was you?"

And there it is. My opportunity.

"I'd heard about them," I say. "There was a video online that everyone was talking about." Which was true. When I was sneaking on the church laptop trying to learn about Gabriella's condition, I had seen clips of ballet schools with wheelchair dance classes.

"But people see videos of stuff all the time. What made you start the class?"

Opportunity again. But I'm too scared to do it.

"One of the girls in the class, Gabriella, had just been in a car accident. Her father died in the crash. I thought the class would be good for her. Her mother Gwen had a hard time. I wanted to help."

"That's really amazing." He squeezes me.

I hold my breath, waiting for him to remember that this is the same girl he thought was my sister, a question I never answered. But he doesn't. There must be so much going on in his life that this little connection isn't clicking in his mind. So I let it go.

There will be a time to tell him, but it isn't now.

"When do I have to send you back to the castle?" he asks.

"If they haven't noticed I'm gone by now, then they won't for a few more hours."

Blitz keeps his arm around me while he fumbles with the clock on the side table. "I'll set an alarm for 4 a.m. Does that work?"

"Sounds good."

I don't really want to sleep, but I snuggle into Blitz, and my eyes are so heavy.

## Chapter Twenty-Six

When the alarm goes off, I'm momentarily confused. Blitz silences the noise and moves my hair away from my face. "You're more than a princess in the morning," he says. "You're a goddess."

I sit up, holding the sheet to me. "I seriously doubt that." I try to run my fingers through my tangled hair, but they get stuck.

"You're otherworldly," he says. He pushes aside the covers. "And somebody agrees."

I glance down, my face heating to see him erect and waiting.

He must have gotten rid of the other condom at some point. I reach out to touch him. He is hot and hard, and he takes in a deep breath as I slide my palm along his length.

"Come here," he growls, and before I know what is happening, he's got me on my back.

"Somebody's looking for a second helping," I say, then gasp as his fingers slip inside me.

"I'd have a third, fourth, and fifth if I had my way," he says. "But I know we can't tarry."

My hand smacks his back. "Did you really just say *tarry*?" My laugh comes out as a snort, which makes him crack up.

"Well, we are talking about princesses and castles," he says. His hand shifts, and I cry out from the pleasure of it. He has me figured out.

I'm feeling bolder than last night, and I catch him off guard by shifting sideways and rolling him over.

Then I'm on top of him.

"Well, then," he says. His hands are free and he grabs another condom package off the side table.

I lean down to kiss him as he tears it open, then sit back to give him room to roll it on. I watch it with interest. This is something I should have known about before. Something I should have insisted on five years ago. But I hadn't. Young and foolish.

Blitz grasps my hips and lifts me up. "You ready for this?" he asks.

I nod and then cry out as he thrusts upward into me. He moves me over him, rapid and unrelenting. I can't even think, sparks are shooting through me so fast. I gasp and try to find some sort of control, but it's nowhere and before I can even figure out what he's doing, I'm over the edge, spasming around him, and calling out his name.

He pulls me down against his chest and rolls us over in one smooth movement. Now he's on top again and his rhythm is hard and fast. I'm still trying to recover from the last orgasm when he adds his fingers and I feel it again, forcing me back into that space, pushing me, making me want more than I think I can bear.

This time when I cry out, he goes with me, pumping straight through it, until I see colors bursting out like an explosion. When he finally collapses on me, I feel so exhausted I don't think I'll be able to move.

But he gives me a quick kiss and withdraws. "Rise and shine, Princess. We have to cross the moat and get past the guards."

I groan and try to dive under the sheets. Blitz laughs and pulls them away. "Now, I'm more than happy to load you on a plane next to me and haul you to LA. But if you want to go home, we have to get you back."

I lie there a moment, thinking. What do I want? I picture myself riding off in the Ferrari, walking onto an airplane.

But I know I can't. There's his show. My SAT. Parents. Toe shoes. Gabriella.

I stick my head back out. "Fine. I'll get my clothes."

"That's my girl."

There's no time to spare now, so we move to the living room and dress quickly.

The atrium is dark and silent as we head down, although a few early travelers are in the lobby.

Blitz's car is out front and waiting for us. The vent blasts cold, though, so I rub my hands together as we take off for my neighborhood.

"So when do you go back to LA?" I ask.

"In four hours," he says. "I was sneaking a day away. There will be hell to pay for skipping this morning's rehearsal, plus yesterday's."

"I didn't know you were supposed to be there!" I say.

"I couldn't concentrate. I had to know that you were okay." He reaches over to hold my hand. "It's just ten days until the finale. I'll declare a winner and end the show. Then hightail it back here for whatever's next."

He's coming back here? For me?

"Is that okay?" he asks. "Do you want me to come?"

"Of course. We can figure out a way to introduce you to my parents," I say. "They might flip, but they can't keep me locked up."

"Why haven't you left?"

"I've been pretty sheltered. I don't know anything about finding a job or supporting myself. I don't even have a driver's license."

He shakes his head. "I can help you." He parks at the same spot he left me in the rain, a few houses down from mine. "This work?"

I nod. "I promise to keep my phone on. I won't ignore you again."

"It's going to get pretty intense in the next few weeks. They're going to start airing some segments to promo the live finale. They might be hard for you to see. Don't give up on me." His eyes are pleading. "No matter what you see. No matter how well I play the role, believe in me."

"I will," I say. "I have faith."

"Okay," he says. He leans over to me, and I meet him halfway for a good-bye kiss. Except that it isn't really. I'll see him when all this is over.

I open the door and take a deep breath.

"Should I wait until I know you're okay?" he asks.

I peer down the street. My house is still dark. "Nobody's up," I say. "I can get in."

"Call me if anything goes wrong, okay? I can come get you."

I lean down and smile at him. "I will."

But as I cross the carport and open the door to a dark, quiet house, I know I've made it.

And I also know my days here are numbered.

## Chapter Twenty-Seven

Blitz writes me constantly. Between taping promo segments. During breaks in the dance rehearsals. I rarely go more than two hours without hearing from him.

I'm starting to believe this could be real.

Mindy comes on Thursday to take me to the park. We watch old *Dance Blitz* episodes. I witness how he goes from a dancer to a philanderer to a jerk. It's all there. The explosion in the ratings. The comments on the episodes. They love it. The crazier he gets, the more they love him.

They created him.

But he let them. He went along.

The one time he seems like himself is during the finale of season one. He's supposed to propose to one of the finalists, or at least offer to be their partner. I pause the footage, zoning in on his expression, the lift of his eyebrows, the tightness around his mouth.

"What are you seeing?" Mindy asks me.

"I'm seeing someone who doesn't like who he's become," I say.

She squeezes my arm. "You're still talking to him?"

My phone chimes and I hold it up. "Every few hours."

"That's amazing."

We do searches and read gossip. There are no limo images, no dates outside of filming. Everyone is speculating that he's actually in love with one of the finalists and wants to have time alone without cameras. They try to guess who it is.

Only I know.

"The finale is December 10," Mindy says, scrolling through links.

"That's the same day I take the SAT."

"You should be done by then, though, right?" she asks.

"Oh, yes, a little after lunch." We double-check the listing. The finale goes live at 8 p.m. our time.

"You going to watch it?" Mindy asks.

"I don't know how," I say. My father appears in the corner of my eye and I tuck my phone under Mindy's leg. The park is quiet, but the weather is back to warm again. I wave at Dad. He walks on by.

Mindy leans in to talk softly. "Come over after the SAT. Spend the day with me and we'll watch it together."

This is a good idea. I might need the support. "I'll talk to my parents about it," I say.

"I'll have my mom call yours."

I stick my phone in my pocket, and we walk through the playscape.

I see Blitz everywhere. Pushing Daisy on the swing. Pulling up in his red Ferrari. I miss him. I cling to our night in the Presidential Suite. I wish I could walk up to the hotel and just gaze at the entrance. But it's too far.

At least I have my memories.

On Friday, I know it must be time for my toe shoe assessment. Danika said it would be this week. I bring the *pointe* shoes in my string bag and head into my ballet class.

Betsy greets me with a smile. "Can you stay after class to be assessed for *pointe*?" she asks.

I nod. This is it!

My stomach is a ball of knots as we go through class with the other students. Most of them are younger than me, some of them waiting to be old enough for toe shoes even though they qualify in years.

When the lights finally blink and class is over,

Betsy says good-bye to the other girls, and I stay behind.

I'm filled with doubt. What if Danika was wrong and I'm not ready? What if I snap a tendon the very first time I try *pointe*? It can happen if you're not strong enough.

My belly flutters with nerves as Betsy closes the door and comes back to me. "Ready?" she asks.

I nod.

"All right," she says. "Come to the barre."

Even though I've taken dance with her for over two years, I'm nervous as I approach the barre.

She notices my anxiety. "Don't worry, Livia. I'm sure you'll do fine. We just have to make sure you won't injure yourself when you try *pointe*."

I place my hand on the barre.

She comes up beside me. "All right. Show me your *demi-plié*."

I drop into the position. I know she is looking for proper turnout in my feet and hips.

"Good," she says. "Now sixteen *relevés*."

This is not as easy as it would have been before doing an hour of ballet rehearsal, but I manage them okay.

"Nice," she says. "I know you're probably tired." She steps a little farther away. "Show me your *passé* balance at *half-pointe*."

I move into place and hold. She squats down,

checking my form, my calves, my feet. "Arch your foot a little more," she says.

I feel her hands on my feet.

"Roll your feet for me," she says.

This is what Danika had me do earlier this week, and I move from flat feet to *demi-pointe* over and over.

"Fix your turnout," she says.

I adjust my knees.

"Did you bring the shoes?" she asks.

My heart hammers. Does she mean I can put them on? "Yes," I say.

"Let's see how they fit."

I hurry to my string bag in the corner and pull out the pristine shoes. I haven't cut or sewn them yet, as I didn't want to damage them in case we had to exchange the size.

Betsy heads to the shelves and rummages through a bag, returning with two small toe socks. "Put these on first. You want extra protection and support until you are secure *en pointe*."

I roll the socks over my toes. Then I pull out the shoes. I haven't put them on, even to check for fit. I was afraid I would jinx my chances.

The shoe goes on perfectly. It makes me think of Cinderella trying on her slipper.

"Looks good," Betsy says. She squeezes along my

toes, arch, and heel. "You'll want to sew this." She sticks her finger in a small gap.

My feet are extra long in the shoes. They have a padding of glue and fabric in the toes. It's a strange feeling.

"Let's go to the barre," she says.

I know she's going to have me do my first *relevé* in the shoes. "Can I get my phone to record it?" I ask.

"Sure," she says. "It's a big moment."

I tug the cell phone out of my bag. I set the camera to record a video and lean it against the wall, using the selfie mode so I can see what it is capturing.

"Okay," she says. "Take care in your first *relevé*. Do one foot at a time, no weight on it, and get a feel for the shoe. Fourth position."

I move into the pose, one foot in front of the other, toes in opposite directions.

"Now go to the toe with your right foot," she says.

I do the movement, feeling my foot slide against the base of the shoe.

She squeezes the shoe around my foot. "Good. Now the left."

I repeat it. It feels solid. She checks this one as well.

"You ready?" she asks. "Let's *relevé* with both feet. Shift to first position."

I take in a breath and move my feet so the backs of my ankles touch, toes out.

Then slowly, I rise, feeling the strange pull on my arches as my feet lift higher, up onto the bulk of the shoes.

I look down. I'm *en pointe*!

"How does it feel?" she asks.

Tears squeeze from my eyes. "Amazing," I say.

"Come on down," she says. "Go up and down slowly a few times in first position, then go back to fourth, this time rising up with each individual foot."

I follow her instructions. Every lift onto the shoes is like ascending a staircase. I watch the mirror, admiring my own feet, the arch, the beauty of the shoes.

"That's enough for today," she says. "Congratulations, Livia, you've moved to *pointe*."

I wipe my eyes with the back of my hand as she hugs me. This is the biggest thing I've ever achieved. I pick up my phone and stop the video. I can't wait to share it with Blitz.

## Chapter Twenty-Eight

All weekend I practice my *pointe* form at home. I improvise a barre with a closet rod, cramming all my clothes to one side.

Blitz sends me a video of him watching my shoe video, the cutest thing ever. He's so proud and happy, but sad he wasn't there to see it in person. But I'm fine with that. I can't imagine how much more nervous I would have been if he were there.

Both Mom and Dad stop by my room when they spot me in the toe shoes, admiring the form. There's something about a ballerina *en pointe* that is enchanting and magical. They treat me a little differently, like I'm someone who has actually accomplished something. I feel myself moving from the shame of the family to the pride of it.

On Tuesday, Janel doesn't mention my *pointe* to

the girls, which makes sense. It is something they may never do. Seeing Gabriella after this achievement strikes grief into my heart. She will never dance *en pointe*. For a while, I'm back into my regret and misery.

When I come out of class, the girls gone with their mothers, I find Suze and Aurora and Jacob huddled around the computer screen at the front desk.

"What's going on?" I ask.

They look at each other like they don't want to say.

I come around to peer at the screen. Suze has paused a video clip of *Dance Blitz*. It's a new promo.

"You don't want to see this," Suze says.

They don't know anything, so I shrug casually. "I think it's cool he got his show back," I say. "Hopefully he isn't still Tweeting naked chicks."

I'm impressed by my ability to sound completely calm and indifferent. Suze watches me for a moment as if trying to decide if it's okay to keep watching, then hits the play button again.

Blitz shakes his head at the camera as if he can't believe it is following him. It zooms close on his face.

"Don't let Mariah see this," he says.

"Who's Mariah again?" Aurora asks.

"One of the finalists," Suze says. "She's the fan

favorite. Nobody wants Giselle after the scandal, and Christy is a total skank."

I control my smile at her assessment. I know the contestants by heart at this point. I've watched all of season two and seen how Giselle, Mariah, and Christy were selected by Blitz to be finalists. All that was before we met. But this segment is new.

I remember what he said. No matter what I see, to have faith in him. I fully intend to do that.

The camera pans up and shows the sign on the shop. It's a jewelry store.

The scene cuts to inside. It's a promo video, slick and polished even though it's supposed to look spontaneous. I know all this is scripted. Blitz is playing a role.

It's still hard to watch. A woman on the other side of a glass case asks him if she can help him pick out something. Blitz tells her he wants a gorgeous engagement ring for the perfect girl.

"Please say it isn't for Christy," Jacob says.

I want to laugh. They are so caught up in it. But Blitz is good. His expression is absolutely sincere as he looks at rings and discards several as "not good enough for how amazing she is."

He looks straight into the camera and says, "I can't handle it if she says no."

I want to laugh. He's so good. But the others are

completely bamboozled. Aurora squeezes my arm. "You okay, Livia?" she asks.

I don't know what to say. I can't tell them how things really are.

The scene cuts away with a voice-over that says, "The finale of *Dance Blitz* will air live in just four days. But the fun won't end there. Once Blitz has proposed, we'll follow the happy couple for three intense episodes where they perform in Paris, meet her extended family for the holidays, and the first important planning session for the big wedding."

What? There's more after the finale?

Now I can't catch my breath. Blitz said he would declare a winner and be done. But there's more scheduled! There's air dates and everything! That can't just go away. It's got to be contractual. He's obligated. This could go on for months.

Jacob notices my distress. "Shut that mess off," he orders Suze.

She immediately complies.

Jacob envelops me in a hug, his tall solid frame surrounding me. "I'm so sorry, baby girl," he says. "He's just a man-whore preying on the innocent."

I know I promised Blitz I would have faith, but I'm not sure I can. He hasn't told me about the extra episodes.

Why hasn't he?

I back away from the desk, planning to head

home. Walk through the park. Okay, maybe not there. Take a random street, one with no memories.

I need to think. Why wouldn't Blitz tell me about those extra episodes? That he can't come get me. Can't come back to San Antonio to live. Can't keep his promise.

I'm just down the steps when I realize why.

He isn't going to do them.

He's going to blow it on purpose.

It's a live finale.

And he knows how to get thrown off the show. He's already done it once.

I whirl around and dash back up the steps.

Jacob, Suze, and Aurora glance up at me, but I dash past them to Danika's office. Please, please be there, I pray. You have to.

When I get to her door, it's open. Danika stops tapping on her computer keyboard when she spots me. "Why, hello, Livia. Come in. How is the *pointe* work going?"

I plunk down in the chair opposite her desk. When she sees my face, she says, "Are you all right? Is something the matter?"

"Blitz is going to do something terrible on live TV," I say. "I know it."

"Whoa, whoa," she says. "What makes you say that?"

My words come out in a tumble. "He told me to

believe him that he was coming to get me after the finale. That no matter what I saw about the show, he would make it happen."

"What makes you think he'll do something rash?"

"There's supposed to be three more episodes! He didn't tell me about them! He would have told me if he planned to do them. He's going to say or do something horrible on the live show so that they fire him." I can barely breathe.

I expect her to argue with me, to say that I don't know him that well or that I'm overreacting. Maybe even that he lied to me.

But she doesn't. Her face is full of concern.

"Let's call Bennett," she says. She pushes the speakerphone button on her console and dials.

"The man who built this place?"

"My son-in-law," she says. "He knows Blitz personally. He funded his training and is one of the producers of his show."

My mind buzzes as the phone rings. "How?"

"Bennett always watches out for hometown talent. He saw Blitz's potential when he was still here at the San Antonio theater."

The line picks up. "To what do I owe this lovely surprise?" a man's voice asks.

"Bennett, I'm on speakerphone here with Livia."

"Is she okay?"

I'm so confused. How does the wealthy patron of the academy know who I am?

"She's concerned that Blitz might do something on live TV to get out of the contract for the bonus episodes. What do you know about that?"

"The contract always had a clause calling for post-season coverage of the couple. What does she think he will do?"

"Livia?" Danika says.

My voice doesn't want to work. After a few stutters, I finally say, "He already knows how to get fired."

"Damn it," Bennett says. "You really think he'll do that?"

"You know what he was like when he asked to borrow your plane," Danika says to the phone.

"He did?" I ask.

"Last week," Bennett says. "The publicity has gotten very intense. He can't go anywhere without a horde of reporters and photographers. He wasn't sure he could even drive back to Texas without drawing attention to you."

"So he is planning to come back here?" I ask.

"Yes, but I don't see how he is going to have time," Bennett says. "The filming for the bonus episodes is already set. The only variable is which girl he picks."

"What if he doesn't pick any?" I ask. "Would there still be episodes?"

Bennett is quiet a moment, and Danika looks down at her hands.

"What?" I say.

Bennett speaks first. "Livia, he has to choose a girl. His contract is very specific. And there are fail-safes in the show ensuring that one is chosen."

Danika sighs. "So a girl will be chosen."

I lean forward. "I'm sure he knows that. So he'll try to get fired. By being the jerk the show has made him out to be."

Everyone is quiet again.

"What do you propose we do?" Danika asks me.

"I can call him, I guess," I say. "Talk him out of doing something rash."

"He might do it anyway," Bennett says. "He was pretty anxious to get back to you."

My heart swells at this, but I won't let him lose everything when we can find a way. "So take me out there. If I'm at the finale, watching, he won't do it. I know he won't."

"Can you get away?" Danika asks. "Your father is pretty strict."

"I'm taking the SAT on Saturday," I say. "I can just skip out. That will make it hours to get there before anyone knows I'm gone."

"Will he call the police?" Bennett asks.

"I'll go over there," Danika says. "We can talk to him together."

"No," I say quickly.

My father moved our entire family once to avoid our shame. I don't know what he might do with this.

"I'll leave them a note. They will know I left."

"We can call them from the plane," Bennett says. "And I'll have someone alert law enforcement that you just went on a trip."

"This is crazy," Danika says. "That boy is a mess."

"But he's our mess," I say. "We'll help him."

"I'll send a car to your SAT site," Bennett says. "Have Danika forward the information to my driver. We'll get you to Blitz."

"Thank you, Bennett," Danika says. "And what was it that Blitz told you when he asked for the plane?"

I can hear the smile in Bennett's voice as he says, "That he's madly in love with the most perfect ballerina and nothing will stop him from coming back to her."

"I thought so," Danika says. "Thank you, love. Kiss my daughter for me."

"With relish," he says.

Danika cuts off the call.

I feel like all the air is out of the room. Blitz said that? About me? That he's madly in love? I grip the sides of the chair. I want him now. I want to get to him right this moment.

"Are you all right, Livia?" Danika asks. "This is a lot to take in."

I can't even answer. She comes around the desk to kneel beside me. "Are you ready for the break from your family?" she asks. "It's been coming."

I'm not really sure. I think of Gabriella, my little brother, my parents. I'll figure out how to have them all. Once I get Blitz, we will find a way.

It's like Blitz told me. Have faith.

## Chapter Twenty-Nine

When Mom brings me to the SAT testing facility Saturday morning, I turn to her and say, "Only students are allowed on the testing day." I pull out the confirmation letter Dad gave me. I knew this was a rule, but also that I wouldn't tell her until the last minute, when she'd be flustered and more easily convinced not to try and make an exception.

It works. She stares at it and peers into the room.

"Please don't get me disqualified," I say. "We're just going to be taking the test."

She hesitates. "All right. I'll wait here in the hall."

I need her to go home. Bennett's car is already waiting for me to bring me to his plane. I have to get away. It's been so hard not to text Blitz about our plan, to beg him not to do anything crazy on television. I have to leave now. I can't take it any longer.

"Mom," I say. "You'll be so uncomfortable. Why don't you just come back in a few hours?"

"I couldn't do that," she says, heading for a wood bench a little ways down. "Your father would come and then there really would be a scene."

She settles down with her book. I look back in the classroom. There is only one way out, other than the windows. I'll do it if I have to. I'll go right out one of them.

I've left the letter propped on my mirror. No one will think to look there until I'm gone. I'm not taking anything more with me than the few items I've stuffed in the backpack I'm holding. It's the biggest risk I've ever taken in my life.

I head inside and get my materials from the proctor. Bennett said the car would wait for me however long it took to get away. Seated at a desk, waiting for the proctor to give us instructions, I'm not sure how I will make my escape. It seems I might be taking the test after all.

BY THE TIME I'M THROUGH THE FIRST SECTION OF the SAT, I don't have any better idea how to get past my mother. I could just leave, I guess. I don't think she would tackle me and hold me down.

But I'm not sure.

I'm not as distracted as I had imagined I would be. I felt like the test would be wasted.

But once I'm involved in the questions, my brain kicks into gear. Blitz, the finale, the escape, and the plane ride all fade away.

During the first break I check on Mom, still sitting on the uncomfortable bench.

"How is it going?" she asks.

"Great," I say. "Just the math and the essay portions to go. You sure you don't want to go somewhere more comfortable? I'm just going to be in there."

She shakes her head and opens her book again. I head back to the room, feeling anxious. I'll do the math portion, and before the essay starts, I'll just escape.

My throat feels thick. Lying. Running away. It's all happening again.

We take our seats and I have to work a little harder this time to focus back on the test. At the next break, many of the students turn in their papers and gather their things. Only the essay students will remain.

Then, life cuts me a break. The biggest break of my life.

"Essay students, we'll be moving to a smaller room," the proctor says. "Remember, do not turn on your cell phones or any electronics during this transition. We're just moving to a room around the corner so another group can use this larger one."

We're moving. If I do this right, I can get away.

Everyone picks up their bags. Students who aren't doing the essay portion head on out. The rest of us cluster together for a moment, waiting on the proctor.

When he moves out, we follow.

"Are you done?" Mom asks, checking her watch as other students file past.

"No, we're moving to a room down the hall," I say. "Just fifty minutes to go!"

"Okay, let me know if you need a snack. I have some in my bag."

"I'm good," I say, my heart sinking a little as I realize I'm about to hurt her. She really did try to be a good mom through all this. She forgave things that seemed unforgivable. She has been a role model despite the adversity.

Impulsively, I reach down and hug her.

"Well, okay!" she says, a little taken aback. "Write a good essay!"

I'm afraid of saying anything else. I might give myself away. I head down the hall quickly, catching up with the other students.

As soon as we turn the corner away from Mom, I run.

## Chapter Thirty

Bennett's car is outside. He told me the driver would be there the entire four hours of the test, waiting for the moment I could escape. I'm relieved to see it, flinging open the back door of the black Mercedes and diving in.

"Good day, Miss," the driver says. "Glad you got away all right."

I feel like a criminal on the run. I resist the urge to say, "Step on it."

Mom won't notice I'm gone until the essay is over, almost an hour from now. But I will have disappeared. Hopefully they will find my note quickly, before calling the police. I might call home, just to ward all that off. I'm so glad they don't know anything about Blitz and can't involve him.

When we arrive at the airport, I stare out at the

jumble of terminals and parking lots. I've never flown. But considering the rest of what I'm risking today, traveling by air seems insignificant.

The driver takes us out on a flat space where smaller planes sit waiting near a huge outbuilding. We're stopped by a security man next to a tiny station, then waved through.

I clutch my backpack to me. I'm so far out of my element now. I've walked away from my entire life for someone I've known six weeks. I tug my phone out of a side pocket and power it on. I had to turn it completely off for the test.

There are a few early morning texts from Blitz, the last one warning me he'll be in rehearsals all day for the finale. He still hasn't mentioned the extra episodes.

I still haven't mentioned I'm coming.

The driver opens my door and I fairly fly out of the car. I only get a few steps away when I realize I have no idea where I'm going.

"The Claremonts are waiting for you on the plane," the driver says. "This way."

The wind whips my hair. It's warm again, and we're headed to Southern California, so I haven't brought a coat. The sky is bright white, gleaming off the airplanes. We head toward a long stealthy-looking one. A set of steps has been rolled up to the door.

I ascend carefully, holding the rail. Inside,

Bennett and his wife Juliet are seated in leather chairs. Bennett stands up. "You must be Livia," he says. "We've been in the same room before, but I don't believe we've actually met."

I shake his hand automatically, feeling anxious and unsure. I'm going to ride with two strangers to a place I've never been to stop one of the most famous people on television from wrecking his career.

"I remember you from some of the classes," Juliet says. "Come sit."

She leads me to a cushioned bench opposite their chairs. My hands are trembling.

"Poor girl, she's scared to death," she says to Bennett. "Go get her some tea."

Bennett heads to the back of the plane.

She sits next to me. "I've done some pretty crazy things in my career, but this one is right up there," she says. "It's no wonder you're anxious."

Bennett returns, followed by a young woman in a crisp khaki skirt and white shirt. "Excuse me, Miss Juliet," she says, and reaches between us to press a button. A tray slides out, and the woman turns it down and out to make a small table. She sets a mug with a tea bag on it. "Let me know if you would like something else."

"Thank you, Penny," Juliet says.

Bennett settles back in his chair. "Everything is

on course in LA," he says. "Dress rehearsals are going well. We are all set."

"Does anyone know who he's going to pick?" I ask.

"The director should know, and probably a couple of wardrobe people," he says. "They have to be ready, as Blitz will do a final dance with the winner."

"He got a wedding ring," I say. "Is it scripted for him to propose?"

"He's not proposing," Juliet says. "All the shows have a segment where they look for a ring, but it's rarely used. Twenty seasons of the *Bachelor*, and only one proposal. In fact, I think that six-carat monstrosity is just on loan, right?" She looks to Bennett.

"It's not even on set," he says. "It never left the jewelry store." He laughs. "The producers have to sign off on anything worth more than half a million that needs insuring."

I begin to calm down with their banter. This is going to be okay. I check my watch. The test will end in ten minutes. That's when Mom will realize I'm gone. Dad is out with Andy. I wish she had a cell phone. Will she call the police before she even leaves? Or will she go home? I should have thought about that.

"What's on your mind, Livia?" Bennett asks.

"I'm just worried Mom will call the police from

the SAT site, before she can get my note. I'm not very good at planning this escape thing."

"I've already put in a call to my friend on the force," Bennett says. "But it's best if we can prevent her from notifying them. I can't guarantee the dispatcher or officer who is called will know anything."

"Doesn't an adult have to be missing twenty-four hours before they do anything?" Juliet asks.

"Technically, I think that's true," Bennett says. "But I'd rather avoid the whole thing if we can."

"Mom doesn't have a cell phone," I say.

"You want to leave a message on your home phone?" Juliet asks.

I can do that. I pull out my cell phone and shakily dial my home number.

Then the worst happens.

My father answers.

For a long moment, my voice is stuck in my throat.

"Hello?" he says again, his voice gruff.

I finally manage to squeak out "Dad?"

"Livia? What is it? Is your test done? Is your mother okay?"

"Dad." I pause. This is hard. "I left Mom at the center. I'm not there."

"Then where are you?"

"I'm taking a trip away. I took my test. It went fine. Other than the essay part. I skipped that."

His voice is a roar. "LIVIA MASON, WHERE ARE YOU RIGHT NOW?"

His anger helps me rise up to defend myself, makes me stronger. "I'm doing something for myself, Dad. I'm on an airplane," I say. "I'm leaving."

"Get off that plane right now!" he shouts.

"Dad, do you hear yourself?" I ask. "I can't do that. I'm leaving for a while. You can't stop me."

I rush on before he can yell again. "But you can stop me from ever coming home. And I don't want you to do that. Don't make it so I never come home."

The line is quiet, then he says, "You're breaking this family's heart all over again."

I don't know what to say to that. He was the one who broke it first. So I just say, "I'm sorry, Dad. I'm sorry for all that I've done. But I have to go."

I hang up.

The phone rings again almost immediately and I realize he's done the dial-back thing. I click ignore.

Juliet reaches over and squeezes my arm. "I'm sorry, Livia. I know that was hard."

I feel numb about this encounter with my father. But it had to happen. One way or another. And I have the best reason. Blitz loves me, or so he told Bennett. And I'm not going to let him hurt his career for me.

The pilot comes over the speaker. "Our flight path is approved and we are cleared to take off in twenty minutes," he says.

Juliet glances over at Bennett. "I have an idea of what we can do when we get there," she says. "But you'll have to talk to the director."

When Juliet explains what she thinks will work, I know she is absolutely right. I just have to have the guts to do it.

## Chapter Thirty-One

Bennett is on the phone the moment we land on the ground in LA. Another Mercedes drives us off the tarmac and Juliet directs the driver to a shop on the way to the studios. She wants to pick up an outfit for me.

As we pull up to the doors, I know it's not going to be like anything I've ever shopped in before. Huge glass doors surrounded with gold make it look like a jewelry store. Or a bank.

Bennett is still in the front seat talking to the people on the set of *Dance Blitz*. My heart is probably not going to stop hammering the rest of the day. I'm just having to adjust to the nerves. It's like the excruciating moment before you go onstage for a recital, feeling like you might faint from the pressure.

Only instead of it being just a few seconds, I'm dealing with it all day.

The driver opens the door, and Juliet leads me out, leaving Bennett behind. "I told them to bring out everything they had in white," she says.

A woman is expecting us and leads us to a back room where a rack of white outfits is already set aside for me. I run my fingers through them. Some of them sparkle, others have some shine. One is more sheer.

"We don't have much time," Juliet tells the woman. "Livia, do you see anything you like?"

"They are all beautiful," I say. "But Blitz likes me in pale blue."

Juliet nods and the woman says, "I'll go pull some."

She is back in a flash with three blue dresses. I choose the simplest and take it into a room with red velvet curtains.

I stare at the mirror as I change out of the red shirt and black skirt that I wore on our first date to the San José Mission. My family is so angry. I may never see any of my other clothes again. I'm glad I wore my favorite.

I slide the blue dress on. It fits perfectly, long sleeved and fitted at the top, then floating across my hips. A hint of sparkles begins on my belly and intensifies as the skirt begins, then it disappears again in the flow of the fabric.

I step outside.

"Turn for me," Juliet says.

I make a quick circle, feeling the air rush against my legs as the skirt flies out.

"Yes," she says. "This is good." She feels along the shoulder and under the arm. "Fifth position," she says.

I lift my arms. She checks everything again.

"All right," she says. "Excellent quality all around." She turns to the saleswoman. "Ring it up, and bring me a light cover or coat or wrap of some sort. She'll wear this out."

I head back to the fitting room and gather my clothes. Another young woman arrives and provides me a pretty satin bag to carry them in.

"Thank you," I say. "Are the tags cut off?"

"Our dresses don't have tags," she says.

I guess in shops like this, you don't care about the price.

When I make it out to the main part of the shop, Juliet has already paid the bill and takes the bag from me. "Put this on her," she says, passing a thin silk cloak in pale gold to the woman who has been helping us. "I don't want to give anything away."

The woman wraps the cloak around my shoulders, fastening it at the throat with a loop around a rhinestone button. It floats around my body like a mist, but is opaque enough to hide my dress.

"Perfect," Juliet says. "Now, hair and makeup." She checks her watch. "And we're heading straight into LA traffic. We should have taken the helicopter."

Helicopter!

We hurry back out to the car. Bennett is finally off the phone.

"I don't think we're going to make it in time," Juliet says as we settle in the backseat.

"We don't have to make the beginning of the show," he says. "Only the end."

"True," she says.

The drive is stressful and long. Traffic is jammed. Sometimes we don't make any progress at a congested light. I check my watch. It's 7:30 Texas time, so 5:30 here. The live show starts in half an hour.

It's been a long day of testing, escaping, flying, shopping, and driving. Thankfully we had a nice meal on the plane, or I'd be dying.

I press my face to the window like a little kid when we finally make it to the gates of the studio. We're stopped and then waved through. There's a parking lot off to one side.

"This is as close as we get?" Juliet asks.

Bennett laughs. "I'm nobody here. Everyone is rich and the talent gets the perks."

She leans forward to speak to the driver. "Don't park yet, drive as far down as you can."

He nods.

Bennett turns to look at me. "You ready for this, Livia?"

"I think so," I say. We pass people pushing rolling racks, and clumps of others talking earnestly as they hurry from building to building.

"This is it," Bennett says, and the car slows to a stop.

He opens his door, and I open mine, too anxious to wait for the driver. We step out into the cool air. Evening is about to fall and lights are starting to pop on overhead.

"This way," Bennett says, taking my arm to lead me to a rather ordinary-looking building with a loading dock and a side door.

We enter a hallway and a young man standing nearby looks up from his iPad. "Hello, Mr. Claremont," he says.

"We need to see Devon," Bennett tells him.

"He's probably on set." The man glances at a big digital clock on the wall. "They are just about to go live."

"We'll find our way. Thanks," Bennett says.

We follow him down a labyrinth of corridors. Signs along the way say "Dressing Room B" or "Caution: Live Shooting." Some of them have red or green lights over them.

We turn down a hall and Bennett takes us inside a door. It's a nice room with sofas and a buffet of food along one wall. Inside, several people are sitting and watching a large screen mounted in the corner.

"It just started," says a blond woman in a gorgeous red dress.

I look at the screen. The *Dance Blitz* logo is lit up over a stage and a man who often narrates the show is talking. Everything else is black. No Blitz. I'm dying to see him, but anxious because this is his world, not ours.

"Thanks, Tina," Bennett says. "Where is makeup stationed these days?"

A petite woman in black leggings and a tank covered in hundreds of little circle mirrors turns. "I can take you."

We head back out in the hall and enter a room a few doors down. My nerves are jangling so badly, I can barely stand it.

Inside, a half-dozen dancers are getting hair and makeup done. I panic for a moment, then quickly realize none of them are the three finalists. I don't think I could handle coming face-to-face with any of the women who have probably slept with Blitz, and certainly not Giselle, who definitely did.

A man steps in. "Chorus dancers, you are on in five!"

The movements get frantic as the makeup girls do their last touches, spritzing and tucking and sending them on their way.

When they are gone, the makeup artists all collectively lean against the long mirrored counter.

Juliet approaches them. "Which one of you can get this girl ready to go on?"

They all look at her. One of them asks, "Who is this? Those chorus dancers were supposed to be the last ones."

"A surprise dancer," Bennett says. "Trust me, you want her."

They all look at each other. The woman says, "I don't know if we can do this without Devon's okay."

The mirrored-shirt girl nudges one of them. "Do you know who this is? Bennett Claremont. He's the producer. He's Devon's *boss*."

The girls still look skeptical, but one of them, a tall Hispanic woman with deep blue eye shadow and spiky hair, steps forward. "What the hell. I'll do it."

Juliet gives Bennett a concerned look as she walks me over to the chair.

"So you're a dancer?" the girl asks. "I'm Cecilia. What sort of look are we going for here?"

"Innocent and lovely," Juliet says. "Nothing too dramatic. Just enough for the lighting and cameras."

Cecilia turns my chair. "Got it."

"Where is wardrobe?" Juliet says. She takes one of my shoes off. "We need something else. There should be spare dance shoes everywhere."

"I have my toe shoes," I say. "They are in my backpack in the car."

Juliet turns to Bennett. "Go get them. Quickly."

He hurries out.

The mirrored-shirt girl laughs. "I guess you're the only one who gets to boss *him* around."

"Probably so," Juliet says and takes off my other shoe.

Cecilia works on my hair, and now one of the other girls comes up to tilt my chin to the light. Soon three of them are working, tweezing and powdering and doing who knows what to my face.

Juliet watches every move they make, ensuring she is getting what she wants. "Hollywood is so different from ballet," she says. "We have to do all our own makeup."

"You're a ballerina?" Cecilia asks.

"I am," Juliet says. Then to me, "When did you earn your toe shoes?"

My face heats up. "Just a week ago."

Her eyebrows lift. "Do not be a hero in those, okay? Do not go *en pointe* other than maybe at the very end. If you even dance."

I nod. We have no idea what's going to happen out there. We have no idea how Blitz is going to react when he sees me.

One of the girls points up at the screen. I hadn't

noticed it with the sound off. "Here comes the first dance number," she says and picks up a remote. Now we hear the announcer saying, "And in our first number of the night, Blitz Craven with finalist Giselle Andreas."

The girls turn my chair so I can see. Cecilia is still doing something to my hair, but I guess my makeup is done.

Blitz comes onstage in all black and dances alone, circling a lamppost onstage. He tips the hat he's wearing and looks down like he's lost his last friend.

Giselle comes onstage, doing the same lonely sort of dance, until they bump into each other. They are surprised, then dance together. She's wearing an old-fashioned brown dress and her hair looks like a pinup girl.

"Your hair work looks great, Marie," Cecilia says.

Marie steps closer to the television. "They went conservative with her," she says. "Trying to tone down the tramp."

"Ain't nobody can take the tramp out of that girl," another girl says.

Juliet clasps her hands tightly. I can see she's agitated. But I think it's funny, and a break from my nerves.

They do dance well together. I can see why Blitz picked her, tramp or no tramp. I can't do anything like what they are doing. Lifts and spins and sliding each other across the floor.

"Okay, see what you think of this," Cecilia says, turning me back to the mirror.

The world whirls for a second, then I lock in on myself. I have to stand up and walk closer to be sure it is me. My face glows, cheeks lightly blushed, and my eyes are big and open, the lashes the only decadent thing about me, long and thick. My lips are pale pink to complement the dress.

My hair is very classic, up in a high bun, glossy and black, with a braid that encircles my head. It's beautiful, almost regal. Like a princess.

I impulsively give her a hug. "It's beautiful, thank you," I say. I turn to Juliet. "Now what?"

"We wait," she says. "We wait until it's time for him to choose the winner."

## Chapter Thirty-Two

We watch the three finalists dance separately with Blitz. There are cameras everywhere, following the girls as they head out, and the announcer sometimes talks with them as they go to their individual dressing rooms.

Bennett has brought my toe shoes, and the wardrobe woman sprayed them light blue to match the dress, adding sparkles to turn them into something new and beautiful. I swing my feet to make sure they dry in time, although she assures me it's very fast.

The interviews give the stage people time to change out sets. We occasionally hear people rumbling out in the hall. Twice, dancers dash in to have a false eyelash fixed or a lipstick smear corrected.

"Five minutes until the finalists come in to be prepped for the selection," Cecilia says.

"They're coming in here?" I ask. I've felt safe and somewhat removed from the activity in the makeup room.

"Yes, they have a wardrobe change in their dressing rooms, but they will come here for makeup," another girl says. "Plus Marie here has to totally redo Giselle's hair."

"I have a plan," Marie says. "We practiced the quick change."

"I can't be in here," I tell Juliet, hopping up from my chair. "I can't face them."

Bennett nods. "Probably not the best idea. They will send a camera to get shots of them preparing. We should be out." He checks his phone. "And...legal has just insisted Livia sign some papers anyway." He opens the door. "Let me make sure Blitz isn't out there."

He looks left and right and motions for us to go. We quickly duck back into the room we started in. There are more people now, some standing to watch the show. It's in commercial at the moment.

A man in a suit sits at a table in the corner. Bennett leads me over.

The man doesn't have any formalities but gets straight to the point.

"This document acknowledges that you do not

hold the producers, television station, production company, or any of their subsidiaries liable for anything that happens onstage." He flips the page. "And furthermore, that you agree to allow your likeness to be used as part of this production, and any derivative works that are created based on this production."

I look up at Bennett. "Isn't a contract what got us here in the first place?"

He nods. "It sort of is." He taps his fingers on the table. "Liam, I know you are doing your job, but I'm going to take on the liability for this one." Bennett leans over and signs his own name to the document. "I'm personally responsible for her actions and any actions taken on her behalf as a result of this production."

Liam sighs. "This is not how the contract was drawn."

Bennett shrugs. "Then call security to escort us out."

Liam closes the folder and stands up to leave. "I was never here."

A couple of the people in the room have noticed what we're doing. The blond in the red dress asks, "Is this one of the chorus dancers?"

Bennett doesn't answer. "Let's go," he says. He takes me by the arm, and we head to the door. Behind us, the show starts up again. Blitz is in a room where footage of the finalists dancing is playing on three separate screens. The announcer asks him if he's ready to make his choice.

We head into the hall. There is a screen a ways down. I can see the flash of the light. I want to see what Blitz is doing, but my nerves are on red alert and I'm trying not to freak out.

We pause outside a set of double doors. Blitz glances up at the red light above it, then opens the door.

We're in a very dark area with red lights low on the floor. Ahead, I can see a brighter light. We carefully walk across, avoiding thick bundles of wires and passing the shadows of people who are turned to a screen. This one is dim and surrounded by a black case so that the light leaks as little as possible.

I see that Blitz is still in the viewing room. The announcer is talking to him, but this monitor has no sound.

The show switches to montages of Blitz with the three girls. I've already seen all these moments, so I turn back to the bright light ahead. Now that we're closer, I can see people moving equipment around.

It's the stage.

My stomach twists. We're here.

A man approaches Bennett. "Is this her?" he asks him.

"Yes," Bennett says. "Livia, this is Devon, the director."

"Hell of a thing to spring on me," Devon says. "But this is gonna go viral tonight." He seems rather giddy. "Livia, I'm going to take you to the dance choreographer so we can talk about possible scenarios."

We move closer to the light, and I spot more people standing together. Devon approaches a woman and points me out. The two of them come over.

"Why are we doing this?" the choreographer says. "We already know who he is going to choose and we already have the dance ready to go."

"Because this girl's the real deal," Devon says. "And we're gonna make reality television history."

My stomach flips again. I have to believe I'm doing the right thing.

The choreographer looks me over, stopping at the toe shoes. "You're a dancer?"

"I do ballet," I say. "But if I danced with Blitz, it would be a waltz."

"What have we got rights for?" Devon asks her. "What can we play if this goes her way?"

"I have several," she says. "Slow or fast?"

"Definitely slow," I say. I feel like throwing up. Am I really going to dance with Blitz in front of everybody? We haven't practiced anything.

I gulp in air. I have to have faith. He said we danced well together. I always understood his communication and was able to follow. It doesn't have to be fancy. It just has to be real.

The choreographer starts walking away. "This is nuts," she says.

Devon takes me to the false wall that backs the stage. "So here is how it goes. Blitz is going to be over there at the podium in the center, the one with flowers on it." He points. "And the girls will be standing to his left."

"When should I go out?" I ask.

"Whenever it seems right," he says. "This is unscripted." He turns to face me. "And you don't have to do this, you know. The show can run as planned."

"I know," I say. "I'll only go out if I think he's going to do something terrible."

He pats my shoulder. "I knew something was different about him when he came back to rehearsals. I wasn't surprised when Bennett called me about you."

A guy in all black comes through, saying, "Back in three." All around me, people move into new positions. Cameras roll around. Hushed commands are spoken into headsets.

"Let's get you out of the way," Devon says. He grabs the arm of a girl dressed in black. "Hide her until everyone is onstage, then bring her right back here."

The girl nods. We walk deeper into the dark, where we stand beside a fake section of fence I recognize from the second dance number.

A flashlight shines and a man walks through. And I see him. Blitz!

He looks focused and anxious as he follows the other man to the stage. They put him in position by the flowers. I try to read his expression, but he's concentrating on something.

There's more movement and the three finalists walk by. They are dressed to the hilt in splashy dresses and full makeup. The woman leading them stops at the edge of the stage, still out of sight.

A big red set of numbers counts down on a screen at the foot of the stage. I can see the audience, movements out beyond the light.

Then music, loud and startling, the show's theme song.

The announcer is out front, brash and a little over the top in his dark brown suit and spiked hair. He speaks to the audience. "This is it, folks. The big moment. After an entire season one with no success in the end, Blitz Craven will choose his partner. For two broken hearts, tonight was their final dance with the man they have all fallen for. One lucky lady will become his partner, and maybe even get that ring."

He turns to our side of the stage. "Giselle, Christy, Mariah, come on out!"

The audience cheers as they walk onstage. When they are in their positions, the girl next to me leads me to where they previously stood. I take off the gold cloak and hand it to her.

I don't know what Blitz can see from the bright stage, but I am directly in his line of sight if he looks this way.

The women all hold hands as Blitz picks up the bouquet of flowers.

"What are your thoughts as you make this decision?" the announcer asks.

That's when I see it. Blitz's expression changes. It's hard. He's ready to do what he has to do. Something crazy. Something horrible. Something to get him fired.

And I couldn't stop myself even if I wanted to. My feet carry me out on the stage.

## Chapter Thirty-Three

Blitz takes a step back when he sees me. "Livia? What are you doing here?"

I run up to him as the audience gasps and murmurs. My body moves, but my voice is definitely paralyzed.

He sets down the flowers. Cameras shift around us. I can hear the three women talking to each other in hushed tones. Even the announcer seems unsure of what to do.

I force air to come out, and then words. "I think you should dance with me right now," I say.

Blitz looks around, toward the finalists, then out at the audience, and finally back to me.

And that's when the music begins.

*Thank you, Devon.*

"Well, it looks like we have a surprise dance," the

announcer says. "Let me be the first to tell you that this is completely unplanned." He turns to Blitz. "What is going on?"

"I think we're just going to go with it," Blitz says.

A woman in a glittery dress comes out and leads the three finalists off the stage. A girl in black comes to move the podium with its flowers out of the way.

The announcer steps off to one side, seeming unsure how to narrate what is happening.

"Did you pick this song?" Blitz asks.

"It's a waltz," I say. "It's what we do best."

He takes my hand. "I'm going to step on those toe shoes."

This makes me laugh. "You are just a damn amateur."

He pulls me in, grasping my hand. His smile is huge and genuine.

The position is familiar and calms me. We begin the steps, one-two-three, easy and simple. When he turns me out in the first spin, people clap. I don't know what the audience thinks, how simple this must look compared to the big productions they saw earlier. But my eyes are on Blitz, and he's looking at me. I have to make that be what matters.

Our steps get longer and more sweeping. We swing to the beat, and I feel my skirt flaring out. Then he turns me to face away from him, his hand on my thigh, and I remember this move and let him lift me onto his shoulder, just like that day in Studio 3.

I roll over his back and cartwheel out. The crowd cheers, and we come back around to each other. He lifts me up again, this time rolling me in front of him like he's done so many times before, his hand on my thigh to sweep me into a downward position. I remember to keep my arms and hands pretty.

Another cheer.

We're doing it. Unscripted. Us.

He lifts me back to standing and spins me in close, so our faces are right next to each other. We're both breathing hard. We stay here a moment, hearing the shouts from the audience.

He curls me out from him and lets go of my hand. He takes a few steps back and then, he does it, a *grand jeté*, just like I taught him. I throw my head back and laugh. "Perfect!" I tell him.

He comes back to me and holds me by the waist. "Turn for me," he says.

I spin the way we did before, then move away from him into a whirl, my arms starting low and spinning higher and higher as the world becomes a blur.

When I come out of it, Blitz is there, kneeling with one leg back. "Show me what you can do now," he says.

I know what he means, and I *relevé* into *en pointe* and take tiny mincing steps toward him. He grasps me around the waist and turns me in a lazy circle. "You are incredible," he says.

"You told Bennett you were in love with me," I say.

"I did," he says.

"You didn't tell me about the extra episodes."

His expression shifts. "No, I didn't."

I stop turning and sit on his bent knee. "You didn't plan to do them, did you?"

He shakes his head no. "Is that why you're here?"

I smile. "Somebody had to save Benjamin from Blitz Craven."

The crowd erupts at that and I realize microphones are picking up our words. Somebody in the audience shouts, "Kiss her!" and that's all the encouragement Blitz needs.

His lips land on mine, and I melt into him in our familiar way. My hands come to his hair, so lacquered and shiny that I almost laugh. But then his kiss gets deeper, more serious, and steals my breath.

The room erupts. The announcer shouts, "Who IS this girl?" over the noise.

Blitz turns me out. "This is Livia!" he says. "And she's my choice for my partner." He turns to me. "In dance." He twirls me out in a circle and then back into him. "And in life."

He kisses me again. And I don't know anything

else that happens because all I can see or feel is Blitz Craven.

~*´♥`*~

WE STAY THAT WAY UNTIL THE LIGHTS GO DOWN. A man shouts, "And we're out."

The room goes wild.

Audience members rush the stage. Whatever security is there can't keep them back.

We're surrounded. Cameras zip overhead, recording the scene even though we're off the air. I have a feeling my face is going to be everywhere tomorrow. I wonder if Mindy will see it. If my parents will.

Blitz keeps his arm tight around me. "I've got you," he says.

Eventually four burly security guards muscle through the crowd and lead us offstage and back into the hall. Juliet and Bennett are there, excited and happy.

"Was this your doing?" Blitz asks Bennett.

Bennett holds his hands in the air. "I just bought the jet fuel," he says.

Juliet embraces me. "You looked beautiful up there. It was perfect."

"Not too amateur?" I ask.

"It was just fine," she assures me. "Let's get out of here before the place is mobbed any worse than it is."

The four of us hurry down the hall. But when we turn the corner, there they are.

The finalists.

All three.

Giselle lunges at Blitz. "What the hell was that? One more humiliation for the road?"

Christy is crying. "I thought you were going to pick me!" she says.

Mariah has her arms crossed. "I was told that you had chosen me. My dress was the one that matched the final dance set!"

Giselle and Christy turn to Mariah in disbelief.

"Really!" Mariah says. Then she spins and walks away.

Blitz seems like he wants to say something, but I think it's best he doesn't.

"I'm sure you will all have wonderful careers," I say and pull on Blitz's hand to move us away.

"I can't believe you fell for a two-bit amateur ballerina!" Giselle says. "I always knew you were a loser!"

"Okay," Bennett says. "That's enough playground trash talk." He waves at the security guards to move the girls away.

Soon we're out of the building and into Bennett's Mercedes.

Juliet, Blitz, and I squeeze into the back.

Juliet sighs. "This is about the craziest night I've had in a long time."

Blitz holds on to my hand and kisses my fingers. "You came for me."

"Of course I did," I say.

"I didn't deserve it."

"Of course you did." I press his hand to my cheek. "I saw a prince who needed to be rescued."

The lights of the studio flash by as we make our escape. Behind us, we leave everything to be sorted by the staff. The crowd, the show, Blitz's old life.

Now it will simply be us.

# Epilogue

Blitz and I stand in the wings of the recital stage as the girls wheel out into the light. As soon as they appear, the audience claps for them.

Janel hurries down the steps so she can cue them from the floor. I hold Blitz's hand as the sound tech starts the music.

Gabriella is near the end, and my eyes are on her as the girls go through their Nutcracker dance. It's not flawless, as Daisy in particular gets stage fright and forgets half her turns.

But it's adorable and emotional, and I wipe tears from my eyes as they finish the song and take their bows.

"We'll get them in tip-top shape for the spring recital," Blitz says. "Now that they have a performance under their belt, they'll be old pros."

We step aside as the girls wheel off the stage. Blitz gives each of them a high five.

"I still think Gabriella is the spitting image of you," Blitz says. "She must have taken after her father, because she looks nothing like Gwen."

I hesitate, thinking it is time to tell him, but we're so close to all the others. I can't do it here. They might overhear.

We follow the girls through the path made through the storage room since there isn't a ramp down from the stage. We let them get ahead, walking slowly through one of our favorite spaces. As we pass the racks, Blitz picks up the top hat from our first time together and places it on his head.

"You haven't changed one bit," I tell him, and bump it so it tilts sideways.

He gathers me in his arms and kisses me thoroughly. I giggle and take his hat, placing it on my own head, then back on the rack.

We wander back down the studio hall. Each room is a staging area for the classes, and the whole place is crazy with excitement and nervousness. Blitz threads his fingers through mine as we skirt around kids getting their costumes straightened or lipstick applied.

Jacob sees us and nods, trying to tighten a hat string beneath the chin of one of his jazz students.

The foyer is quiet. I've already done my performance, so we don't have to stay. Still, we linger by the front desk, looking over the programs laid there for the latecomers.

"I'm sorry your parents didn't come," Blitz says.

I shrug. "I didn't expect them to." When we got back from LA last week, I went by my house. My father refused to open the door.

Mom came out the back and walked around. She hugged me and told me to give him some time. She asked if I was already pregnant.

I said no.

Blitz got out of his car and stood next to it, waiting to see if I wanted him to come forward.

My mom asked, "Is that him?" and I told her it was.

"He must have money," she said, and then she went inside the house.

I waited a little longer to see if they would come out again, but they didn't. The curtain moved, and I saw Andy wave at me. I blew him a kiss.

I would give them time, like she asked. Hopefully one day they would come around.

Some of the girls from our class wheel out and head across the foyer to go watch the other recitals. After a minute, Gwen appears with Gabriella. I lean down to give her a hug. "You did great," I say.

They go out the front doors and I stare wistfully

at them as Gabriella zooms down the outside ramp. How I wish things were different.

When the foyer is quiet again, Blitz puts his arm around me. "So, how do you know her? I mean, you set the class up just so she could come."

I glance around. There's no one near.

I close my eyes and gather my courage. "Blitz, she's my daughter. I had her when I was fifteen, and my parents made me give her up for adoption. She doesn't know I'm her mother."

Blitz pulls me close to him and presses my head to his chest. He smells like expensive clothes and after-shave. I want to get lost in the smell, forget what I've just told him. It's unbearable, waiting for him to say something.

"Do you want to get her back?" he asks quietly. "I can call my lawyer."

I pull away to look him in the eye. "No," I say. "Gwen is a wonderful mother. I would never do that to her."

He nods. "Okay. Then I see we'll really have to stay in San Antonio." He puts his arm around me, and we head for the doors. "Gwen could probably use some help. Let's see if she'll let us have some private lessons with her very beautiful, very talented daughter."

My eyes smart from tears as we head out into the

chilly evening and walk to his red Ferrari. This man gets me. All the way.

"Let's do that," I tell him. "I'll bring it up to her next week."

"Until then," he says, "let's go back to the hotel. There has got to be some part of you I haven't yet memorized."

I laugh, and he picks me up to cradle me against his chest.

I kick my legs, the pale purple tights of my recital costume a blur as I try to escape.

"Don't even try it, my princess, my sugar plum fairy, my love," he says. "Because now that I've got you, there is no way I'm ever letting you go."

He sets me down in the parking lot of my favorite place, the Dreamcatcher Dance Academy. I glance back at it as he opens the door. My life changed at this place. And it's only going to get better from here.

I HOPE YOU ENJOYED *FORBIDDEN DANCE*! WHILE this book can stand alone, in the next book Wounded Dance, Livia faces the ultimate threat: the father of her secret baby. Get book two or splurge for the entire Lovers Dance Boxed Set.

## Also by Deanna Roy

### The Forever Series

*A young couple reunites in colleges, four years after the death of their newborn.*

*Book one* Forever Innocent *is FREE on all venues.*

- Forever Innocent (Corabelle & Gavin)
- Forever Loved (Corabelle & Gavin)
- Forever Sheltered (Tina & Darion)
- Forever Bound (Jenny & Chance)
- Forever Family (Corabelle, Tina, Jenny)
- Forever Christmas (Corabelle & Gavin)

- Boxed Set: First Three Books
- Boxed Set: Final Three Books

- Stella and Dane (Standalone)

## The Lovers Dance Series

*A sheltered ballerina is lured into the life of a brash TV reality show star.*

- Forbidden Dance
- Wounded Dance
- Wicked Dance
- Tender Dance
- Final Dance

- Lovers Dance Boxed Set

- Billionaire's Dance (a standalone prequel)

## Other Books

- Conversations with Little Dude (Nonfiction stories with her son who was adopted from foster care)
- In the Company of Angels (A fill-in-the-pages baby record book for babies lost to miscarriage or stillbirth)
- The Magic Mayhem trilogy of action/adventure books for children ages 9-12.

---

## If you prefer your romances with no graphic love scenes or coarse language

You will love Deanna's pen name Abby Tyler. As Abby, Deanna writes funny, feel-good small-town romances with a recurring cast of feisty senior citizens and the couples they push together, by hook or by crook.

**Deanna** is the six-time *USA Today* bestselling author of romance and women's fiction.

She is a passionate advocate for women who have miscarried. She founded the web site Pregnancy-Loss.info in 1998 after the loss of her first baby and continues to run both online and in-person support groups for women who have endured this impossible loss.

She is a foster mom, an adoptive mom, and a baby loss mom. She lives in Austin, Texas, with her family.

Learn more about the author at
www.deannaroy.com

---

Join her email or text list for new release notices at
Deanna's List

facebook.com/deannaroyauthor

twitter.com/deannaroy

instagram.com/deannaroyauthor

goodreads.com/Goodreads

bookbub.com/authors/deanna-roy

# Bonus Scene by Blitz

You've read the entire book from Livia's point of view. Here's a bonus scene where Blitz shows us how he's feeling in a key moment of their relationship: the consummation in the hotel. *Enjoy.*

---

DAMN, IT'S COLD OUTSIDE TONIGHT.

I ease my foot off the accelerator, allowing the Ferrari to roll along the curb in front of the park where I met Livia last time. She's told me she'll get here as soon as she can.

It's late for this neighborhood. The houses are all dark, the occasional flash of a TV screen the only light in any of the windows.

Leaves circle in front of me like a mini-cyclone,

and I see someone hurrying down the sidewalk, head down in the wind.

It's her.

I inch forward, watching her huddle in on herself in the cold. Her hair streams behind her. When the Ferrari gets to her, I reach over to open the door from the inside.

"Oh, Princess, it's way too cold for royalty to be out in this weather," I say.

Her teeth chatter. "I'm fine," she says.

I'm surprised she can talk, she's shivering so hard. I crank the heater. Her bare legs have to be freezing in that skirt. I swear I'm going to buy her an entire wardrobe when I get the chance. I don't know what the hell her parents have done to her, but she's obviously been through enough.

I ask her if it's okay if we go to my hotel. I don't want her to think I'm trying to lure her somewhere. Even after the movie theater, she seems so innocent. I don't want to push her too fast. I sense somebody did that already.

But she says, "That sounds perfect." And from the tone of her voice, I believe her.

The fog is crazy. She asks me about my parents, and the tough times after my stupid Tweet went viral. I give her the basics, only half paying attention to my own voice, focused on getting her warm.

Then she says something about her bra size, and

my brain fires off an alarm. Just like that, I'm back to her body, her innocence. I think she just needs an escape.

"Princess," I say. "You're tempting me sorely, and my intentions are strictly honorable tonight."

She gets quiet after that, and it's like I figured. She's scared. I don't want her scared. I want her to feel safe with me.

We get to the hotel and head up to the suite while I try to figure out how to keep her feeling comfortable, not like she's been lured into a trap.

Livia's adorably naive about the secure floors and how the elevators work. I step back while she plays with the screen inside, even though just the sight of her so close to my private room makes my blood beat.

She's definitely not safe with me.

I'm trying to figure out how to cool my jets when we arrive on our floor.

I pay zero attention to the bartender in the private lounge until Livia whispers, "I'm underage."

"Nothing right now, thank you," I tell the guy. Livia has this fresh-faced youthfulness about her, all loose hair and no makeup. But she's old enough. I checked. I can't seem to stay away from her, even if I wanted to.

I've gotten jaded about fancy hotels, but Livia's

reaction to it reminds me how rare it is for people to stay in a place like this.

I see the white sofa, the fireplace, the piano, and the big windows through her eyes now. And she's right, it's beautiful.

I set down our coats and watch her head to the bank of windows overlooking San Antonio. She's a vision, slender and graceful, her long black hair flowing down her back. She presses her hands to the glass and looks out with big, awe-filled eyes. I've forgotten what it's like to feel that inspired by the ordinary world.

I come up behind her and sweep her hair off her shoulder. "You okay with getting away?" I ask.

She shivers, and suddenly she does seem anxious. I withdraw a little and take her hand. "Come sit with me," I say.

She lets me pull her close on the sofa, and I ramble on about the dance show and the contestants until she starts to relax. I think she's calm, but then I say, "The winner will be better off than I will."

"So you have to do it?" she asks. "Choose a winner?"

She's hung up on that, probably because of all the hype that I'm going to propose marriage to one of the girls. I most definitely am not.

I explain that television is driven by ratings, and being an asshole made the show outrageously popular. But none of it is real. Well, other than me being an asshole. That's probably true.

"But you still have to choose," she says. She's really stuck on this point.

"I choose this." I squeeze her hand.

"Well, it's really inconvenient right now," she says.

This makes me laugh. I want to reassure her, but keep it easy. I turn her cheek so I can get to her.

Her lips on mine are soft and responsive. I think this might be as far as things get when she presses ever so subtly against me, her mouth parting.

And then I just take over. I want to taste her, all of her, feel her body shudder around my hand like it did during the movie.

I'm too hungry for this to wait, so I shift our positions. My fingers brush across a strip of skin on her belly and she sucks in a breath.

"Sensitive, Princess?" I ask, even though I know the answer. She's mine, all mine.

I work my way up her delectable skin, then remember she said she hasn't worn a bra. I'm instantly hard as a rock. "You made it easy for me. God, that is hot."

I want to know every inch of her, and her taut breast in my mouth is a feast. I'm a greedy bastard now, and I pay attention to both perfect nipples. I could only do so much in that movie theater seat, and now I'm going to have all of her.

I work my way down. "What else am I going to find?" I ask, mainly to let her know where I'm headed. She could stop me if she wanted, but the way her back is arching, I'm pretty sure I'm going straight to where she wants me to be.

My body skims hers as I reach her legs. I kiss the inside of a knee and nibble my way up. The dancer in her is obvious, the muscles taut. Her skin is impossibly smooth.

My nose pushes the flannel skirt out of my way as I move up. Her breathing is ragged. We're still good.

Then the skirt shifts, and I see her, soft and pink and exposed. No panties. It takes every effort not to bury my face there straightaway.

"You're perfect," I say, so close to her that I can feel my breath against her skin.

I slip a finger inside her. She's warm and tight, and my groin is ready to explode. As she moves with me, her body shifting with my touch, I watch her upturned chin, listening to her little sounds.

When she shifts down closer to me, I know what she's after. And I give it, tongue inside her, smiling as her hands grab my hair.

Then it's all movement and tension, her muscles showing me the way. I'm working her, thighs at my ears, loving every moan and cry, then she calls out my name and the pulsing begins.

It's glorious and strong, like waves lapping at me

on a shore. I slow down as she does, getting more gentle, then slowly withdraw.

Her skirt is bunched up on her belly. I move to straighten it when I see a tear slip down her cheek. She's trying to cover her face.

I pull her to me. "You okay, Princess?"

She nods against my chest.

A worry starts to seed that I took this too far, that she's regretting being here. Maybe she thinks I'll force her into more now that we're alone in a hotel.

"Hey, talk to me."

She shakes her head. "Just old stuff."

And that's when I get it. Somebody did something to her. This is taking her back to bad memories.

"Did somebody hurt you once?"

I'll kill them. I'll pull their spine from their bodies.

"No," she says. "Never. No. It's just been a long time."

I'm relieved a million times over. I cradle her to me. "That's all right. We don't have to do anything else." And we don't. I've had enough fast women for a lifetime. Going slow is fine by me.

But she shifts around to face me. "I think we do," she says. Her voice is shaky but then she kisses me, and there is no hesitation in that.

And I'm there. I sweep her up and get her in the bedroom, pronto. We're going to do this right.

She laughs about the princess bed, but I'm pretty intent on getting her naked, immediately. I lay her on the bed and get that skirt off her.

Then I take my time. I want to know every inch of the body I've held so many times in dance. I've lifted her, turned her, held her in my arms. But now I've really got her. Naked, lit by the bathroom light, just for me to see.

I run my hands over her, starting with her jaw and neck, down those beautiful breasts, and along her ribs. I frame her hips with my palms, my thumb dipping into her belly button. She smiles.

My hands fit over her thighs, down her knees, to her strong ballerina's calves.

She's perfect.

I stand up and get my clothes off as fast as I can. She watches me, taking me in. I see her expression soften, like she might cry again. Now I'm unsure what she wants.

She sits up. "Can we dance?"

I kick my clothes under a chair. "A naked waltz. Now that's an idea." I'm happy with slow. Happy with anything involving her naked body.

I pull her up from the bed and shift her into a waltz pose. I swear we never actually dance to music. But it doesn't matter. She follows my lead as we move across the room. The feel of her breasts against my chest makes me insane.

She's impossibly beautiful, and I tell her so, then kiss her. I can't bear any more waiting. She's too precious, too perfect. I need her.

I lift her by the thighs to straddle my hips. She's right there, and I could just take her, but this has to be perfect. The way she'd want it. I walk us over to the bed and lay her down on the sheets.

If it's been a long time, she's probably unprotected on her own. "Condom work for you?" I ask. I can gauge if she's really ready for this by her answer.

She nods.

For a moment, I can't find my damn pants. I kicked them in some dark corner. After a frantic search, I extract my wallet and the condom. I make sure I'm ready to go before I get near her again. All control is gone now.

I crawl over to her, touching her, kissing. It seems like forever that I've known her and wanted her, waiting for this. I separate her knees, and she lifts herself up to meet me. She's there, ready. We're heading here together.

Slipping inside her is like a miracle. She cries out, eager. Her joy is beautiful and unexpected. I feel my jaded heart cracking, not that she hadn't already dealt it some serious blows. She's authentic. This is really her, showing me how she feels.

"My sweet Livia," I say. "How I have pined for you."

I'm damn overwhelmed by this, swamped with the sweetness of her below me, how real it all is. No agenda. No manipulating me or trying to get something out of me.

Nothing but us here. The real deal.

I reach between us. I've already learned her, know what she needs. Her eyes widen like she didn't expect so much tonight, and as her sounds start to come, I'm flooded with everything about her. She's everything. I can't live without her.

Her eyes meet mine as she lets go, crying out. This gets me, and I'm unleashed. We hold still, our bodies locked together. She touches my back, my waist, my skin, as if she has to reassure herself that I'm not a figment of her imagination.

I know how she's feeling. How can this be real? I carefully withdraw and draw her next to me. There's no sound but our breathing. Nothing penetrates our perfect world.

And I swear I will do whatever it takes, quit the show, disappear from the media, anything I have to do to protect this. I am already hers, and I will move every mountain in our way to make her mine.

## Sneak Peek of Wounded Dance

Blitz takes my hand as I stand up from putting on my shoes. We head down the hall of Dreamcatcher Dance Academy, which is filling with moms and little girls for their classes.

We cross the foyer, waving at Suze, who sits at the front desk. A few moms stop talking to point at Blitz. He smiles and is friendly, but doesn't pause, his hand on my back as we head for the doors.

I'm on the steps when my brain stutters. My attention fixes on a man on the sidewalk, looking up, his cheeks ruddy from the cold as if he's stood there a while.

My body gets some message from my brain before I can comprehend exactly what is happening, why I'm feeling a threat. My feet are rooted to the concrete, my chest buzzing with alarm.

Blitz stops with me. "You okay, Livia?" he asks.

His words are what bring the moment into focus. This man in front of me wears a black leather jacket, his layered brown hair flying in the wind.

It's him.

God.

It's him.

Denham Young.

Kicked out of my life when I was fifteen. Gone for good. Lost to me.

My great love. My shame.

Gabriella's father.

He's found me.

In Wounded Dance, Livia faces the ultimate threat: the father of her secret baby. Get book two or splurge for the entire Lovers Dance Boxed Set.

www.ingramcontent.com/pod-product-compliance
Lightning Source LLC
Chambersburg PA
CBHW071424260626
47162CB00013B/2627

* 9 7 8 1 9 3 8 1 5 0 6 1 6 *